The Harbinger

Spectral Hunter Series

Morgan Kessler

A Little Vast Studios, LLC

Contents

Prologue

A neurosurgeon who forgets his scalpel in a patient is criminally negligent; one who leaves behind evidence of murder is doomed. And Victor... Dr. Victor Shepherd is not doomed. He makes certain of that each time he approaches his work. Which is why he prowls this bare-bones health facility for his next subject's eligibility.

"Quite a bit of extra time with Mrs. Wynn this morning, Doc," the nurse behind the admitting counter says.

Victor shrugs off his lab coat, smiling. "My favorite patient."

"More than your own patients?" She raises a playful eyebrow.

"They're not mine yet. One does not take credit until the kinks are worked out of them."

She laughs, and Victor joins her with perfect timing.

It's true. He's not at Riverbend long enough for anyone to be his. They may know Dr. Shepherd as the human interested in the passel of brittle old folks and crumbling staff, but they never know him for long. It's just too bad. He has always had an affinity for the weak, the disabled, the terminal. There is beauty in a brain that refuses to die.

"Is she still in the land of the living?" Victor asks, almost as an afterthought.

The nurse rolls her eyes. "She'll outlive us all."

He's sure she won't. Not in the way they think. She is old, a paraplegic, and silent enough to make an excellent candidate, should he decide.

Victor nods, slipping into his fall coat. "Well, I'll check in on her another day."

"Say hey to the wife and kids!" she calls.

He gives her a wink and an absent wave of his hand. Victor has no wife, no kids, no loose ends. He will not be doomed.

He steps to the door, and the world quivers before him. The air thickens with a disquieting charge. There's a glimpse through the window—a raggedy man, staring. He is looking back at Victor.

Then he feels it again, a sickening brush of the uncanny against his skin. It prickles at first, crawling over like a swarm of invisible insects. The sensation is unsettling. A tremor of unnatural awareness ripples through the air. He steadies his gaze, focusing on the man, his unkempt beard flecked with whatever had missed his mouth. The grubby scarecrow in a blue woolen cap stands there swaying, hollow-cheeked and tattered. Still staring back at Victor. Still watching, like he knows. As their eyes meet, that eerie sensation magnifies, intensifies, engulfing him in a wave of utter dread.

Insistent. Unexplainable.

He does know. Somehow, that drifter knows! Victor abandons the door, slinking into the bathroom until the eeriness finally dissipates.

Rushing to his car, head down, he is confident in being unseen. Yet there he is, watching from across the lot. There's no mistaking it now. That vagrant, whatever this crawling sense is on his back, it arises from him. *I should deal with him before his awareness spreads. Before someone believes in what this one knows.* But that's how the careless get caught—by reaching too eagerly, too visibly. By mistaking obsession for necessity.

Victor gets into his car, though he doesn't take off.

The man remains on the far side of the lot, a threadbare silhouette against the gray sky. He makes no move, just stands with all the time in the world. Victor flicks on his cell phone, thumbs the keys as if arranging important business before pulling away, giving him one last glance.

He hasn't budged. Like he has a purpose. Like he's waiting.

The thought of being anticipated by someone like that is both infuriating and alarming. He has had the slightest inkling that something has been off since completing his last experiment. *But I've been careful.* And this is one unexpected twist he will not allow to develop any further.

He drives slow, anticipating him around every corner, every stoplight. Victor circles the long way around to his apartment, the vacant suburbia of it, the eerie silence and the gray clouds low to the rooftops. Surveying the street, no vagrant. No chill tugging on his hairs.

Surely if he had an accomplice, another watcher, they'd have revealed themselves by now. He allows himself the thought that his awareness might be as derelict as his appearance—an unlikely accident, easily dismantled. Inside, Victor scrolls through his notes and sits in numb quiet.

A thought occurs. As bizarre as the notion is, a subject with such peculiarities might yield fascinating results.

This time he laughs alone.

It's been five long years since his hiatus began. That lull which was pressed upon him by his patron has gnawed while his research starved. And now, Victor is already considering something unprecedented. There's an undeniable allure to it, a sense of reclaiming his momentum. To locate this subject, to verify his vulnerability, could it only require his hands remain steady? He might even enjoy the challenge.

He stops the laughter with a sharp breath, honing his focus on the weeks ahead.

Nothing will go awry. Not when he can feel it again, the obscenely thrilling whirr of possibility.

Chapter One

Searches in the Blind

E ach morning starts with a black coffee, a systems check, and thirty silent seconds peering into that bedroom, which hasn't changed.

June's singsong voice still echoes in her mind, a ghost of bright, unwieldy energy. Her daughter's pink room holds its breath just like Evie herself, waiting for life to spring back into it. "Perfectly Unfinished"—lettered on a mirror she can barely look at. The words are a taunt she cannot erase. Clues, pieces of the unknown, all laid out in her mind's eye—a purple scarf, the one left behind, now you see me, now you don't. Those touchstones seem only to haunt. Evie went out one afternoon, came back, and June was gone, a vanishing act without the logical conclusion she so desperately needed.

With a step back to the hallway, Evie seals the room as it was.

She maneuvers through her hours with a tenacity rivaling any machine; her mind a precision instrument slicing through the weight of disorder. Each action is an orchestrated movement in her symphony of control. The mundane becomes her fortress. She moves from her desk to the kitchen counter and back, the rigid structure insulating her from the past's chaotic echoes. Dishes are rinsed and dried, each rhythmic motion another tick in the day's march from morning to night. She knows how to keep memory from creeping in, how to stave off the spontaneity that once filled their home. Her solace is pattern, repetition. January, February, March. Socks, shoes, coat. Chaos is an enemy she has learned to outmaneuver. Routine is her shield, and hiding behind it feels safe, familiar.

The expected. The logical.

Before Evie's hand disturbs her computer's slumber yet again, she catches her vacant reflection from its darkened monitor. Her wraith-like image blinks back with her own eyes. Hollow, a shadow of the woman who once moved with brightness and ease. Hair pulled back, no-nonsense, those dark curls she kept tamed and disciplined. She gauges her small frame, a vulnerability of such slightness. She used to wonder if maybe she was disappearing as well. But it is only enough to give her pause, then disappears with a tap as the device hums to life.

Her desktop reflects her discipline: approved FBI wallpaper, minimal taskbar with BureauMail, Evidence Tracker, and "SIGINT," plus a widget showing real-time case statuses. Folders are precisely organized by case codes, dates, and operation tags. An open, encrypted notes app displays time-stamped observations, as it should.

She clicks through files, cataloging data with cool detachment. The spreadsheet she scans is a tangle of numbers that others might see as chaos, but to Evie, they're a balm. Patterns emerge where others see only scattered fragments. She navigates the columns with swift precision, digits bending to her will. Her mind wraps itself around each detail until she finds what she's looking for—another anomaly, another thread.

Algorithms can be trusted more than people—people lie, break, and disappear.

The papers arrive at noon. Delivered with casual disregard, they land on her doorstep with an arrant slap. She knows what's inside before picking them up—a familiar weight, a familiar grief. The envelope feels thin but heavy, a new end to an old story. Michael's looping signature traces the edge of his resignation, an elegant mark of certainty. It tells her what her husband wants, what she already knows, and what she's tried desperately to avoid. Closure, where she would rather not.

Evie slides its contents onto her desk, its presence an unwanted inclusion of her space. With a turn, her hand goes for the phone. Maybe this time. She will compose better words in her head, a logic draft which won't dissolve into emotion. *You win. We both lose. I can't believe this is happening. Let's talk.* But every approach seems hopelessly flawed, a repetition of what they've been over so many times before.

The phone lingers silent, unmoved by her indecision.

Another outreach to her husband wouldn't change a thing. However, she could focus on something she could impact—her work.

She gathers the details of her financial anomalies, ready to pitch. Picking up the receiver, she dials his number. "Boss, it's Evie," she began, her voice steady. "I've come across something on a financial crimes case, some pretty interesting patterns. I'm looking for some feedback and possibly a hand-off."

"Hi, Evie. Why yes, I'm still alive. Glad to hear from you are as well," Supervisory Special Agent Haden remarks, a gruff hint of sarcasm. "Home life keeping you busy these last several months?"

Evie sighs with a twinge of guilt. "Apologies, sir. I don't mean to be so... It's just... I've been catching up with everything, trying to manage on my end. You know. Doing my best." She takes a breath. "That's why

I've called. This recurring anomaly... It rounds itself back to a series of transactions that appear connected. It's like someone is laundering money through shell companies but with a twist—they're hiding in plain sight."

Haden releases a breath of his own into the phone. "No doubt it's impressive, Evie. I know you are not one to disappoint," he says. "At the same time, I am glad you called. I have been mulling over whether or not I should send a car out your way. I've need of expertise on something else—potential serial activity. Can you be ready in thirty?"

"Yes," urgency prickles at her skin, "I can be ready." Glancing at June's door, the weight of grief mingles with this unexpected call to action. *Could I be ready?*

"Good. I'll have one of our fresh faces swing by. See you shortly." The line disconnects before she could chance a second-guess of herself.

Well, best get to it.

It has been five long years since June, about three of those spent within the four walls of her home office. Days spent at the hum of computer fans and clatter of keys, a stark contrast to the bustling office she once knew. If not for Evie's unwavering precision and the clockwork regularity in unraveling financial crimes from afar, surely the Bureau would have lost faith in her long ago.

Leaving the unsigned papers, Evie heads to her bedroom closet. Her suits hang like soldiers. She enlists a pale gray one, its soft fabric a calculated contrast to her rigid exterior. Other than court appointments, she still hasn't much use for them. Brushing her hair into a tight bun, she stands before the mirror. Evie can't help but fumble with the clasp on a bracelet—a Mother's Day gift. Before allowing herself to acknowledge the memory, she snaps it off and replaces it in her keepsakes drawer.

The door knock downstairs interrupts as bad timing, an unexpected crack in her schedule. They aren't due for another ten minutes. Is this a tactic, something to catch her off-balance? Of course not. Don't be silly. She opens the door to an obvious NAT (new agent trainee), slick-haired, feigned confidence in his practiced eye-contact. He reaches into his jacket, his hand haphazardly producing an ID.

"Mrs. Cross? I'm Mitchell... Mitchell Colins, here for—"

"Special Agent," she corrects. The words flip out sharper than intended. "I'll be ready in fifteen." He stands awkwardly, pocketing his billfold, the SUV idling at the curb. She will let him wait, coolly closing the door and resetting her pace. Lists and rules. Order and routine. She inhales methodically—one, two, three—and pushes thoughts of Michael, of June, into the farthest corner of her mind.

In her bedroom, she recovers a small hardened case, her Glock 9mm nestled inside as it should be. It feels like a reminder of the person she once was. The weight of it in her hand is surprisingly familiar. Next to it, her FBI badge, glinting with quiet authority. She hesitates, withdrawing it with the lanyard containing her building entrance card. Useless and forgotten for so long; it's a relic she hadn't the need for. Evie holsters and pockets appropriately, a soldier gearing for readiness.

Giving herself a once-over, ensuring everything is in its place, she makes her way to the front door.

Agent Mitchell stands outside, shifting in uncertainty. This time he addresses her with the correct formality. "Special Agent Cross... ready?" he asks.

Evie offers a curt nod.

With a turn of the deadbolt, she rounds herself to face the day. A Virginia-chilled afternoon seeps through her thin suit. The world outside expands, widens like a chasm as she takes a moment. Evie catches Mitchell assessing her, perhaps sensing hesitation. Quickly she straightens, her movements automatic as she takes her place on the passenger side and closes the car door.

From her window, sunlight echoes through their interior. Evie watches the young agent drive fully attentive. She can almost feel his questions, his curiosity about this slight woman who doesn't quite fit the fed profile. "Something you want to ask?" she says.

He blinks twice before replying, "No, ma'am. Just... we weren't sure you'd be available, given your leave."

Her clipped laugh is more punctuation than humor. "Work doesn't stop, regardless of the circumstances. We all need to make our way these days."

He nods. "It's good to have you back, ma'am. Agent Haden's been, well—he'll be pleased."

They lapse into silence, the kind which stretches, as she allows Mitchell's comment to sink in. *Haden's been what?* The glass fogs with her breath, the scenery a blur as autumn trees strip their leaves in resignation. Their drive feels too long and not long enough, a contradiction she's learned to live with. Evie's fingers find her temple to press. This reopening of the world, this crack in her careful isolation—it's an adjustment which needles at her in anticipation and unease.

Chapter Two

Return to the Fold

Quantico rises before them, an immense concrete testament to order. This sprawling behemoth of procedure and protocol was once Evie's stage where her identity took form. Now, the same walls feel like they're looming, emphasizing her fall from grace. Memories wash in as the car proceeds closer. The late nights spent analyzing files until theories became conclusions. Then, after months of training, her promotion to a full special agent status. The commendations came with almost predictable regularity until it fell apart. It feels like a lifetime ago.

Maybe it was.

The building swallows them as they enter, a church of glass and stone.

Recognizable faces meander through the corridors. They pass by with nods she can't decide if respectful or wary. Perhaps they're both. As they approach Haden's office, she can tell the briefing has started.

Their voices are already leaking through the door. Evie steels herself. The young agent opens the door and announces her like a diplomat.

"Special Agent Cross," he says as if it's an answer to a question no one asked.

Supervisory Special Agent Thomas Haden looks up, his eyes reflecting the seasoned investigator. His grizzled hair frames a face marked by decades of experience in law enforcement, each line a testament to unraveling human darkness. As he breaks into a grin, he conveys something more paternal than professional. "Evie." He stands, stretching his arms as if he's going to hug her, only to stop short.

Pulse skipping a beat, Evie manages a small smile. "It has been a while," her voice steady yet cautious. Turning toward the others, she glosses over Marcus Vaughn's self-satisfied smirk, Elena Reyes's usual intensity, and Cassandra Webb's unassuming quietness. The warmth that Evie musters is unexpected, a camaraderie she thought had been buried deep. "Glad to see the Bureau and department are still standing." The words are an olive branch extended across the gulf of her absence.

"Let's catch you up," Haden says with a clap, motioning to the wall. It holds a map pinned with photos and notecards. So overwhelmingly analog in this digital world; a theatrical crime board Evie can read from the doorway. Yet, an oddity hovers in the middle. One city, one death, and now Haden summons her? A single death doesn't scream serial killer.

So why am I here?

"Marcus," Haden says, "why don't you fill Evie in on what we briefed?" He drops his chin toward the man.

Vaughn leans back, arms folded. "Five years, Evie. Five years and it would appear we're being haunted by a ghost. Thought it fitting I lay it out on a map for you."

Evie's stomach knots. "Didn't that deceased killer, Barnett, close this case?"

Vaughn leans against the wall, his voice an unsettling mix of pride and disdain. "A month ago, they found our new Jane Doe in an abandoned warehouse along Route 1, close to Dumfries. The body was pristine—except for a few off-putting details: clean shaven, no eyes, no brain." He let his words sink in. "I know. Vaguely familiar, but not exactly the same."

Elena Reyes steps forward, her brow furrowed as she adds, "The original victims had partial brain tissue left behind. But this one? It's like every part that mattered was meticulously carved out."

Evie's pulse heightens, each beat echoing her dread. "But you think this is only loosely linked, right?" A myriad of questions swirl in her mind. "Are we looking at a copycat?"

"You'd think." Vaughn scoffs before turning serious again. "That'd be the smart call, my first call at least."

"Then why am I here?" Evie asks, frustration riding under her calm.

Haden steps forward, placing a reassuring hand on Evie's shoulder. "We need you to see this firsthand," he says. "The coroner will show you what he found—maybe then we can understand why this case has resurfaced. We've done enough here. Let's reconvene at the morgue. Move out."

Badges click and gear rustles as the team gathers. Marcus closes his notebook and falls in step beside Evie en route to the elevators.

"Here's what we know," Marcus begins quietly. "Victim was found discarded in a vacant lot by homeless copper scrappers. They go around ripping out drywall in old buildings. Anything for a buck.

Temperature was just above freezing—decomposition is slow. Forensics confirm no brain, no eyes, clean cranial cap. Victim is female, mid-twenties, no ID, no signs of struggle. According to the Doc, whoever did this sedated her first."

Evie nods, scanning Marcus's face for uncertainty. He offers none. She tugs on her suit jacket and follows him down the corridor, already bracing for what awaits at the morgue.

The autumn chill takes on an antiseptic note as they descend into the Prince William County morgue, a solemn transition from the frenetic energy of the Bureau. Its fluorescent lights cast a harsh, unforgiving glow that bleaches everyone to a clinical pallor. Metal gurneys align in rows, each a chilling reminder of abrupt ends. Their footsteps break what would otherwise be an oppressive quiet.

This gray-haired, middle-aged man's coroner badge reads as Emmitt Corwin D.O. "Was beginning to wonder if I should place her back in the fridge, sir," he says, with a wave toward a table.

A sheeted figure lies in stark repose.

Evie edges closer, bracing herself, a thin veneer over exposed nerves.

The coroner withdraws the sheet, loosely placing it on a counter. A young woman's form is revealed—skin pale, lips blue, an unmoving shell. Then there was the real expected sight: a clean removal of her scalp, surgical and precise. The skullcap rests in a metal tray alongside.

"At first, I considered the body as familiar, having worked on other Cartographer cases. But notice the bone separation," coroner Emmitt says, gesturing with a pen. "Clean and identical to the originals, down to the burr holes. I know you suggested a copycat, but this is exact."

Her mind races, wrangling with implications. "Burr holes? How's that—"

"Ah, yes!" Emmitt flipped his pen toward her. "You see, brain surgeons use a perforating drill to place between three to five holes from which a craniotome can pneumatically saw the remainder of the skullcap off. This body has four holes aligned in an identical way to the original killings. As far as I know, that detail was never released to the public."

Vaughn interjects, "Okay. So why the difference in what they took? Why no brain this time?"

The coroner shrugs, the gesture resigned. "Five years is a long time. Killers evolve. Maybe they refined their technique."

Haden, steady and sober, cuts through the unease. "According to all our compiled research, approximately 30-40% of serial murderers still never end up being caught. You four are my guys—" Evie glances at Reyes and Webb. "...my team. Make damn sure this one isn't among them."

Her pulse quickening, Evie notes her own unspoken confession. She helped orchestrate his escape, so now she has to help catch him. "Agreed," she responds, pushing back against the irony.

Reyes's pipes in. "Then let's get to work. We start with the MO and revisit our earlier assumptions." She maps it out with a finger as if the air is made of coordinates. "We should examine what didn't match the first time. Victimology, geography, tools. Anything overlooked."

Vaughn's brow furrows. "Overlooked? We had this cooked before. Let's not go off on wild tangents. There could be subtler explanations."

Evie knows a thinly veiled dig when she hears it. "We consider every possibility," she counters, keeping her voice level against the condescension.

Haden's watchful eyes move between them. "Let's get the paper-work started on this latest vic. Cross, I expect insights. Vaughn, bring her up to speed with Reyes."

Evie turns to the coroner, a question hovering. "When can I get a full report?"

His pen taps the clipboard, a subtle metronome. "Give me till morning. I'll have everything ready by then."

The team disperses, fingers pressing keys on phones; a muffled clamor of footsteps and voices. Evie lingers, staring at the young woman's hollowed expression. It's a face not unlike her own daughter's, or what she imagines June's might have been. Now, this killer is speaking to her, reaching out from behind the mask of a dead girl.

She turns, mouth dry, finding Haden still with the coroner. "Boss," she says, riding a careful line between certainty and doubt. "I'll go over everything tonight. You can expect my brief before Noon."

He turns, studying her. "You're not sticking with the team?"

Evie tenses, anticipating the conversation. "I've been able to man-age outstanding results from home. Right?"

Haden's face shifts from expectation to a resigned understand-ing. "We're going deep this time, Evie. Full throttle. I need you fully plugged in."

She takes a breath, holding his gaze. "You'll get what you need. Allow me my way for now."

He hesitates, a battle of wills playing out in silence. "Alright," he concedes, his tone softer. "But you keep me in the loop, Agent. Un-derstood?"

A nod, a relief. "Will do."

Their words linger, half promise, half truce. The echo of her own guilt follows Evie as she exits the building.

If they only knew.

Chapter Three

Team Efforts

Buzzing office lights and ringing phones assault Evie before the revolving door completes a single spin. Quantico agents dodge each other and part in hurried halls. The place was always chaos. That hasn't changed. Vaughn gives Webb and Reyes the quick and dirty: victimology, cross-checks, reports by end of day. Evie's head is already splitting as she follows Haden, no doubt to round up her NAT ride home.

That's when Building Security cuts them off. The guards flank a derelict, half-deranged male, his beard matted into ropes, clutching at plastic bags. Layers of mismatched clothing hang on him like rags. "Sir," the first guard shouts over the din, "we told him to leave—"

"We did," the other guard adds. "At least six times. But he's been here since you left. Claims it's urgent."

They continue to ward the bagman, as he glares through the mix of suits between them.

Vaughn and Haden exchange knowing looks. "More every year," Vaughn is unable to contain his smirk.

"So quickly?" Haden replies. "The crazies have a fixation on these things. But man, that was fast."

"Should I call in the butterfly nets?" a guard responds.

Haden shakes his head. "No need. I'll take care of it."

As they close in, the vagrant fixates on Evie with sudden clarity. His burst of movement startles, pushing past Security and agents alike.

"I see them!" he shouts, words spitting urgency. "Their spirits. They follow. They know!" Ragged hands thrust outward, ammonia seeping from grime and desperation.

Haden stops Evie short. "Wait." His tone she didn't recognize, almost gentle. The air thickens. Agents fall silent, their previous clamor collapsing into gawking attention. Evie is abruptly at the center of a messy, judgmental universe.

"I'm not crazy," the bagman insists. "You hear them too. Yes. The whispers. You know I'm not crazy!"

The pause is too long and too heavy, this wild man—his eyes pleading at hers.

Evie rotates her head, a slow denial. "No. Afraid I'm not hearing anything."

Haden breaks the moment. "Let's get you the help you need, sir," he offers, his voice calm but distant. "I've some connections at Quantico Community. Let's give them a call. Sound good? How about a coffee while we wait?"

The bag man jerks his head and shakes with defiance. "You don't understand," he replies, hands fumbling through every layer of his coat. "They chose me to deliver. But I'm not enough. They need more, someone... stronger." This time, he turns to her. Direct. Intense. He pulls out a crumpled piece of paper.

Evie's hands twitch, a traitorous response.

He thrusts the wad forward, but Marcus is quicker. The paper flutters just as the detective gives it a snatch. "Enough of this," Marcus spouts—full stop.

Security grabs the bag man. He offers no resistance as he's dragged back. They haul him toward the door, while office voices hum back as if they had never stopped. At the exit, the vagrant twists, continuing his protests over Security's heads, "You don't get it! They'll find another way!"

He becomes a vanishing act, spit out by glass and stone.

Wading back through the office, Vaughn leads the way, trash in-hand. Evie pretends not to care while he escorts back to her old desk. Dustless yet barren, that corner holds court among the other's more colorful workspaces. Lives exist here and everywhere else in the building. Just not at hers.

Marcus lingers, as if her silence requires intervention. "It's great to have you back, Eve." He waves back toward the absent bag man, saying, "Try not to let the loopy-loops spoil your return." His look of her hovers. "You're not buying into any of this, right? I mean, you are the logical one here."

Evie reaches over and plucks the crumpled paper from him. With a flick, she tosses it into her desk's trash bin. "Not all data sets are equally valid," she counters.

He smirks, triumph in his eyes. "Good to hear. We can't have everyone chasing after wild theories."

"Don't need a genius to figure that." Evie's words taste bitter, almost not escaping her mouth.

Marcus leans on an elbow, eyes on her. "Guess we can add crackheads to your list of obstacles, Special Agent. From serial killers to stock portfolios to lunatics. We cover it all these days."

She glances at the wastebasket. Her own eyes betraying her. "Always have."

"Well, no need of a debrief from my end." He spins, heading off to the others as if a report were already written.

He thinks I'm onboard.

With everything.

If only.

Evie reaches for the paper, an unconscious twitch of fingers hovering over its crumbled edges. The vibrations of her phone break through with familiar intrusion.

MICHAEL: I'm at the house. We need to talk.

She slaps the phone onto her desk, careful not to crack the screen. Evie's head is still caught in her daughter's empty room, an infinite regression of absent answers. Outside her fishbowl, no one takes notice as she sits, silent. Fitting back in isn't as easy as they think. Especially when the ground keeps shifting. Vaughn throws a stack of papers down on a desk three rows away, motioning like a conductor to the rest of the group.

There is an expectation to know the tune.

Time to gather things and play along. Evie shoots one last glance at the trash bin before leaving it all behind. Security is outside the conference room, chatting over coffee as she searches the office. She finds Mitchell, his suit too pressed, his steps too fast. All that potential, unmarred by trauma. She takes a long breath. They don't stay green forever. "Special Agent Cross," he says, almost relieved when she catches up. "Are we headed back already?"

"Ready as ever I'll be."

He opens a side door, leading Evie out to the rear lot. The air nips, biting against her jacket. Thoughts of June wisp from her every breath.

The house, a crypt of memory. Michael is waiting. What could he want that all the years, a thousand arguments, and a set of unsigned papers haven't already said?

Chapter Four

There but Not

The man waits like a scarecrow, eyes raw against the evening sun. The way he paces before spotting the car, she imagines he's been there a while, his every move loose and frayed. His fragility heaps a layer to his once deliberate nature, to the confidence she once knew. Evie dismisses Mitchell with a curtness and approaches from the driveway, each step a contest of their shared grief. "Michael," she says, voice taut. "What are we doing here?"

Searching his face for an answer, he exhales, gesturing with an envelope. "I thought I'd save more postage," he says. The attempt at humor dissolves into weariness. His shoulders slump under the expectation.

"An email would've sufficed," Evie counters.

Stepping up onto the porch and past him, she unlocks the door, cracking the door ajar. They both stand on the threshold, unmoving, quietly demanding something beyond conversation.

"I said the documents would be coming," Michael says. "Was hoping you'd just pull the Band-Aid off quickly. Get it over with. Wasn't expecting you'd not to be home."

Evie meets his intensity with a cool detachment. "You know me. I go where needed."

He looks at her with a twist, as if to say her words barely pass. "Not talking about us, are you? Do you think I'm here about your work?"

"You might be surprised, actually. It truly is impressive," Evie adds. "An algorithm I've developed is turning heads. Potential embezzlement scheme. Haden is trying to pull me back on site." Maybe her matter-of-fact tone may shift his, redirect them to something manageable.

Michael grips the envelope. "This again," he says.

A pause hangs, as if his squeeze has its own voice. Evie busies herself pulling the keys from the lock, a moment of false industry which lets her avoid his stare.

"I've signed my copy," he presses. "Once you sign yours, we can sell the house and I can get my half of the equity."

Evie stands for a beat, then two. He holds the papers out, but she does not reach for them. She knows where it goes from here. The repetition, the circular arguments. "There's no need to rush this," she replies.

Michael's expression hardens, that stubbornness they both share.

Stepping inside, her hand tightens around the knob as she holds the door wide. Their home reveals itself in crisp lines, an arrangement without sentiment. All decor and no picture frames. Surfaces wiped clean of emotion and history, meticulously curated. Free of pain. She turns to face him, aware of how exposed they both feel standing here.

He lingers, eyes flicking past her to the hollow interior, to what they once had. "The walls must be closing in," he observes, "now that it's just you and what's left." His tone is edged, searching for a reaction.

Well, he's not wrong. Doesn't mean she has to admit it.

She avoids a flinch with a shake of her head. "I've identified a pattern," Evie continues, her detour transparent. "In these Westlake accounts. It's keeping me—"

"Occupied?" He finishes, voice rising. "I can see that." There's a fracture in his composure, frustration at her deflection. He will not let this go. Despite avoiding his gaze, Michael's silence is more accusatory than his words. She knows his thoughts before he speaks them. "You gave up on *us*," he reminds. "You're going to give up on this too."

He moves, closing the space she's trying to create. The scent of their time together lingers between them, a mixture of spice and bittersweet happier days. This nearness—a reminder of their history, of wounds still too raw to heal.

"There's nothing to give up," she responds.

He backs away, adjusting his hold on the envelope. "I won't give up." Michael's defiance leaves him gaunt and breathless. His conviction stings; a barb meant to hit deeper than the matter of unsigned documents. He's making this about more than he says, and they both know it. She sets her jaw, clinging to the distance that her logic affords.

Tipping sideways, Michael searches her face. "Just sign the damn papers, Evie. It's all I need from you now." His plea leaves a slow fading echo. She anchors herself to the doorframe, everything in place except for them. Evie knows he'll leave this time as empty-handed as before. They stare each other down, each unrelenting, each with something to lose.

Evie swallows back an explanation she's made a hundred times before. There's no point now; he wouldn't hear it. "That's not what you need," she insists. "That's what you think you want."

"Think?" he challenges.

"I know," she says. Her insistence is brittle, ringing hollow even to her own ears.

Michael drops the envelope to his side. "How long do you plan on holding out?"

"Why don't you still care?"

That's all it takes.

Evie looks away, toward the white, clinical room. The way he says nothing shows it matters less to him with each passing moment. Without a reply, Michael shoves the envelope into her hands, turns, taking to the porch steps. Those words remain as he heads off.

It's all I need from you now.

It's never as easy as that. At the open door, Evie watches him walk a sharp line away. She holds the papers tightly, imagining they've always been signed, and he just refused to see. Maybe that's why he keeps pushing—still with so many false memories left to blame her for. Michael will never give up, not until everything is exhumed. Not until he has her admit that she buried them.

She steadies herself, unsure what to do with these papers as well. This confrontation should have made things clearer, not more complex. They can't leave it like this. She has to try.

"Michael," she calls.

At the sidewalk, he pauses, glancing over his shoulder with wary deliberation. Michael purses his lips, then resolves to march back.

"Had a change of heart?" His voice is too sure, as if he expected her to break.

Evie musters herself, straightening with a look up at him. "What are you going to do with the money this time? The same as before?"

Michael glares back. "You still don't get it. I need that money. That's the difference."

"Another detective won't find anything we couldn't," Evie says.

"Then why keep it from me? Just to prove a point?" He waves his hand angry, sad, uncertain.

Evie's eyes speak of the despair her voice has not the words for.

Michael catches himself. With a shake of his head, he steps closer. "I'm not giving up on her. Or on you. We need the funds. There's no closure without knowing the truth."

"You really think that?"

"You already know that." His hands tremble with the insistence of a man who won't let go.

She blinks up at him. "I meant for you. Do you really think that?"

"Hope is a dangerous thing, Evie." Michael's eyes glint back at her, sharp and broken. "You said it yourself."

He waits for a sign she will relent, for any crack in her resolve. Her response surprises them both, perhaps more than if she had signed. "Come in," Evie says, "I'll make tea."

He shakes his head. "You really think you can play house?"

"It's not what you want too?"

With a huff, her husband uprights himself. Thus going from wounded to clearheaded in a heartbeat. He assumes the stance of the man he once was. "Let me know when you're ready to live in it," he replies.

That familiar chasm opens, a raw grief that grows with each syllable.

"Why? Is that another thing you'll accuse me of giving up on?" Evie counters.

"How about this? Where's your line between personal and professional these days?" Michael holds both accusation and empathy, but without cruelty in it. "Seems you've found a way of solving one by discarding the other." He unfolds a photo from his jacket. Not offering it up, but keeping it for himself. It hurts knowing, even from this glancing angle. June's smile is bright and impossibly innocent, much like it was on her last birthday.

Evie's mouth goes dry. He holds her eyes, then the picture again, weighing which is more telling. She wonders how many copies he's kept. How long he spends comparing each for hidden meaning, for a trace of who's to blame. Why can't he understand? She just couldn't bear to see them anymore.

Evie shifts, self-conscious.

"It's been five years, Evie. Five. I can't keep pretending. I can't keep waiting."

Her mouth opens to respond, but can't.

He turns with a finality, his shoes loud and determined against the pavement.

With that, Evie closes the door with a click and turns. She finds the house empty, yet full of all she wants to avoid. Alone now, she draws the envelope near, weighing her certainty against the inevitability of loss. Her own hollow words return. He's gone again, she repeats, wishing she could hold on to him.

The divorce papers stay as before: unsigned, as unrelenting as the absence that still fills her every waking moment.

Chapter Five

Price of a Lie

E vie remains alone, house empty, amber whiskey in a tumbler. She fixates at the end of the hallway, on June's door—only ever viewed from that doorframe. There on the verge has been enough. Tonight will be different.

Fingers hesitating on the cool doorknob, she pushes it open. The reverent museum of a bedroom appears stilled in time—stuffed animals, clothes still in the closet, and her "Perfectly Unfinished" mirror beckoning. Catching a sob, she inhales its staleness as she enters.

Wavering memories unfurl like a tapestry, dragging Evie back. The old ghosts of their FBI's Critical Incident Response (CIR) team manifest with methodical precision, their sterile equipment stark against the pastel walls and whimsical decals of June's room. Forensic technicians snap photographs of the crimson-stained bedding. They capture every sign of violence coloring the fabric. A blade's incision mars the comforter, a stab hole in its once soft surface.

Evie stands in the doorway, her face a mask of professional calm despite the chaos within. Her eyes stare without seeing. Behind her, Michael paces with restless energy, his footsteps reverberating on the wooden floorboards. His voice rings out in sharp demands for action, but each word betrays his unraveling composure.

The CIR team rushes through the house, as immediate as the incident itself. All angles, all procedure. Technicians set up in pairs and take careful stock of their surroundings. Details are committed to notebooks. Evie takes it all in with a detachment born of desperation. She wraps her arms tight and breathless, her body edging around the room. Michael lingers behind her, his silhouette raw against the bright hallway light. Voices and sounds overlap, filling the spaces, snapping open and shut like the cases filled with sterile equipment. Someone mentions the missing knife. Another dusts for prints.

Her husband stomps—head in his hands. It takes every technique that she can muster to keep from coming undone. Evie doesn't quite know yet how useless it all will be.

Childhood innocence clashes with the relentless investigation, each vying for dominance in the room. A mother's love pierces Evie with ruthless clarity, the juxtaposition sharp. Michael's voice cuts through the air, urgent and raw. "I need answers!" he bellows, his eyes wild as he moves toward a stocky woman snapping photos at the crime scene. She stumbles back from the bed, startled by his intensity. "What aren't you doing? Is that my daughter's blood? Tell me something!" His breath comes in ragged gasps with every demand, his hands clutching for the blanket-shrouded bed.

Michael trembles under his unanswered questions. He's understandably unraveling, like a father with little that he can do. That's why it's on her. Evie stands firm, holding him back from those who orchestrate the operation. June's room remains a crime, silent beneath the onslaught of certainty that only careful documentation might unravel. She understands both sides—the desperate father and the methodical professionals.

"Michael," she interjects softly, stepping into him with a steady gaze. "They're doing everything they can." Her voice is a lifeline tethered between urgency and calm. Frustration consumed the man, demanding urgency from an unyielding process that offers little solace.

But that was just the first day.

Their shell of a home swallows her whole, flushing her around the times ahead. Evie becomes lost as well, floating through hollow spaces emptied of purpose. Chores are managed. Family embraced. The Bureau updates her in small bits, pieces of news progressing nowhere. She commits to the laundry. Michael sorts the garage. They dine on tasteless suppers, with barely an appetite between them. When Evie sweeps the entry, she discovers the manila envelope just under the front door mail slot, a note taped to the outside.

Her hands shudder as she sees the words. It still takes her moments before their meaning registers. Typewritten stabs which orchestrate a demand... their threat. "Some symphonies are meant to be played out. If you want what remains of your daughter, see to it the case you are on does not lead to its Maestro."

Unspooling the red string holding down its flap, she feels something shift as she upends its contents. The ponytail tumbles forth, a single dark coiled braid, settling into her palm. Evie's breath catches on her scent, a sharp intake that quivers through her entire body.

The name slips from her lips. "June."

It's hers. The same hair she'd braided the mornings before school, the same hair she brushed while squirming in impatient giggles.

This piece of her daughter is so solid, so real, it hurts. She backs against the wall as if from the force of a physical blow. Her knees buckle, but she remains upright. Michael suddenly appears by her side. Their despair writes itself out in patterns few would have predicted. Disjointed words and halting spaces grow over the sight.

"What the hell is that?" he demands, already knowing what she can barely accept. "Tell me. Goddammit, tell me!" It's enough for them both to hold on to a maybe. A perhaps.

"I need time to think," she whispers. They'd both been waiting for the very thing they feared most. For something more. For anything. Each hour after her disappearance finds her without a plan, without consolation. Evie pushes him and everything away until there is only herself. She has to have the answers. She refuses to break, not this soon.

"What does this mean? What's it mean, Evie? What are you thinking?" Michael's eyes widen, voice swinging from hope to accusation. "Is there something you're not telling me? You know what this is." It's all he can do not to grab her by the shoulders and shake the truth out.

She sets her jaw, muscles rigid. "Michael, I need to think. I just need time."

"Time? Time? What are you going to do about it? Tell me you have a plan."

Her breath is shallow. "I said—"

He cuts her off. "I know what you said. I want to know what *we* are going to do."

The kitchen provides a freezer bag. Evie seals the braid tight within. No additional contamination. The rules of evidence are basic, so she makes do. She finds herself less steady as time stretches, afraid of what comes next. The Bureau will need to confirm what they both already know about it. *It is hers.* She'll turn it over right after—right after she's done.

Then there is the note.

Has this made the FBI no longer their refuge? Is she no longer that person?

"We should be working together," Michael tells her, reaching past his pain and across her measured barricades. The truth, a sewing thread she doesn't want to pull through. "We should…" His words never finish their way to her ears. He doesn't need to. Evie is right there with him.

She buries herself, clutching every resource with desperate precision. The blood, the trail, the way they were failing her and the way her team never would. That slip of paper held before her. Letters and lines find their patterns, rearranging a set of incompletes. It forms in front of her, not according to any investigation. But according to him, and according to their wishes. A promise to her husband she doesn't need to make.

There is little else to do but that.

Assuming her place before her computer, Evie assembles the facts and her strategy. First, she compiles them: two files that meet and another one they never released, building toward a new inevitability. Next, a refinement, giving each a sign of his will, this Cartographer that says so little yet takes so much. The shifts are slight. A word, a trace. A reference, a thread, all buried in the coding. So few as to hardly suggest direction, but the changes extend toward one clear conclusion: another suspect, another man. So it's known, so it's certain, someone will claim credit. Another someone already dead will assume the destruction, and she will recover their daughter.

Hope is a dangerous thing.

Her knuckles blanch. They bruise with cold doubt in that dark room. She does not give up on this. Not yet. As Michael loses another kind of faith, Evie gives the final piece of herself to him, to June. Each keystroke aches. Her resolve stretches thin. Evie tells herself this and only this: *she must.*

The screen's glow pulses, a tide lapping at the edges of her will. Before she commits, there is a moment. Evie's finger suspends an inch above the key. *Am I doing this for her, or for myself?* She could feel the blood rush in her ears, feel June's absence like a live current. 'Fraudulence' hovers behind her eyes, an accusation from her own mind. This was a plea bargain with a devil she had never believed in—not until it asked for her daughter back, piece by piece.

With a finality more careful than her loss, Evie saves what matters: the data that isn't true and the certainty of uncertainty. It moves from the falsified data of his precision to the very files which Marcus Vaughn will take over and lay claim to. A tribute, this kill that doesn't belong. Evie sacrifices and submits in the process of making him sure, and leaving herself...

Knowing.

Days bleed into weeks. Evie fills the empty hours with artifice, answering every hollow ring before it can reach the second. The home's delivery slot gapes at her, postal and barren. Maybe tomorrow. Yet, only ghosts and emptiness usher forth. No more envelopes. No further demands. No June. No more point. No more anything. Her professional fortress shudders, then collapses. The DNA came back positive. Marcus' diligence succeeds in closing the Cartographer's case. She holds a bright stuffed bear to her chest, rocking back and forth as the hours lose track of her.

Just like hope.

It all loses to the vanishing of her logic, and the logic of the vanished. Evie drops and nearly crumbles as she lets go. This transition is from month to empty month. No whispers, only ghosts.

Nothing.

"You never came back," she sobs now, flashes of the past and the weight of the present collapsing together until there's no air left. No breath, no measure. "You never came back," over and over again. Evie repeats softer, slower, until it is a whisper against her heart. Her body shakes, spent and folded, the old bear clutched to her chest. Tears fall onto its tattered fur, staining it with the weight of all she's lost. Of all she has done.

When the tears finally fade, when her pulse calms, she is left with the shell of her resolve, a decision she can no longer reclaim. Evie recovers, wipes her cheeks, and places June's bear back onto the bed. It sits there like a witness, an old absence. She straightens and stands, gathering the pieces of herself as best she can.

Willing herself, Evie reaches the hallway. The house breathes an empty sigh as she departs, leaving the past to linger behind that closed door.

Chapter Six

Ghost of a Life

The cereal and coffee seem to taunt her, like so many other items on the store shelves. Evie selects them and navigates the grocery aisles like a well-considered scheme. Instant noodles, frozen dinners. Single portions insulate her from the world of families and multi-packs. Visions bloom painfully in her mind—pigtails, ribbons, a fresh-picked apple in her lunch bag. A memory so vivid she avoids the fruit section, conscious of the peculiarity. What does she know of a life this honest anymore?

Her fingers trace the shopping cart, recalling how smaller hands would clutch its edges, begging for snacks and candies. She lets these thoughts wrap around her until they almost tighten, then she drops them in pursuit of other items. A sack of rice, batteries, milk. Back in the dairy section, she finds a half gallon—if nothing else, her life was supposed to have the order Evie so carefully maintained.

That was before.

She relives the moment: the braid, and the secrecy of a single sheet's offer. If not for the jeopardy of exposure, if she hadn't been so very calculated. Evie knots with the illogical of it, with how it insists on being the one thing she can never scrub clean. The past is not a variable she can control.

Protocol required her to turn over her daughter's hair. She'd followed that rule. But the note—Evie concealed the note, tucked into a drawer, its demands unspoken like her plan. She could see the way it all would have gone. A single miscalculation, and she would have been the one under investigation.

What might have gone wrong? An exposure of her tampering, of the note itself, and of the way it would have left her. Any gain? None. Evie imagines their words, their certainty that she would never chance to overplay her hand. A bad decision. An error in her code. None of that happened. The data fell into place. The Cartographer case was closed. But no June.

Never June.

She still believed back then. Believed she could connect it all, the note's typewritten stabs with the same coordinated precision that she once had. And maybe she still does, Evie thinks with some irony, as she collects a dozen eggs and lets them settle into her sparse cart. Arrangement. Pattern. The logical sequence should lead somewhere. She stares down the refrigerator aisle. One more piece of data. That's all she needs.

The grocery store glares under garish fluorescents, its rows a testament to her isolation. Unlikely suspects refused to show, not even the real Cartographer. Especially not him.

Her mind turns back to those exhaustive weeks, to her own analysis.

She spirals through "what if" and "why not" until it closes in again with the force of so many impossible choices. The note was outside protocol, she justified. Risked her and June's future. But it was something. The only thing tangible from the moment they found the braid, from the moment she received the threat.

Her checkout station beeps, its conveyor rhythm a testament to how life moves forward, regardless. Summer, Fall. Christmas, spring. Hope is a dangerous thing. If only she'd gotten results.

The clerk bags her groceries without comment, but the pity in her eyes is unmistakable. Single bags. Single life. Evie pulls out her wallet, fingers fumbling through credit cards.

She steps outside into the dying light of another autumn day, more crisp than warm. It shivers through her thin jacket. She maneuvers through the parking spaces, remembering her Ford Fiesta's place. Canned soup, generic bread, and an extra blanket all sit neatly in the passenger seat.

A roughshod array of tents and tarps huddles on the fringe where the parking lot meets the woods beyond. These homeless are swathed in ragged layers, a vivid contrast to the pristine glass facade rising behind Evie. She pauses, her mind flickering back to the one from the Bureau—his eyes wild with an indescribable intensity. His voice was urgent and raw. It seemed an unnamable pull had reached out from him to her, one she never acknowledged. Now, these figures in the distance gather like wounded phantoms.

She stands frozen beside her unloaded cart. The realization is a vise tightening in her chest. Her head swims with a thousand abandoned hypotheses: following rules, breaking them, neither matter. Nothing has brought her daughter back. She is suspended between two worlds, each as empty as the other. The scent of autumn fills her lungs, drawing her toward another season's end.

A voice snaps her back. "Lady, you gonna use that cart?"

Evie shakes herself from the fog. A man in ripped layers eyes her from the edge of the lot. He gestures at her cart and waits for a response.

"Take it," her voice is distant.

He hoists the cart, his sinewy frame nearly vanishing under it. "Bless you," he mutters, wheeling it away with the urgency of someone who knows how quickly fortunes change.

She lingers there for a moment before closing the door. Evie unconsciously touches her wedding ring. Her fingers, unsteady. June. Michael. This family she can barely name as her own. She stands unmoving, the sight of them gnawing at her.

This too will pass.

This too she can forget.

Evie snaps back into motion, pulling the door shut. The car's heater cranks to a hum, pushing back the chill as she pulls out of the parking lot and from the past. The homeless blur in the rearview, a smudge of color and movement.

Chapter Seven

Familiar Victim

Hours later, the darkness of her home wraps Evie like a cocoon. She moves from the office to the kitchen, her shoes echoing against the silence. It's good to be back, she tells herself—a lie she almost believes. Her previous evening with Michael, the weight of his accusations, pulls at her. Perhaps his head has cooled. She goes to dial his number, changes her mind, and hangs up. She can try again later.

The light from her monitor flickers to life as she returns to her office. Her opening number: Whiskey. Work. Rest. The order is always the same. Evie pours herself a glass and lets the liquor burn its way through her system, bracing against the chill. She checks her phone.

MICHAEL: Stop avoiding.

She squeezes the device. Just like him, she thinks. Everything she can't escape. Everything he'll not allow.

Her desktop embodies order, standing firm against life's chaos. Folders are arranged, color-coded for expediency. Evie opens the one labeled CARTOGRAPHER, letting its details spill over. Numbers. Patterns. The logic of the vanished. She embraces the data, churning through the files with a mechanical ferocity. She taps out commands with practiced ease. Dissecting the data, she sifts for a narrative to emerge.

The phone buzzes, jolting her from the cocoon of numbers. Another of Michael's unresolved needs?

> HADEN: Need you on this. Potential victim in Alexandria. Homeless male. You will recognize him.

Evie's chest constricts. She re-reads the message, disbelief coiling into unease. Her mind is calculated, cautious. But a flash of recognition strikes and sticks. The desperate man. The one they had dismissed with a smirk of Vaughn's?

The phone vibrates again.

> HADEN: Our team is en route. Can you make it?

Evie's fingers hover, uncertainty branching in every direction. She types back a word before she can think better of it.

> EVIE: Yes.

The data remains on her screen, waiting patiently for her return. But the urgency of the text, the implication of her oversight, pulls her away. She knocks back the rest of her drink, its warmth failing to dull her guilt. How quickly could these things happen? Evie's hand trembles as she grabs her coat and exits the sanctity of her home, the door clicking shut behind.

Her car engine protests the cold before it turns over. She accelerates, the tires slipping on the slick pavement. Evie merges onto the highway, traffic thinning as night spirals into darkness before her.

The scene, a narrow alley tucked behind a flickering neon-lit convenience store, is unsurprising. She approaches, where her solemn team huddles around forensics and a shrouded form. The air is thick with refuse and damp concrete, a blanket that clings to her skin. Yellow police tape flutters in the night air, a bright scar across the scene's monochrome bleakness. Portable floodlights stave off the shadows, illuminating the grim tableau. Haden stands with his team. He looks up, his expression shifting to relief as he catches sight of Evie.

Marcus cocks an eyebrow her way. "Thought you'd make the smarter call and wait for the reports to come in," his voice laced with familiar condescension. "Not much left to see."

Evie ignores his taunt, her eyes fixed on Haden. Her boss steps forward, the weight of his attention grounding her. "I've got to admit," Haden says with a nod, "wasn't sure you would show."

"Some things are worth another set of eyes," Evie responds, scanning the scene. "What do we have?"

"Par for the course," Haden begins, glancing toward the covered figure, "local PD found him about two hours ago. Homeless male. No ID. No signs of struggle. But most importantly, no eyes, no gray matter. From what I gather, looks to be the same one who showed up at our doorstep. See for yourself."

Evie winces at the implication.

"What I don't get," Vaughn interjects, "it's only been weeks since his last kill. Didn't the old Cartographer hit every three months or so?"

Haden draws himself up. "Original cases did have a longer cooling-off period. But this recent activity suggests an acceleration. That means we are either catching up—or whoever this is is taunting us." His voice is sober, yet urgency runs beneath.

"That's assuming it's the same killer," Vaughn argues. "For all we know, it could be an entirely new player working off the old script. Maybe someone with direct access to the case files, hmm?"

Evie tenses at the accusation's edge. "What's the coroner say?" She steers the conversation, seeking facts.

"Corwin? He calls the bone separation clean. Identical to the previous one," Haden confirms. "He just got here and is about to give us the rundown."

They step closer as Corwin flicks the tarp back. The body's familiar yet hollow face strikes Evie with a chill. The man's skullcap lies like an overturned bowl on the concrete. Where eyes should be, cavernous sockets stare up at the sky. She struggles to keep her composure. This new Cartographer's signature is undeniable.

"Like I said," Vaughn's voice cuts through, "weird it's happening so fast. Even for a psycho like this."

Corwin adjusts his glasses, unfazed by Vaughn's commentary. "The pattern is eerily exact," he states, pointing with a gloved hand. "Tissue around the scalp and bone cuts are meticulous, no sign of struggle. It's as if the same hand from five years ago performed the surgeries. Same skill, same precision."

Evie leans closer, her mind churning.

A quiet rage builds within. She should have listened. He might have lived. She should never have altered the case files. None of this—no deaths, no home leave of absence—might have come to pass. Her fingers curl, barely containing the fury. "Any other evidence?"

Corwin shakes his head. "Nothing obvious. Just the body."

The victim's eyes are deep wells of black, the floodlights finding no purchase within. She stares into the void, unsure of what she'd expect. Bile percolates at the edge of her throat. To their killer, this man was just meat for whatever sick wants. Quietly, a fire ignites within her.

Then... she sees it.

At first, it glints impossibly distant within his eye socket—as if from six feet under. Faint blue whispers of something barely there and yet not. She leans in closer, inches apart. Evie's teeth clench as the glimmer intensifies. She squints in at it, unyielding, ice cold. *Is it staring back?*

In a shot, it springs.

Leaping the gap, like an electric arc, something preternatural crosses over. Her own vision flashes—a spark of ice blue. Evie recoils, pressing palms to her eyes. Somewhere behind them, she feels it burrow. A chill streaks through her mind and down her spine. It spreads, branches of unseen electricity, across her chest and down her limbs with unbelievable clarity.

The force pulses with terrifying purpose, as if delivered by the dead himself. Evie's pulse hammers against her temples, the icy torrent clashing with the heat of her blood, charging every nerve with chilling intensity. A ringing overtakes her ears, drowning out all sound but her own quickening heartbeat. Surely this is her guilt-ridden imagination, her emotions in mutiny against logic and science.

It can't be real.

Slowly, the muted voices of her team tunnel their way back to her. Their analysis and strategy are still ongoing. Elena offers, "I'll get to canvassing the homeless in our area. See if we can nail down who this guy was."

"No doubt, running down his prints will get us that faster," Marcus countered. "Corwin, shall I grab the kit?"

What!? Had they not noticed?

Evie rises, stumbles, nearly collapsing as her muscles struggle to pay heed. She braces against a nearby wall for support, her breathing shallow but steady.

"Evie?" Haden's voice pulls her back, tentative but expectant.

She straightens, burying what surely is some fantasized dread under her professionalism. "I'm fine," she replies, the word brittle. "Just fine." She resists the urge to press her fingers to her brow, where a faint throbbing cold persists.

Vaughn hovers, suspicion mingling with arrogance. "Sure about that?" His skepticism a thin veil for the challenge he is too eager to make.

"I said I'm fine." Evie's response firmer, her resolve solidifies. She's not about to share. Not with Marcus. Not worth letting it shake her.

Haden regards her. "Alright," he says, turning back to the others. "If you say so."

Evie swallows her knot of fear. Her hands steady. She tentatively returns to the body, refusing to let the other's sense anything amiss. Just a trick of her mind. Just the pressure, the stress, the horrible certainty of how close she is to blame.

She refocuses, vague accusation into committed certainty. A wave of energy fuels her. It calls to her need for order, bending the chaos into some semblance of results. How quickly could these things turn? Evie breathes deep, finding composure. She takes a moment before any of them have a chance to question. Then she engages, pushing back. `

"If this is a new player," Evie says, her voice regaining its edge, "we should consider all scenarios. Maybe it's someone who feels they need to finish what was started." She lets the strategy build. "Maybe they had an accomplice?"

Haden nods, taking her lead. "Sounds plausible. It could explain the activity. And these new details. But what's their motivation?"

Evie narrows her eyes, a thousand possibilities flashing by. "Unlikely they're collecting trophies; it's more like they're seeking something. But what? Why again? We dig in, and we find answers."

"Well, let's see how that plays out." Vaughn's confidence rings hollow.

"Be ready to eat those words," she fires back, turning to leave. Her vision's chill still lingers, as does a renewed purpose. If the Cartographer wants to taunt her, to set himself up again, then Evie will pick up the pieces—no matter the cost.

Chapter Eight

Answer the Call

It's late. While Quantico is never empty, the wee hours do maintain a very skeletal crew.

Evie feels him watching her, gauging her resolve against the shifting shadows. Haden's office light pulses with a steady, electric thrum—mirroring the tension between them. She can't help but scan the files spread across her boss's desk, each photo of the Cartographer's victims a failure to stop. Her mind traces the angles of their conversation before it begins, mapping the probabilities, anticipating moves to come.

Haden leans back, his chair creaking. "I want you on the team, Evie," he says, his voice both a command and a plea. The paternal note beneath the professional request cuts deeper than he could know. "You're our best at this."

Evie's gaze flickers to the picture of the vagrant, his hollow eyes meeting hers with their own unspoken question. She braces against the flood that threatens to overtake her, blue whispers still vivid in her mind. "I'm not so sure I am, sir," she replies. "Maybe I never was."

Haden meets her words with a pause, measuring their sincerity. "You've never been anything less than brilliant. No one else sees cases the way you do. Hell, anyone ever accuses you of being a savant?"

"Savant?" She laughs. "You mean reckless. We both know what happened." She swallows, the truth like shards in her throat. "Appears Barnett might not have been our Cartographer."

"You don't know that." Haden turns, side-eyeing her. "We've re-opened the files. Have been over them for days. Marcus closed that case because the puzzle pieces fit. The case was strong. It just seems we may not have had all the pieces."

Evie's fingers tap ever so slightly against the desk's edge. "I'm not ready," she says, her posture rigid, her words measured. She avoids Haden's searching gaze. Any deeper involvement might expose her past, her tampering. "This feels different," she adds. "I think even someone like Marcus knows it. I'm not sure I have it in me, not anymore."

Haden's eyes narrow, chewing on her admission. "I don't believe that for a moment," he says, his voice unwavering. "But if you're not ready to face it this way, let me know how you can. I'll take what you can give."

The offer pulls at something within her, the need to make it right, to unsay what's said. She exhales, her breath heavy. "Then allow me to assist, without being fully in. At least until..." she hesitates—until it's safer, until her secrets are assured, until that specter of exposure lies dormant.

Haden nods, a reluctant assent. "I hope you'll see it through all the way. I'm holding the space on our team should you change your mind."

The words cut deeper than he knows. Evie stands, forcing a smile. "You'll have my insights by morning, sir." She walks through the door, her footsteps echoing her confusion. Old loyalties press, still wanting these fragile new ones.

She straightens her jacket and takes deliberate steps toward the exit, passing the desk where she tossed the vagrant's crumpled note. Her gaze lingers on the bin as she rounds through the office, a silent acknowledgment of ignoring his plea.

Nearly out of the building, Evie pauses in the lobby. She presses her back against a wall and looks to the illuminated garage. A coolness trickles down the hairs on her back. It slinks along several vertebrae until fading across her skin. For a moment, she allows herself to consider the impossible—was tonight not just a projection of her guilt?

She shudders.

Evie pushes off the wall and steadies herself. She is the logical one. Her mind sorts through the day; her decision to stay on the periphery is probably best. She knows what she must do; her resolve will not be determined by urgency and whatever is gnawing at her.

Hand on the exit handle, her phone buzzes in her jacket.

> HADEN: Remember, you're not off the hook.
> Don't let it rest.

Evie thumbs a reply with the speed of someone who knows better.

> EVIE: I won't.

Thrusting out of the building, she strides past the rows of parking spaces. Evie gathers momentum, not about to give it rest, not about to let Vaughn, Haden, or herself impede her decision. The faint fumes of a day's work hang in the garage as she strides across the concrete toward her compact car. The palm of her clenched fist digs into her keys, resolving to follow wherever the evidence leads.

Whatever she felt back there in the alley, however illogical, it has become a taunt. A signal. The vagrant's wild eyes and outstretched hands tug at her memory. Ignore me and they'll find another way. He foretold something. Whether or not real, this became 'another way.'

She should have listened, should have known better. She will not lose more than she already has.

Chapter Nine

Tenuous Approach

A sense of stillness hangs in the morning air, as if her house braces for what Evie must uncover next. Her slippers pad on the hardwood floor. She places the divorce papers on the kitchen counter, allowing them to breathe like a decanted whiskey. They stare back like all the emptiness she refuses to name. A stack of unopened mail joins the papers. Unread, unprocessed, she leaves them as companions for later. There are more pressing matters, more important griefs. She's got less than two hours before Haden expects an update.

Then, squared against any uncertainty, she retrieves a warmed compress from the microwave and holds it to the back of her neck. She needs only a moment, long enough to dispel the chill.

Evie scans her home office; its organization clinical. She powers on the laptop, her hands warmed against the keys. A strange prickle teases her fingertips, shading urgency with doubt. She pushes that aside, like she does all feeling. Routine. Structure.

Chills will subside given time. Just give in. She notates the VINAP files Haden is expecting. They'll get delivered soon enough. Evie opens the CARTOGRAPHER folder, and another marked TRIALS. She burrows through the contents of each with mechanical efficiency. Her mind is an instrument of precision and detachment, threading one element to the next. She assembles the possibilities and then dismisses irrelevancies. Point, counterpoint. Facts and flaws.

There, yet not there.

Evie turns the possibilities over. Could there be an absent accomplice? If so, who? Whoever leveraged her, of course. She pauses to consider, words hanging in the air. Theories bleed into more theories. Time is short. She must get this right. Tie it off to something real.

Those five-year-old threads should have been enough to catch him. Why else would they steer her away? Was someone just toying with her? No, whoever they were, they went too far. That wasn't a game.

A cool tide surfaces within, then recedes. It flows with her breath, almost deliberate, affirming. Evie banishes the logic in that. Her screen fills with reports, scans, possible leads. She cross-references case notes, holding back a vague unease. There must be something there, somewhere. *Where are you hiding?*

The room stills, life outside fading into a quiet expanse. Her periphery shuts out the room's subtle drift of shadows. Focus, brushing it off. Still, the sensation clings. A faint digital flicker catches her eye, drawing her attention back to the laptop. She stares at it blankly for a moment, her fingers hovering over the keyboard.

It's way too early for fatigue.

Close your eyes, take a breath, and begin again. She complies, shutting out everything around her. Yet, drawing in a breath elicits a stir—something cold, foreign, something that wasn't there before.

Evie opens her eyes.

Her laptop—this laptop—is no longer an isle of structure. Chaos unfolds as old files flood the screen. They self-populate, sprawling like untamed weeds. Evie's eyes widen at her own connections, her own crime, consulting her from the past. These files pulse, unrelenting. Everything she has sought to keep buried. What the hell is going on?

Her breath catches, ice gripping her fingers. She knows she's alone, but the sensation is oppressive, something invasive, beyond rational. Her pulse quickens as she leans closer to the laptop, a moth to the flame.

A smear moves across Evie's screen, slipping from one victim's photograph to another. It enlarges stains on carpet—details overlooked. Digital manifestations highlight a sequence of muddy footprints leading from a window, something data-driven analysis failed to uncover. The temperature in the room drops noticeably. Evie's analytical mind races for rationales—a computer virus, a stress-induced hallucination, someone has hacked her system.

Each document shuffles its way to the forefront, a litany of guilt. There's no order in the emergence, no predictability. It takes a moment to register, a moment to accept the impossible: no. This is not random. Evie's heart pounds. She struggles to keep pace with the files as they shift, as if directed by unseen hands.

She glances down. Her hands! Frenetic tapping of keys, sharp gestures along the touchpad. She's doing this. No, that's not right. It's not — The idea takes hold, a thorn against her logic. She needs it gone; needs this intrusion to stop.

Seizing control, Evie slams the laptop shut and leaps to her feet.

The cold recedes.

Just my imagination. Just stress. There is comfort in the lie.

She reasserts herself, dragging her hands through her hair. She remembers that the coffee in the kitchen is still hot. That's what she needs. More caffeine.

In the time to pour a mug, Evie feels her pulse steady. She returns reluctantly to her office only to immediately part the curtains, allowing the in the cloudless day. Nothing strange awaits. No shadows, no flickers. The room is as it should be: deliberate, sterile, precise.

Her laptop is dull and blank, mirroring the darkened monitor's reflection.

Evie embraces the bitter aroma of her mug. Its warmth seeps into her fingers, bringing with it a heartiness needed to get things done. Rubbing the back of her neck, she finds her resolve. Her boss is waiting. The team is expecting. Evie is the one least expected to let anything go. Taking a breath, her logic claws its way back. She brushes the touchpad, then uses a strong finger to hold firm the power button. She'll find what she needs to put this case to rest.

But first, reboot into safe mode.

Nothing is going to get in her way.

Evie drops back into a familiar cadence, cataloging each scan, each report, until the anxiety settles into a hum at the base of her skull. Maybe this is just one more test of her reliability, she considers. Maybe it's her own tangle of guilt waiting for the next line of code to untangle it.

Whatever it takes. One way or another, she is going to bring their team a conviction.

Chapter Ten

Maybe

With her FBI reports submitted to the team, Evie can refocus on that oddity and begin again. She reopens her operating system's log files, convinced she'll find a rational explanation for the morning's unearthly bizarreness. Beyond all her expectations, the logs did turn out to be as they should be. Theories. Assumptions. Code and filters. Her calculations are all there, waiting with indifferent stoicism.

Each troubleshooter builds on another, her puzzle resolvers ever expanding.

There should be comfort in this. Order in the chaos. But the lack of logic in the morning's event weighs heavy. Cold, strange. A tiny knot forms in her stomach. Evie wonders if it could be a breach. Certainly felt like some sort of one. What was that? The flurry of wild photos, the way those pixels smeared.

Is this what madness feels like? What losing your grip means? She pushes the thought away, unwilling to entertain it. A final, desperate conclusion: it is the stress doing this; the long hours and pent-up anxiety are enough of a cause. Stress. Just stress.

She pinches the bridge of her nose and exhales.

Resigned but undeterred, Evie shifts her focus. She opens the JUN_1556 folder, the one that would always be June's—the one that never was. No logic, no patterns, no conclusions. Just loss. There at the top—a digital photograph suspends her breathing. The ponytail. Torturously familiar. She fixes her attention on it, dark strands that still haunt like her poor daughter's ghost. It curls in June's familiar way, with its red ribbon binding the evidence so tight.

Evie numbly taps at the keyboard. The details are nothing new. How this evidence always differed from the Cartographer's other victims. Speculation, too much of it. There were no other victims like hers. Nothing in their department could connect them back to. She knew her daughter was only leverage, the only victim without a body. The Cartographer's others were all adults, culled diversely. There was never hair left at the scene. Nor a knife, so unlike a surgeon's scalpel.

Evie ricochets through a thousand considerations. Who else would send the ponytail? What sort of someone would protect this monster, someone with greater reach? Someone with the power to dip into their lives, into her daughter's? She grips onto her facts, a lifeline tethering her to what's real versus what's not.

It had to be someone else. Perhaps... someone who cares?

Not for June, of course. But, is it so far beyond the pale to imagine another might harbor something for this Cartographer? The notion coils around her reasoning. It slithers along the sort of mind which might go to those lengths. Someone with knowledge of their department, able to steer outcomes through her.

A child only a mother could love.

"Ha!" Evie snorts, resting her head in her palm. "That'd be quite a mother."

No, it'll be something else. Someone keenly accustomed to leveraging others, getting their jollies at pulled strings. Considering the note, at the very least an appreciator of the arts—for orchestras.

Clean reasoning. That's what always carries her to the finish line and lands those convictions.

Why can't her husband see that?

Michael would argue against her. Maybe June is not dead. He's a doctor. He saw the evidence for himself. There wasn't enough blood on the bed. The timing's too perfect, too staged. Maybe it is the Cartographer passing himself off as someone else? Maybe we're not fated to know. Maybe...

No maybe.

Stab wounds don't always bleed heavily. The knife can act as a plug, sealing the wound and preventing blood from escaping. Especially true if the blade is deep and closes off major vessels. Victims can bleed out internally. Michael is a doctor. He also knows that. He just doesn't want to know.

He could never accept she was gone. Evie had to... had to in order to claw her way back. She rubs her temples; the memory leaves her drained.

"Maybe." Her voice mocks.

She leans back, eyes unfocused, trying to stave off exhaustion and doubt. Another restless night, another round of questions with no answers. She gropes for some certainty to hold on to, some fact to wrap around her mind. Each time she thinks she's close, it slips through her fingers. The laptop light blinks at her, as if to say, 'Still here. Still waiting.'

Evie closes the JUN_1556 folder. Surely there is a rational explanation for what's happening. Her laptop, her life, their daughter. The alternative: that she's losing her grip is too terrifying. Her fingers drum against the desk.

She stands, pacing the small room. Too much time alone. Too much time in her head. Her eyes land on the kitchen, on his decanted papers. A jury for her life. Judging, accusing. Maybe Michael is right; maybe she shouldn't have given up. At least then they could be together in desperation.

She forces herself back to the task at hand, back to the logical, back to the present. Theories. Assumptions. Code and filters. It's the only way she knows.

But connective strings tug behind her eyes, and she can't stop the pull. Evie fixates on a blank wall, its empty surface a temptation. She has always dealt in logic, in the calculated precision of data and outcomes. But this—this crime is different. This is something she never lets herself fully consider: a conspiracy not of evidence but of people.

If it works for Marcus and the Haden...

Spurred by impulse, she moves. Evie prints photos and reports she has already. Pins and tacks become her new allies. She creates a map of the unknown, a network of everything uncertain. The wall becomes a mess, a madness, an unexpected cooling comfort. Lines of red twine connect the impossible, winding and intersecting like veins. Notes scrawled by her own hand take on an erratic constellation.

"Why protect a serial killer?" one asks.

"Who silenced them all these years?" says another.

"What's the connection to June?" taunts a third.

She takes a step back, evaluating her creation. Her eyes move from note to note, thread to thread. There's a rawness to it, a haunting imperfection which she can't ignore. Chaotic questions leap out, each a challenge to her neatly ordered world.

Evie feels a thrill, a fear, a pulse of something chilling. She allows herself to consider—no, to truly believe—there might be more than she's let herself see. The thought is intoxicating, terrifying. It takes root.

She returns to her desk, her mind a flurry.

Conspiracies such as these are a testament of a mind unraveling. They become physical manifestations of wild thoughts, of her fears. As she stares at the map, something within begins to fray.

"Find the evidence. Make your case, Evie." Her voice drops to a whisper. "There has to be something." But even as she says it, the logic eludes.

She returns to run fingers along the threads, the papers, the pins, as if touching them will anchor her. Her knuckles are cold; the room colder. She backs off; the walls becoming close, rebounding off her doubts. Too much to process, too much to bear.

Taking uncertain steps back, an easiness slides over her shoulders, cooling strained muscles. What makes her think the world is just chaos and certainty? Maybe there is something more. The notion presses back at her logic, giving her distance—breathing room. But if not evidence, then?

Drawing a long inhale, Evie collapses back into her chair.

She'll find answers when she's ready. Just maybe not tonight.

Chapter Eleven

Waking Dreams

Her dreamscapes grip with a gnawing intensity, refusing to let go.

Clawing out of sleep, she finds herself cold, sweat-soaked. The room slowly rounds itself over, as if the world is recalibrating. Evie swallows, her throat dry, her mind tangled in the same relentless loop—June, the Cartographer, the impossible weight of what she's done. It's a conspiracy of guilt. The digital evidence. Lives spent.

Through a haze of half-consciousness, she navigates through the darkened house, down the stairs, toward the kitchen. Her fingers flick on the light, and she squints against its intrusion. This early morning hour isn't ready for the living yet. There's still hours of sleep to be had.

Evie grabs the compress from earlier in the night; its warmth is long since gone. She holds it against her neck, a feeble attempt to relieve her tension. The microwave hums as she reheats it. It ticks. She counts the seconds until it beeps.

The ache is stubborn, lingering. An unearthly chill from earlier? Her delusional grasp. She pushes past it, opens the fridge in search of something stronger than a compress. Her hand hovers over the milk, orange juice. Her eyes land on a squirrelled-away beer in the door,

Michael's brand. It sits among the single food portions, a remnant of his presence.

It might as well be a ghost itself.

She hesitates; the sight of it fixating. Evie's fingers wrap around the bottle, gently lifting it from its door cradle. The coolness seeps into her hand, a contrast to the warmth of the compress. She waits, savoring the bottle until condensation beads on its surface. A droplet trails down, tracing the length of her wrist. Evie can't help but cradle the beer like something fragile, something rare.

This is what she needs. Her eyes flit around the kitchen, scanning the drawers in need of their old opener.

When she finds it, a smile threatens to form. The opener—firm, familiar—like him. She presses it against the bottle's cap. A gentle click, a muted hiss. The aroma of hops rises, a comfort that is instant and bittersweet.

She closes her eyes. A wish his affections were still there, his warmth a counterpoint to the void manifested since their loss. There was a time when they would laugh, his hand reaching for hers, the space between them nonexistent.

On the table, the divorce papers linger. She turns away, clinging to her fantasy. This beer is an indulgence, one Evie is more than ready to allow. Her first sips go down smooth and fast—her fantasy now both inside and out. It is more than a token gesture. Logic backs her up! Beer. What better way to get back to sleep?

Turning from the kitchen, Evie clicks off the light.

The house is a patchwork of shadows, every object an echo of how it used to be. Each furnishing and rug is known all too well. She traces a familiar path through the rooms, navigating without light, a shade of herself drifting through the spaces they once shared.

Her eyes adjust slowly to the dark, the grayness of various shapes: end tables, bookshelves, the love seat he used to read on, curtains allowing in the moonlight. Her car in the drive...

...and the silhouetted figure standing alongside—staring.

Startled, she drops the bottle.

It hits the flooring with a wooden thunk, the sound distantly rolling beneath her. Heart pounding, Evie is not about to take her eyes off. The woman stands there, backlit by the streetlight, unmoving. A gently breeze flows through her dress, playing against her legs. She can't see her face, much less her eyes. But there's no mistaking that posture, that angle. *She's looking right at me.*

Cold liquid seeps under her toes. *Damn.* The beer.

Evie stoops to snatch up the still-emptying bottle, the smell of hops turning her appointed living room into a brewery. She'll need a towel.

Glancing back up, she does a double-take. Her Ford Fiesta is alone now, holding down the drive. The figure—no longer there.

What? Oh, hell no. I am not losing my—

Evie rushes to the window, pressing herself against the glass, breath fogging her view. Frenetic eyes dart in both directions. There—a silhouette moves under the streetlight, a pale shadow in the dark. Her heart leaps to her throat. The figure crosses a neighbor's yard, passing behind a cluster of bushes. Evie notices it now, the awkwardness of her barefoot steps, the struggle.

She pulls back, hand to her mouth. Her pulse ramps up like quicksilver. This is too real, too solid. It can't be a dream. This is someone in trouble.

Sitting the bottle on a table, Evie bolts through her living room. She yanks the door open—the night air bracing her body. She hesitates. The absurdity of herself in nothing but a thin nightgown is just a flicker of doubt.

But not enough to stop her.

She runs out across the lawn, her voice piercing the stillness. The figure is distant now but clear.

"Wait! Miss, are you okay?"

The suddenness of her own desperation surprises her.

The figure slows, flinching to a stop. Evie's heart hammers with an impossible hope. It is not like her to lose herself, to be so unguarded. She is logical, precise, always in control. But this—

Entering her neighbor's yard, Evie calls out, "Do you need help?"

The figure turns achingly slow. Recognition hits Evie like a flash. A visage from days ago, one she'd not forget. White hospital sheet. Metal table. That woman now stands before her, dreamlike, pale, with those hollow eyes. The depths of those sockets stare out at Evie, an imploring sea of darkness. Her cheeks are lifeless—her face ashen and unmistakable.

The victim.

The Jane Doe from the recent autopsy.

It can't be.

Momentum carries Evie forward across the lawn, her eyes go wide, mouth gaping. The dead woman nods back at her, the motion deliberate and slow. Yes. She raises her hand, a wad of paper outstretched.

Skidding on wet dew, the ground gives way under Evie. Her bare feet come out from under her as she gasps backward. Wetness seeps through her nightgown, a shiver rippling across her skin. She winces, eyes pinched tight against a graceless landing.

A moment to steady herself—to find her breath.

When she looks up, the yard is empty.

Evie's pulse thunders in her ears, the night air sharp against her cheeks. Her body is heavy and damp; her disbelief heavier. She struggles to her feet, craning to see—anyone, anywhere.

But there's nothing.

Her breath streams out, a chilled mist condensing and then vanishing. Evie's hands shake, cradling her ribs as she wraps an arm around herself. The pad of her neighbor's yard is soft beneath her weight. She is alone in the dark, and this is all too real.

Whatever this is; apparition, some memory, her past—the dead. It wants her.

Evie shudders, clutching her body, sucking in the cold. "This is happening. This is really..." she rasps, the words an exhale of dread.

She backs up to the sidewalk, stumbling with the weight of it all. The raw cold finds every nerve, chilling her resolve. A premonition pulses through her, electric and foreboding. She staggers her way back to the house, her thoughts a jumble.

Closing the door behind her, Evie slumps against its wooden interior.

The dead want something, something only she can give.

Can this really be happening?

Chapter Twelve

Gut Punch

The stream of warmth running down her back is oddly unsettling.

Under the bathroom shower, Evie still finds the damp sensation doesn't relieve her chills. It winds around her, reminding her of something lurking. Her thoughts circle the impossibility of the night before. The dreamlike encounter with that dead, stalking... What, delusion? She felt the ground beneath her, the wetness of her fall, felt it all.

A ghost. That was a ghost. The word is outrageous, but the woman haunting her invades her memory, filling her with a dread she can't shake.

This wasn't just a flicker on her laptop, not just some silhouetted hallucination. That was the victim, the one from the morgue, as alive as anyone could be without eyes.

Evie has always been the logical one, always the rationalist. But now—the visions, the words of that vagrant, the cold pinpricks against her brain—they are pieces of a puzzle that defy everything she knows. That homeless man, the other victim, he said, 'They follow. They know!'

The water washes over her body, slick and determined. She lets it flow past her shoulders, down her arms.

That wad of paper. She snaps back to the woman's outstretched hand. It was reaching toward her, toward Evie. There was no escaping that message. She knew exactly what that meant. It's been so many days.

Maybe it's not too late?

Evie dresses with care, her movements more deliberate and steady than her thoughts. Navy slacks, white blouse, black trench. She secures her hair in a bun, each strand controlled, a contrast to whatever disorder remained looming. It's far from the shock of last night, but that still taunts her every motion. Before leaving, she slips the Glock onto her hip, a tangible reminder that the world is solid, not just flickering shadows.

The drive to Quantico is overcast, mirroring her uncertainty. Her car's heater presses back the chill as she navigates the familiar route.

Quantico's building is half asleep, lights flicker to a life not quite awake. It is both welcoming and condemning. The parking lot is dotted with the first of the day's arrivals, agents trickling in. Evie steps out of the car and straightens her jacket. The air is crisp against her. She braces herself, unsure of what she will find. Is it hope or something else?

It's early enough that Security greets her with an upward nod, a polite but curious acknowledgment: the prodigal agent returns. Her name lingers in their eyes, the question of how long she'll stay unspoken.

None of that matters.

Right now, she needs to know if there is any meaning.

Evie heads to her old desk. Sure, it's a long shot, but one worth trying. Her vacant cubicle betrays no sign of life; no photos, no files. A barren framework of an agent who once was. Her pulse builds with her stride. What reason would they have to check her space? She's never there. The building janitors would have emptied all the other trash cans. But maybe they'd not bothered with spaces scarcely used, with ghosts of employees.

Evie stops over the bin to peer down.

Crazy hunches are Michael's thing, not hers.

There it sits, crumpled—alone. Hesitant fingers slowly crane it up out of its hollow. Her nostrils flare as Evie controls her breathing. Would it be rational to expect anything of this? Resting it on her desktop, Evie's fingers begin to press and smooth. Each rumple flattens under her weight.

One side, a patchwork of paper creases and stark blankness. She flips it over. There's a faded letterhead above letters scrawled out, pencil lead scritches staring back up at her.

'Perfectly Unfinished'

Her pulse turns to a cold thrum.

Those words. June's words. What were they doing there?

The wreck of her logic crashes against the impossibility. It was on her daughter's mirror. There is no way this vagrant could have known. These words cut deeper than any scalpel, leaving her raw and exposed. It is a dread Evie cannot shake, a twist of both certainty and horror.

She can't breathe. Her vision tightens.

Evie's mind spirals through the chaos; a compulsion to silence the doubts overtakes her. He knew. How could he? She broke every rule. She gave in. Was this what she deserved?

This can't be it! It can't be all there is. No.

Her voice is thin. "Not yet." The words push against the void, to herself, to the dead who mock, who know more than she does.

Evie snatches up the note, leaving her vacant desk. Her movements are determined with a new conviction. She cannot accept that it's too late. Not this time. She forces herself to absorb what logic can't, what her own resolve couldn't, something she might've never have found.

Cutting through the office, she draws the attention of early arrivers. Her presence itself is a strange anomaly. Evie doesn't care. Her pulse drives her. She veers from their path, avoiding the stairs to Haden's office. This isn't a time for permission and oversight. To hell with what they think. There's more for her to find. There's his personal effects collected from the body.

Evie heads down a corridor, certainty biting at her heels.

If he had this, if he knew, then there must be more.

She has to know. Evie won't lose this chance. The note is a weapon. A call to arms. A big screw you from beyond.

Flashing her lanyard, Evie signs for evidence release. The room is cold concrete, metal shelving lined with too many tragedies. She finds the vagrant's box, lifts it with a hefty tug, and moves to an empty table. Underneath is a faint whiff of an old timer's cologne—a warm and inviting aroma in the otherwise sterile environment.

Then SSA Haden entered.

"Evie?" His voice is a calming echo in this hard place. "You're the early bird. Have you come up with something? Need a hand?"

She shakes her head, her focus unspooling the ties on the box.

"Noticed your car in the lot," he says, throwing a thumb over his shoulder. "Glad to see you jumping in," he adds, waiting for a response.

Evie glances up, the weight of unspoken expectations hanging between them. "Something caught my attention," she says, keeping her tone measured. "Nothing solid yet, but I have... something. Not sure I'd call it a lead."

Haden nods. "Okay. Well, keep me posted, Agent." Thankfully, he leaves her to the job.

Evie rifles through the contents; snack wrappers, pan-handled coins, papers, random and scribbled, spill out across the table. Her heart races. She snatches one note, then another, unfurling each. Each addresses another victim, another crime. Each scrap, every scrawl is an impossible, forlorn message of loss, just like June's.

They know. They follow.

Her mind ignites with possibility. The room feels alive with presence, the whisper of lost souls bearing down. She gathers everything, her resolve more solid than it's been in years.

Evie grasps the note with June's words. Its presence is a taunt, a cruelty. The temperature drops, like a breath from the other side. She flinches at the familiar chill, at the sense it conveys. Her wrist feels the grip of something unseen, a tightening insistence she can't ignore. This time, the force is stronger, more determined. It wraps around her, squeezing, conjoined with her. Refusing to let go. Yes. We are not letting go this time.

It's what she needs.

Evie closes her eyes, surrendering to the certainty pulsing through her. She allows it to flow, to seep into every doubt, until it becomes a part of her own will. A perverse sense of direction fills her with purpose. She breathes through the chill, opens her eyes, and looks at the papers scattered before her.

They know, and now she will too.

She clutches the note.

The ghost of a smile peeks out. "Alright, then." She exhales. "Let's see where this takes us."

Evie departs the evidence room, her heart pounding. She feels it driving her, this force, this presence. Her pace quickens as she exits the building. Haden and the others probably wouldn't understand, but she is going to damn well try to. She's going to more than she dares admit. This is a lead like nothing she's ever had before.

Chapter Thirteen

Other Natural

From the kitchen, she stares intently at her landline. A cliché—a musical refrain plays in her head. She knows who to call, and it's not supernatural pest control.

Evie returns the phone back to its cradle, disconnecting before the call can even begin. Her mind follows a familiar thread, leading her to where she doesn't want to go. Ohio. It is the gravity of a God-fearing upbringing. Her voice would crack with confession. They'll say she needs to find her faith. They'll tell her she's strayed. Evie runs her fingers through her hair, undoing her bun. Her parents believe in angels and demons, in a world that her logic has always dissected and dismissed.

But maybe they'd be right.

Maybe it is something so outside her framework, so far-reaching that it's what she has left.

The phone stares back, unblinking.

She could call, could risk their judgment if it means another way forward. Before she ventures into wherever, whatever this is, she needs a solid footing—a foundation to start from. Steadying herself, she reaches for the only explanation she knows they'll offer. Their voices already echo in her mind, a chorus of warnings and scriptures. These elements are all too familiar, given the dark places her career path leads. Her father's stern belief, her mother's quiet concern. They never tire of being certain. Her fingers hesitate, but she doesn't. In one motion, she dials.

A single ring. Then two.

Her father booms with immediate recognition. "Evie? That you?"

"Yeah, Dad. It's me."

"Finally," he replies, his voice a righteous echo of knowing. "Your mother and I are happy to hear from you. Thought you'd be too busy. Thought you'd be—"

"It's never too late to call my folks," she interrupts. "Just been a lot to manage."

"How are you holding up, Evie?" Dad asks. "We've been praying. And praying. And praying. Even for Michael, why he's giving up, I'll—"

"Dad," Evie cuts back. "You know I'm trying. Neither of us is ready to call it over. He..." she hesitates, careful with the words. "He even came by the other night. We talked."

"Talked? Well, that's something," says her father, earnestness reaching across the line. "Was it about you getting back together, or was it more of his nonsense? The minute you let this become final, he's going to regret it. I guarantee."

Evie pauses, her thoughts a tangle. "He did say it's all he needs from me now. Those papers. Signed."

"Then don't." His certainty rises. It is almost a challenge. "You've always been the smart one, dear."

Her mother's voice cuts in from the other line, gentler but with its own force. "Honey, you know your father's right. We worry about you so much. We were getting ready to call if we hadn't heard from you by tonight."

"I know, Mom. I know."

"So tell us then, what's really going on? You sound… not like yourself," she presses. "Are you doing alright? We can come out and see you if you need."

Evie swallows, measuring her reply. "I'm doing okay," she begins, the build of logic before emotion. "Just been reassessing things. Getting a clearer understanding."

Her father reverberates back. "If that means you're taking this time to get right, I say it's about time! We've been worried about how your work could come between. It's not like that's ever happened before."

This chorus was all too familiar. "No," she says, "it's not about work. It's about—something else I can't quite explain."

"Try us, dear," said her mother. "Understanding is what parents are for."

Evie exhales. "I've been seeing… signs."

"Signs?" her father blurts. "What sort of signs?"

Her mother takes a more tentative tone. "You mean higher signs?"

Running her fingers through her hair, Evie let it settle. "Maybe." She falters, then rebuilds her logic. "Maybe it's something trying to tell me what I've missed."

"What Michael has missed, you mean." His rebuke is harsh, insistent. "Evie, when will he learn? I don't think he's ever understood."

Her mother chimed back, softer but no less sure. "You're made of stronger stuff, honey. We've always known."

Rolling her eyes, Evie moves on. "It's something else. Hard to say what. Just feels… I don't know, outside myself. Like I'm being guided. Pushed."

"Finally," her father says, relief mingling with his righteousness. "You're coming around. What have we said all along?"

This was all it took, this shift in language. A divine reference. She had them in a safe space.

"Take these signs as a blessing, dear. Take them as—"

"I am, I am," Evie cuts off. "I'm just not sure I understand what they mean yet."

"It's a start," Dad replies. "You'll get there. See it as a turn for the better."

Her mother intervenes with a mix of caution and encouragement. "Evie, this change, is it what you need? Does it feel fulfilling?"

Now it was Evie's turn to be cautious. She didn't have to share the rest. Didn't have to say it all. Is her silence more telling than her words?

"Higher signs are never wrong, honey," her father goes on. "Maybe what you've been through isn't either. He works in mysterious ways, as we all know. Could be guiding you back. You'll see."

Keep it together. Don't get swept up.

"Listen to your mother, dear," says her father. "Be sure you're on the right track this time."

Her mother's concern slips just under his. "Evie, I know your spirit. If this is something you're unsure about... Well, don't stray so far that you lose yourself."

"I'm trying not to."

"You need to be careful, honey. Don't be misled," Mom replies.

Evie presses the phone to her ear. "I don't think I'm losing it. It's hard to explain," she insists, her voice cracking. "This feeling... It's real."

"Then you welcome it. You go to church," Dad says. "You find a pastor or a priest, someone who will give you guidance. That's where you start, not just with a call."

Her mother breaks in again. "Where else can you go to get right? You need to know what you're dealing with."

"I thought I'd start by talking to you. By letting you know."

Dad rides over his wife. "You know what to do. You've always known. You'll see the bigger plan, and then he'll be the one calling you."

"She wasn't talking about Michael, dear," added her mother. "You just take care of yourself. You go there, and you'll find suitable answers."

Evie's resolve holds steady. "You just might be right. Will do. Love you. Love you both."

Evie hangs up, her mind echoing with their words. Her mother is so sure, so certain. Their voices linger as she slips into her coat. The morning is gray, the sky a sheet of indifference. The suburbs slip by as she navigates her way through town. Her heater's warmth is more than physical—a comfort, a release.

The turnoff feels like it's too soon, just off the main highway.

She parks in the back, out of view of the parish office. Her parents would be thrilled to know she's following their advice, so pleased to welcome her 'back.' Cool detachment wraps around her, embracing her objectivity. Evie is unsure she's ready to share her desperation, how quickly she's falling into the very mindset she once mocked.

St. Francis of Assisi Church rises solemnly, its brick and stone facade cresting the hilltop. She hesitates, watching as the faithful come and go, their movements certain. Her parents would have called this holy ground. To Evie, it's simply an unknown.

A data point from which to start.

The door reverberates against the interior silence as she enters. Light filters through stained glass, casting fractured shapes across the pews. Evie stands awkwardly, her presence a disruption to the quiet. She steps lightly as she moves past rows of carved wood, eyes scanning for some form of authority. This feels exposed; such an open, hard place which lets too much in. She catches sight of a stooped figure lighting candles on the far side, his movements deliberate and slow. He pauses, then turns, sensing her.

The priest is older, kindly looking. There is a comfort in Evie's approach, as though he could recognize her unbelief. She summons the courage and feigns confidence. His eyes widen as she stops short.

"Father," Evie starts, breaths uneven. "I wonder if you might hear me out. I'm not really part of the—" She gestures around the church, looking past her own doubt. "—the congregation, but... I don't know where else to go."

The priest nods with patient warmth. "Of course, my dear. Ask, and I'll do my best to help."

Evie searches for words that won't betray her, revealing only enough. "I'm not even sure how to say this. It's strange." She shifts on her feet. Then, finding her hand in her pocket, she withdraws and flashes her badge. Honest, yet so unlike herself. "I'm a federal agent. Just sharing that for context. I'm here on my own time. Someone I'm close to has been seeing things. And... it seems it might be... Oh, hell. I'll go ahead and say it. Spirits. Something not of this world."

The priest's eyes steady on her, not with the harsh judgment she expects, but merely a tempered invitation to go on.

"These spirits seem to push for something," Evie says. "Pushing them. To take action."

The priest takes a moment before answering. "And your friend, have they invited these spirits?"

Evie considers, careful. "They're not entirely sure what they've done. But there are reasons. They may have borne false witness once. But, for a good cause. For something they thought would protect. Now, it seems to come back at them."

"Ah," he says, nodding as if seeing this a hundred times before. "Even if it was to protect, was it the moral choice? Denying the truth hardly ever lands on a just side."

"It's hard to say." Evie pinches the bridge of her nose. "Their intent—it wasn't to hurt anyone. It was a hope of saving someone in return for turning a blind eye. They've been living with the consequences ever since. With the guilt. Now, someone may have died as a result."

"Then perhaps making amends is the right path," he offers gently. "An act of honest contrition. You see, as for spirits... I'm afraid the church views ghost tales as superstition. In even rarer instances, as demonic tricks. Heh... I hope your friend is not one to resort to seances or other such practices."

"The Bureau is more objective than that," Evie says. "Besides, these phenomena seem more like a question of faith."

The priest smiles. "Confession may certainly help, even for the most logical. But if your friend is not ready to turn to the church..."

"Can you think of historical cases where this... Where ghosts were involved?" Evie presses, her words cautious. "Academically speaking."

His brow furrows, considering. "I have heard old rumors of souls believed to revisit, especially those whose lives ended violently."

"Like?"

The priest pauses, his voice lowering in reverence. "There were tales from the Spanish Inquisition. During some of the more brutal years, many innocents were lost to awful conversion methods. Some who inflicted these methods claimed sanctuary against spirits who returned to testify, chasing those inquisitors responsible."

Evie assembles a framework. "So history… might repeat?"

"Perhaps," the priest says. "Are you investigating an inquisition underway?"

"Possibly, of a type. We're not as superstitious at the Bureau though," she replies. "Doesn't mean I'm not… they're not worried." She wavers as her logic searches for footing. "What if they can't make amends?"

Candlelight glints off the priest's eyes. "Purgatory is a space for souls that have not fully embraced the divine. They reside in a place in-between to achieve that goal. I sometimes wonder. What happens to those who cannot find grace? When Purgatory is not enough. If what you say is true. If your friend cannot make amends… then perhaps we are dealing with something more. Perhaps a harbinger of things denied."

His words send a chill through her.

His voice falls to a low murmur in the vast space. "If enough souls bear witness, say in a genocide, part of me wishes they might become something more. Then, perhaps your friend should tread carefully. They may become a focus. But of course, such a thing would be an extreme, to say the least."

"What could I do?" she asks, fear creeping in.

He offers a measured nod. "Take refuge in God. Take shelter in what you've dismissed. That is the best advice I can give. Otherwise, your friend risks being overwhelmed."

Evie tenses, absorbing the implication. She knows it firsthand.

Reaching into his robe, the priest pulls out a set of beads. "Do you know the rosary?" he says, placing them in her hands. "You can look it up on Google. It's a little involved, but powerful when appreciated. Wherever your friend is, whatever their struggle."

Evie accepts, fingers fumbling slightly.

"Wronged beliefs can be relentless. Your friend should find strength beyond themselves. Sometimes the answer lies closer than we think," the priest adds. His gaze shifts to her hand, noting its ring. "What does your husband think?"

Evie recoils inwardly. Her mind is a cacophony of guilt and desperation. She slides the rosary into her pocket; its presence is some comfort.

Chapter Fourteen

Two Paths

The Tidewater Grill is a blur of clattering dishes, waitstaff maneuvering around the lunch rush like choreographed dancers. Their table is small; it would be intimate under different circumstances. But today, there is a chasm, wide and unrelenting. Evie traces a crack in the table with her finger. Michael watches her, with a mixture of hope and resignation hanging over the unsaid.

"I don't know if I have much of an appetite today." Evie settled the napkin across her lap, gauging Michael's pleasant demeanor. "Shall we cut to the chase?"

He shifts in his seat. "We're here because... I thought you were reconsidering." He glances at her left hand, the ring she couldn't bring herself to leave behind.

"Maybe I signed them already," Evie says. Her words not quite a lie.

Michael's jaw tightens. He's not about to let it go. "Then we can move forward?" he asks. "We can sell?"

The waitress appears, her presence a pause in their tension. "What can I get you folks to drink?"

"Coffee," Evie says.

Michael's voice is thin. "Vodka. Cranberry."

Evie's brow raises. "Is that needed?"

The waitress shifts, uncertain whether to stay or go. Michael waves her off. Likely glad to be out of that situation.

"Would you rather I didn't? We just keep going in limbo?" Michael asks defensively but hollow. His eyes meet hers, searching.

Evie says, "You scolded me for giving up before."

He shakes his head. "On us or on your cases?"

"You tell me." Her retort lodges between her heart and throat.

"I can't keep waiting, Evie. I can't keep pretending." He echoes those words, the same ones that sent her reeling the last time they spoke. He leans forward, earnest. "I need to know where you are."

"I don't think you know where you are."

The waitress returns with their drinks, her tentative smile met with grim faces. Evie wraps her fingers around the coffee cup, its warmth a comfort she doesn't feel. Michael stares at the vodka, at the way its red hue refracts. He doesn't touch it.

"I'm right here. Trying to hold on," Michael says, raw and exposed. "Trying to get through to you. I won't let June go like you have."

"Damn you." The accusation slams into her. "That is still your wish fulfillment talking. I'm being realistic here. One of us has to be." She catches the irony of the last few days, of what is realistic anymore. "I'm pursuing things on my end. Just not like you would have me do."

"I've heard that before," he says with an edge. "Your Director's odds. But what was it? Half of all killers go free?"

Evie glares at him over the coffee cup. She hadn't expected this.

He presses, "Thought being out there again would remind you. Even the best investigations come up empty. They never solve these things as well as you think. So you tell me, Evie. Would getting 100% make us better? Would it make us whole?"

She flinches, and for a moment, she has no reply.

Michael doesn't let up. "Would it bring her back?"

The last question cuts through her. It's exactly what she's afraid to ask herself.

"You've always had faith in the numbers," he presses. "I used to have faith in you."

Evie's voice is small, defensive. "I haven't stopped having faith. Not in the way that should matter."

"Then prove it," Michael says. "To both of us."

"How?"

"You know how." His tone softer now. A mix of challenge and plea, yearning and accusation.

Evie remains silent, the weight of his demand hanging between them. Her fingers drum against the coffee cup. This is the Michael she fell for, the one who refused to let anything go. His conviction and his certainty. It's the Michael she can't bear to lose.

He waits, with nothing but the hum of the crowded restaurant filling in the time it takes for Evie to gather herself. Her lips part, a protest rising, but Michael cuts her off. "You're holding out, haunting all these cases. The way you're chasing this one—it's the same as always."

"Are you calling me a ghost?!"

"I'm saying you never stopped being one. You never stopped drifting. I'm saying you're not really here until you're ready to see it through. Giving up on June is as good as giving up on us."

His words echo the priest's, a dismissal of all she now believes. She widens her eyes at him, a flash of anger, of bewilderment. "You don't get it, do you?"

"Then help me get it. Why keep holding on to unrelated cases? Why not focus where you're really needed?"

"I'm not letting anything go," she says, voice brittle. "I'm really starting to think you're the one—"

"Running?" he interrupts. "I know. You've told me. I've heard it a thousand times. But guess what, Evie. We're both running. And we're both going nowhere."

She looks down at her hands, at how unsteady they are. He's right in a way she can't explain. He's right, and it stings. She takes a breath, trying to find the words. "I'm making progress."

"Where? On your cases or with June?"

"With everything," she insists, but her voice wavers. "This isn't how you think it is, Michael."

"Then help me. Help me understand. Or are you waiting for the first 100% closure report before you let me in on it?"

He knows how to hit her where it hurts, how to unearth truths she won't admit. "There's always a chance. We might still—" She stops herself, her own lack of certainty crushing.

He reaches for his drink, bringing it to his lips. His hand is steadier than hers. "Hope is a dangerous thing, Evie. Now we're both saying it."

They lapse into silence, each trying to anticipate the other's next move. Michael sets the vodka glass back down, but he doesn't let go.

"Maybe it's all I've got," her voice trails off.

"Maybe it is," he replies. "And maybe that's why it's still not working." Michael's eyes bore into hers, holding her gaze with gentle determination. "Evie, I need more than a percentage. I need to see you. I need to know we're on the same page."

"And if we're not?"

He leans back, a shadow crossing his face. "Then you're right. I don't know where I am."

A heaviness settles between them. He turns slightly in his seat, looking past the crowded restaurant, past the noise, as if searching for something that's not there. Evie watches, a stir of anger and helplessness. She's turning over his words, an emerging idea taking root.

"If that's the case," she says, "maybe there's more than one way to find out." Evie carries a note of resolve. One where she's about to see where it leads.

Michael takes a sip.

Evie reaches, her hand slipping onto his.

He pulls back, the motion sharp, eyes guarded. His expression shifts, a crack in his guarded facade. He stands abruptly, tosses a ten and a five on the table, leaving his drink half finished.

"Think about it," he says. "Think about what you really want."

Evie nods, but he's already moving, weaving his way through the crowded tables and out the door. She watches him disappear, her heart vainly following. She is going to follow this lead. There's just no way of knowing where it will lead. And Evie is not about to risk what's left of her family doing it.

This is on her.

Chapter Fifteen

Venturing In

It isn't much of a drive back from the Tidewater Grill. Evie tells herself she's better off putting her efforts where they're better served.

She settles in with another mug of coffee, already threading the lines of what logic can unravel. This is where her talents are strongest. And she clearly once got close to catching the Cartographer before. Now, she just needs to retrace those possibilities. Reviewing the coroner's report, what new physical evidence links back to him?

Certainly it is a him. Beyond the obvious majority of serial killers being male, this one would require strength enough to haul bodies around and discard them. Then there's the escalation in the crime, going from partial tissue removal to a need for more challenging outcomes.

Much of that asserts as male.

But apart from that, what does this killer need specifically: surgical implements, conditions to perform these acts, medications or anesthesia to incapacitate? Given the precision of the cuts, might a sterile environment be desired?

Both the Bureau and DEA tightly control and monitor hospital medical supplies. No signs back then or now of missing or altered manifests. Yet, all these things, and likely more, would still be required. Thus, what's needed is a dive into the dark web: discreet shipments, the very equipment needed to carve open a skull and extract minds from within. Her fingers itch to cover this old ground, to sketch out the pathways that will lead her back.

Evie's laptop bathes her in blue light, a glow that cools her logic. It's only a matter of finding a package and following it to either its source or destination. One would point to the other. Even dead drops can be tracked, depending on how far she's willing to go. Muscle memory guides her fingers, each keystroke inching deeper into the digital depths.

A specialized search on the dark web.

Evie's mind spins the code, an algorithm to match her conviction. She recalls the details: The Cartographer used equipment far beyond reach. Burr holes and clean separations. Might have been all it took to lead to a single thread, one left unguarded? If she could find that again.

A sudden chill creeps into Evie's resolve.

What if—

What happened before? Remember that? Those risks are very real. She's already lost June. Could it trigger something just as bad—or worse? Evie stares at the screen, a glaring reminder of what she stands to lose. Michael. The team. Her mind.

She won't make that mistake again.

A deep breath, a steeled gut. Not this time. She'll launch her search from the West Coast. A new account, shrouded and deep-faked. Evie brings up a VPN, hiding her tracks, positioning the search out of Seattle.

The process is familiar, almost comforting in its mechanics as she encodes a bot of her own, specific in its logic. This time, no complicated layers. This time, it looks for overseas specialists; logically in medically sensitive deliveries, a smarter algorithm that covers and masks its inquiries.

If she was getting close, then she'll get closer. It's just a matter of time before the results come in.

She lets the systems do the heavy lifting, her own mind a parallel processor of scattered thoughts. The rosary. The priest. How far is she really willing to go?

How far gone she already is.

The last several days have unhinged her more than she cares to admit. Everything was to be so precise, so careful. Now she's allowing this thing to take root, to pull her strings.

Evie clenches her jaw, shutting out the phantom cold.

She will not let this consume her. Not with some call-of-the-dead driving her forward. They want this. They both need this? Then they're doing it her way. Find the evidence. Make the case.

Her logical mind seeks a pattern, a way to make sense of the senseless, a way to repurpose this inner hunger. Perhaps her parents and the priest weren't so wrong, even if faith was never in her code. Who knows? Perhaps an act of contrition might make this all go away.

Okay, but not before she puts it to good use.

Her mug is half empty, its heat dissipating as her patience wears. Evie waits, monitoring the sweep of her bot in the web, wide and consuming. She allows her mind to wander: the vagrant alley, the body, the arc of ice blue. Start from there. Her logic is in the director's chair. Break the task into manageable pieces.

"Is that what you want?" she says aloud, the house swallowing her voice. "To get under my skin?"

Expecting no answer, she continues.

"Whatever you are, we're going to have to work together. So, let's list out the possibilities. Number one: a disembodied presence capable of subjecting its host to strings of jump scares in order to make a point. *Thanks for that.* Number two: an entity that can exert influence even at the cost of my sanity. Which is pretty friggin' thin already. Number three: some supernatural force that is going to cost me everything if I don't act on your wants. How am I doing so far?"

Evie's words hang in the empty room.

Silence.

She steadies herself, undeterred.

"Number four," she says, "are you a force that isn't as capable as it thinks? A spirit unable to grasp the concept of compromise?"

Evie feels the chill like a breath on her skin. Her fingers wander into her pocket, looping around the string of beads.

"Here's another possibility for you," she dares. "What if I still refuse to play along?"

Silence—her only response.

The laptop screen glares at her, a stark reminder of how long she's been at this. Hours?

Looping the rosary around her wrist, Evie switches gears. She calls up a browser and starts her search; ghost stories from the dark ages, disembodied spirits, paranormal obsessions. Anything that might have a loose connection to her ordeal. All the accounts are overwhelming in number. Each page, each result is a rabbit hole of fanciful lurkers and grim fairy tales. They bleed one into the next. Haunting. Possession. Poltergeist. But not a whisper of something of credence. She leans back, her eyes blurring as she scans. The hopelessness of it seems nothing more than a time suck.

Her logical mind refuses to accept that there's no pattern here. Of course there is. She just hasn't found it. The cold prick of the unknown tantalizes her. Her breathing shallows, the laptop a faint glow that mirrors her own uncertainty.

She pushes with all that she has against both the creeping dread and the possibility that this is meaningless. She will find a way. Just not like this. Maybe there's another approach.

One she hasn't tried.

If she lacks the spiritual vocabulary, maybe she's searching with the wrong terms. Evie types with a new resolve.

'Rituals for contacting the dead.'

The results flood in, a patchwork of ancient rites and modern-day follies. She scrolls, her mouth set as a thin line. New Age. Druidic. Wiccan. Each claiming a path to the other side, each more bizarre than the last. Evie clicks through them, her skepticism warring with desperation.

'Old and powerful,' she reads something druidic. 'Must be performed in the absence of restrictive garments. Do not fear; embrace the unknown.' Hitting print, she snatches up the output paper. It's a simple dance step. Can be performed in a small space.

Evie shakes her head. "What the hell," she mutters. It's not like anyone will see.

Shutting the laptop with grim determination, she stands—visible tension in her slight frame. She will not let the dead have their say, not unless she's the one dictating terms. There must be a way to bend this to her will. A way to make sense of the disorder, to bring it under her control.

She stalks to the bedroom, her quietness gathering momentum. An idea takes hold, absurd in its conception. Evie prepares herself. Retreating to her bedroom, she closes the curtains, and stands before the mirror. Her reflection is a mix of disbelief, determination, and self-deprecation.

Evie's humility pushes in its reluctance, but loses out all the same. She sets lit candles in a circle, their little flames like grasping hands. She knows she might be losing it, but the 'what if' is more than she can bear?

Okay. Here goes nothing. Her blouse lands on her bed, then the rest. She inhales deeply, ready to begin. The beads settling against her wrist, draws back her attention. *Yes. Almost forgot.* Unspooling the rosary, she reaches out to set it on her dresser.

The room shifts. A distinct and icy presence surges inside her.

From the periphery, her mirror image glares out at her. That reflection—a gaunt, skull-like visage with hollow cavities for eyes. She gasps; the force of it electrifying.

Startled, she snatches back the beads, the air thick with panic.

In a flash, the visage recedes, leaving only her reflection, her own wide eyes. Evie's heart pounds in her ears as that gaunt figure sears itself into her mind. She clutches the rosary, its beads tight, biting into her skin. Could this simple act ward off the thing inside her? She's not sure. But the thought wraps around her, a thin and fleeting comfort.

She scrambles for her clothes, the ritual abandoned. Disbelief colors her cheeks. The beads remain looped around her wrist as she dresses, extinguishes the candles, then bolts from the room.

Chapter Sixteen

Reflections

Evie stands in her kitchen, a crucible of doubt and determination. The blackness of her coffee stares back at her, its warmth a more soothing reflection. She sips, looking for the bitterness to drown her terror and buoy her spirit. Her body feels lighter, but her mind bears the weight of so many questions. What the hell is she doing? Can she control this? Will she be enough?

Pressing forward, she sets the cup down, its clatter against the table an uncertain jolt to her wavering resolve. Still, her logic crystallizes: knowledge is power. She has a new data point, but it's still not enough. She'll need more.

Willing her limbs to move, she turns back toward those answers. Evie steadies herself as she takes to the stairs again. June's door looms before her, a silent witness to her doubt. She affords herself a moment, then strides past it, choosing a more dangerous confrontation.

The mirror beckons through her open door, the surface smooth and unyielding. Mustering herself, she marches up to it. "Do you really need this?" Evie shoves down her inner tremble, regaining a flicker of her deeper strength. "Am I really all you've got?"

Her reflection looks back, unchanged.

"Fine," she says, more to the room than to herself. "If that's what it takes." Evie knows the absurdity, the lengths she's willing to go. But she also knows this is beyond reason, beyond the methodical world she's held onto. She steels herself, ready to confront the impossible.

The bedroom looms silent, a waiting void. Evie swallows hard. Her logic tells her this is madness, but that logic hasn't served her well. Not lately. Her hands are steady as she moves to unbutton her blouse.

This is stupid.

It can't really be about... She purses her lips and glares back at her mirror image. This is not about rituals, is it? At least not in that hokey sense. This is more than a physical exposure. It's a surrender.

Bracing herself, she unwinds the rosary.

"What do you want from me?"

Evie waits, her breathing shallow with expectation. She is not the kind to give up, never has been. But her grip of uncertainty is tighter than she allows herself to admit. She remains motionless, a statue of determination.

Nothing.

"Where are you?" Her chest rises, defiance swelling. "I know you're there. I know you want this. Are you going to let this 95-pound broad intimidate you?" The reflection merely mocks back, paper-thin against the weight of all she dares to think.

For a moment, it feels so useless. For a moment, her belief must have been wrong. She's not close enough. Perhaps she's being played—abandoned. Nothing new.

For a moment, she believes.

But then—

The prickling sensation slowly winds its way up her spine, that familiar chill tightens in her chest. Evie tenses. Her skin crawls. There it is, surging outward, pushing back. It's happening, and she is both terrified and relieved. It is icy and invasive, a whisper from beyond the grave.

She steadies herself, reaching for the dresser's edge. The rosary rests just inches away. No. This is what she's asked for. Time to go for it.

Returning her gaze to the mirror, that skull-like apparition glares back at her, its hollow eyes a sea of darkness. It seethes, vacant and indifferent. Resisting the urge to flinch, she dares to stand firm against its void-like stare. The air crackles with a hushed intensity. Her mind races as the cold gnaws at her will.

"I'm not afraid to—"

—but the bravado curdles on her tongue. Her pulse hammers, a sudden spike that pierces her ribs and wrenches her head. Everything slows as the apparition's pupils bloom like twin voids. The world narrows to a pinpoint; her face bloodless in the glass. Its arm erupts from the surface, outstretched and flayed to bone and tendon.

Impossibly cold fingers seize her forehead. She arches with the electricity of it.

And the world contracts.

Evie's mind explodes into a conflagration: flames, screams. They blister her consciousness with a relentless barrage of atrocities. A young boy clutches at his mother, his face a mask of terror as they are swept up in a tide of bodies. Soldiers advance with cold precision, their rifles indifferent to the death they unleash.

The vision shifts.

Homes collapse under a hail of shellfire. Cries piercing the air are snuffed in a plume of flame and smoke. Evie feels their pain, every sound a shard of ice in her heart. She struggles to push back, but the horror is unyielding.

Another flash.

A village consumed in a brutal culling of machetes and bullets. The acrid reek of bodies smoldering is too much. People run with nowhere to hide, their dying agonizingly not swift. Evie's heart pounds a rapid staccato; breathing all but gone.

Thousands of souls. Millions.

A force as old as hate itself.

She gasps against the onslaught, each vision a testament to humanity's darkest. The weight of it crushes her logic, leaving her raw. She is exposed to the seething anger of an entire history's remembrance. This is more than lost souls. More than a single killer. It's an awareness formed from disregard and faithlessness. Vastness she can barely comprehend coursing through her veins.

A Harbinger.

Evie reels, her psyche battered with images of the unyielding, the unforgiving. Of what it has become. She releases a cry, primal and desperate, and collapses to her knees. Her vision blurs with tears, everything a kaleidoscope of despair and fury.

The mirror's surface shimmers, its reality twisting as if the world itself is bending to break her.

No.

She will not break.

Evie's hands fly out in defiance, clutching for the mirror. Her voice rises, raw and unrefined, the words a guttural plea. "Enough!"

A crack splits the air as it arcs across the mirror.

A moment of stillness as it teeters over, then lands with a shatter. Glass fragments burst outward, glittering like shards of her fractured certainty. The cold recedes with a suddenness that leaves her heaving, gasping for air, desperate for purchase. Pulling the rosary from the dresser, Evie crumbles to the floor, beads pressed to her trembling chest.

The room swirls around her, a haze of broken reflections and shattered resolve. She lies on the carpet, the impact of what she's seen, what she's felt, a heavy residue. The chill within her ebbs but doesn't fade entirely.

She remains motionless, attempting to piece herself together.

It wants more than she thought.

This Harbinger.

She climbs to her feet; the rosary falling to her side. Her breath is shallow, but it is her own.

Evie leaves the bedroom, wrapping the beads around her hand, and pauses at June's door. She hovers there in its silence, a reminder of why. Of what she's willing to do. Clutching the handle, she steels herself and opens it.

A coldness flares within her, the haunting chill now a seething ember, igniting her determination. She gasps at the intensity, her limbs electric with new strength.

Evie closes her eyes, and she sees it. The vision, the power. She sees it in some full, terrifying scope. This Harbinger of unforgivable pain. Of vengeful torment. It is a manifestation of all that has been denied. It is strong. More than will, it is vengeance personified.

It can give her what she needs.

Whoever took June... wherever they are... they haven't a chance in hell.

She breathes through the rush, through the vastness and the fear. Her hesitancy fades, but not entirely. Logic calls her back like a distant echo. She lets out a breath, steadying.

Look what it has shown already! Look how quickly!

Evie shudders, disbelief and determination mingling in her mind. She draws a deep breath.

And embraces it.

The beads press against her palm. She squeezes them tight, shutting out everything but what this force can provide. Its presence surges through her like a revelation, potent and consuming.

A fusion.

Evie will not lose herself. She will bring it to heal, not let it take her, not without giving something back.

The cold mixes with her pulse, and Evie sways. She staggers back to the doorframe, reeling from the force within, from her own defiance. Her vision spins. She holds herself upright, but barely.

"You want this?" she whispers to herself, to what dwells within.

Then show me.

Guide me.

The hallway shrinks, her vision closing in.

Her thoughts stagger. Then fades to...

...black.

Chapter Seventeen

Returning to the Scene

The night is wide and unrelenting, a chasm that swallows Evie whole as she maneuvers through the dark. The sparse streets are a maze, a desolate path leading her back to the alley. Where better to begin? Let's see what this force can do. She steps out of her car with measured resolve, her breath white tufts in the November air. The sound of her shoes on asphalt seems so loud.

Haden's old text haunts her: "Homeless male. You will recognize him." Those small data points settle with her as insufficient. That man tried. We didn't listen. She pushes forward, catching herself at the memory of the vagrant's wild eyes, his stark clarity. The dead know.

They need me to.

A pulse urges her onward. Evie feels its icy hand in hers, pulling her to follow around the back of the convenience store. She half-closes her eyes, letting the chill guide.

Is this how it's going to be?

She emerges from the street, turning down the alley where he was found. Yellow tape remains, flapping gently on a breeze. She ducks under it, her footsteps on the damp pavement. The floodlights are gone, with only moonlight illuminating the scene. This is where he was discarded, a victim of no further use.

Evie's pulse skips a beat, her intuition raw and exposed.

What if this is a trap?

What if it's a gift she can't accept?

The air is dense, a blanket of fog that clings to her. She hesitates, pulling at her doubt. An unseen outstretched hand, a silent plea. It won't be in vain. Steeling herself, she feels again for the rosary in her jacket pocket.

A distant glimmer catches her eye.

There.

At first, it seems a trick of the light, a phantom dancing on the edges of perception. Fleeting and faint, a shimmer plays with her vision, toying with her. Dim shadows and imagined shapes seem to move through the woods at the far end of the alley. Is it something, or is it nothing? The shifting blur catches her, teetering between real and not. She feels a jolt. No mistaking, there it is. A figure emerges from the treeline. It comes on slow and silent, an echo of someone. He seems more moonlight than physical. Her heart quickens, but she doesn't move. She stares, unblinking.

Breathe, Evie. You asked for this.

He just stands there, a faint beacon on a wooded verge. Gossamer tangles weave through his beard, empty eye sockets seeing nothing. Vacant, but expecting. She steps closer, her motion hesitant but determined. The same chill envelops, the same pull as before. But this time, she does not flinch.

Is this it?

The moment is a whisper, a thin breath between hope and fear. Evie cannot help but feel a burgeoning sadness as she closes the gap. Where was her compassion when he needed it? When he was living. Her fingertips flit around the rosary, confirming her life preserver is within reach. She wills herself forward, voice barely more than a tremor.

"What do you want?"

The vagrant's ghost stands silent. Is there even anything to share anymore? Can he? She forces another step. Evie settles on a bead to squeeze between finger and thumb.

"What do you want me to see?"

The air crackles with possibility. His specter remains, its presence unwavering. Several yards between, but narrowing. Her fear begins to thaw. Maybe all she needs to do is reach out, connect. Surrender to this possibility, like before. So close now. Evie withdraws her hand from her jacket pocket, extending to reach out.

His head tilts ever so slightly, moonlight glancing off the hollows. Her spine shivers. Then he appears to mimic her move, pulling from his own pocket... a wrinkle of paper. Its edges waver, translucent as a memory.

Evie stares at it. The paper is as she remembers; she is sure of it—the note from her office bin. It's the same texture and size. Her fingers hesitate against it, unsteady. The vagrant's form shifts but holds. This is his message. A last attempt to reach her. Her last chance to listen.

She takes the note. It unfolds before her, glimpsing the momentary letterhead: Riverbend Manor. Then, like the surrounding fog, it fades through her fingertips into nothingness.

Something slides through her, white heat and cold.

He will not rest. They won't.

She staggers back, propping herself against a tree. It is all she can do to contain herself. The night air floods in, returning her breath.

As she tightens her grip, there's a scrunch of wooden fibers. Evie glances to her hold, at the spectral extensions rising from her fingers. The bark is now marred as if by a large bestial claw. That's when she senses the surge flowing through her. A violent energy, a force she can barely name. It is a wave which flows with intensity and then recedes, leaving a tantalizing void in its wake.

Resonance.

Her heart pounds. The magnitude of what she felt... *Oh my gawd.* She can use this! Evie grips the tree again, willing for it to return. The flow washes back—vivid power. The tree quakes, bark splintering under her squeeze. She withdraws a few steps, astonished, breathless.

Is this her solution? What she's been seeking?

Her breath is visible, ragged. The night seems less daunting, less cold. The implications pulse through her. This actually feels more alive than she has in years, a vigor both unnerving and exhilarating.

"Riverbend Manor," the name slips from her lips with a nod.

She repeats it, letting it etch into her memory. This is what the vagrant wants her to find. Her mind spins with the possibilities, with the enormity of all of this. She was right to follow, right to listen.

The evidence she needs is within reach.

Evie looks back.

The woods stand dark now. The trees loom like tall shadows in a dim suburb. His specter having apparently returned to haunt them. This time, however, it is not alone. The night is full of presence, of power. Evie feels it coursing from all around.

The force follows her, a chilling companion as she exits the alley. Her movements are rapid, purposeful. This time she will not be afraid, not of ghosts or of herself. Evie pauses, hands trembling from adrenaline. She lets the magnitude of it sharpen her resolve. Riverbend Manor. This is proof she can't ignore, and she is going to find more.

Her view tips back, taking in not so much the roil of the overcast night above, as the incredible implications. What if each crime left a trace, a haunted presence capable of speaking to her? What if every whisper of evidence was just that—a whisper, the dead's plea she hear them?

Evie races to her car, the night a blur of cold clarity.

She knows where to begin.

Chapter Eighteen

The Lead

Evie slouches into the driver's seat, fingers still chilled by the evening air. She doesn't know what to expect when she enters 'Riverbend Manor' into the search bar, but she can't wait to find out. It appears as the first result, glaring up at her from the phone. She taps the map icon, loading its GPS data: less than an hour away, a simple route across the bridge and then south.

Her mind hums with excitement. She allows herself a small grin. If this is really how it works, she thinks, I might actually have a chance! Considering the magnitude of possibilities, she snaps the phone into its cradle and eases out of the alley.

Fog drapes itself among the trees, thickening as Evie weaves along the winding Virginia roads. It slides along the car with every passing mile. Riverbend Manor—what does it mean? She wonders what the vagrant intends for her to find, what the dead are beckoning her to do.

The car's warmth strains against the night's chill. Her focus flickers between the road and the phone. She steals a glance at the clock: 11:17 PM. The facility probably won't be open to the public at this hour. But who knows? If she times it right, she might be able to slip in during a shift change.

A handful of vehicles dot the parking lot. Evie winds her way around the side, far from the entrance, engine ticking in the silence. She studies the building, its brick facade looming against the dark sky. It looks worn, forgotten by time and funds. With the withdrawal of her keys, she slides out and quietly shuts the Fiesta's door.

Around the building's rear, a service door stands propped open with a towel—a breach she hadn't expected. Judging by the spent cigarette butts in the bushes, the reason becomes readily apparent.

She hesitates at the threshold. The weight of what she's doing settles over her—trespassing here could cost her more than she's willing to pay. The Bureau wouldn't just reprimand her; they'd launch an investigation. She can already see Vaughn's smirk as they pull her badge.

And yet...

She moves inside to the dull hum of fluorescents and antiseptic assaulting her senses. At the hall's far end, a woman in scrubs hovers before a rolling workstation. She's absorbed by the pods in her ears. After a few taps on a digital screen, the nurse rolls off and around the corner.

A sigh escapes her lips, and she presses on. She isn't about to let this lead go, even if she doesn't know what she's looking for.

Evie traverses the dim hall, the overhead lights indifferent to her presence. The span stretches, sterile but stagnant, doors flanking on both sides. The place seems comatose; a waystation for the forgotten. The glow of an Exit sign beckons to her, while another corridor stretches into shadows.

She stands still, the pressure of time and decision building.

Then something takes her hand: an impossible sensation, cooled like the dead. Her bones tense at its touch.

A gentle tug pulls Evie forward, down the shadowed passageway. She moves past empty rooms, beds stripped bare. Some contain patients; in one she thinks she hears a faint sob. A November breeze blows outside, making the walls creak with the gusts.

With every step, her urgency grows—a longing to connect, to know.

Her other hand confirms the rosary in her pocket as she is led around another corner. Evie drifts through the facility, hugging the walls and willing herself to be as unseen as her guide. The lobby opens ahead, and tired voices banter as she draws nearer. She listens.

"Night, Doc," calls an orderly.

Polished shoes make a soft tap as this doctor walks purposeful strides toward the exit. The man is tall with a lean but capable build. A clean, crisp white lab coat covers his dark blue scrubs. He releases a sigh as he waves back to the orderly. Soft leather-gloved hands pull a stocking cap over his head.

The outside fog mingles shadow and vapor against the vestibule. Vague wisps coalesce, drawing Evie's attention. Faded locks of auburn, gaunt cheeks, blue eyes—moonlight giving rise to a specter waiting. Standing out there. The ghost of a woman stares up at the doctor as he opens the first door.

This ghost trembles, a quake of soundless rage.

And Evie feels it: Hate.

The specter fixes on the man. He passes through the vestibule, his calm a contrast to the fury trailing his steps. Her haunting face pivots, empty of anything other than to watch him just walk away. Her mists swirl as she rounds herself back over, returning to look back into the lobby. To look back at her...

...at Evie.

Go on—her expression seems to say.

Evie's logic battles a rush of adrenaline. It's not like she can just walk after him. She'd be exposed! Her career. Her plan. Her family.

Everything. Her body tenses with indecision. Creaking hinges of a chair, the orderly relaxes back grabbing a magazine. The outer door slowly swings shut. Moments slip by.

Now, Evie.

She hears an engine turnover.

Her mind is too conflicted; the need too great. This desire too strong for her caution. Evie draws a breath, a curse, a resolve, and then she bolts after him.

"Hey!" The orderly looms up as he stands from behind the lobby desk. "Who the hell are you?"

She darts past, flinging herself through the vestibule.

Evie plows forward, breathing hard. She reaches for the rosary and looks around. The sound of wheels on asphalt turns to her right. A gray SUV makes its turn from the driveway and pulls off down the road. The doctor is gone. She glances back. The ghost—gone.

She eyes the orderly reaching for a phone through the window, a quick calculation.

The night air closes around Evie. They haven't made her yet. It's not too late. She ducks, moving in low arcs through the lot, reaching her own car.

Evie fumbles the keys into the ignition and fires the engine. The dashboard blooms to life. Tires screech. Gravel kicks. She heads back to the main road and glances in the rearview.

It's still clear; nothing but fog catches her blur.

Yet, something stirs in that reflection. Unseen but there, simmering. More than anger—disappointment. She was this close. She had him in her sights. Her grip tightens on the wheel, her knuckles whitening under the tension. Was that a miscalculation? Certainly not. That was being driven; whatever this being is, it is clearly impulsive. No, not going to make that mistake! She has no proof, nothing to connect this doctor to the killings.

But she is getting closer.

No envelopes. No letters. No threats. The evidence, the lead—it's hers. The dead know! This doctor must be the Cartographer, and she is not about to let him slip away. She picks up speed; the hunt consuming her. Logic grips hold of these events, shifting immediacy to align better with strategy. There's no need to chase after that vehicle, not when she has what she needs.

She takes a breath, aware of this Harbinger's intent.

This is the new plan. Her plan. This time, Evie will follow wherever it takes her.

Chapter Nineteen

Uninvited Guest

Evie sits before her laptop, morning sunlight streaming through the living room windows. Golden hues bathe the room in warmth. Files and cases are distributed neatly on the screen. She pours over them, about the only thing she pours today. The coffee she abandoned two hours ago sits idle on her desk, its heat long since dissipated. The surface collects a film, with Evie too immersed to notice.

Too focused, too consumed to allow any shadows of the past to distract her.

She searches and disseminates. No errors.

Riverbend's service records are a tangle. They're not terribly thorough and tend to bleed together, almost an intentional mess. But then, this isn't the first time she's run into misleading datasets. She untangles them as if lives depended on it. Her lips thin to a line, knowing at some point soon... someone will.

Evie narrows it down: three names.

Dr. Ignacio Flores, Dr. Victor Shepherd, Dr. Simon Fielder.

Many doctors have consulted or rotated through this Manor over the last five years, their expertise spread out over several facilities. They do a tour and then move on. Yet these three were posted most recently.

Shepherd and Flores are neurosurgeons. Fielder a researcher in behavioral science. Her fingers fly, commands intuitive and precise. She digs, she burrows, she mines into their past—her excavation deep and thorough.

But something else feels closer than it should be. She ignores that sensation, keeping at it. Public records. Lawsuits. Anything she can grab, everything she might have been restricted from before.

A soft knock at her door threatens to snap her out.

She's so close. Evie knows this.

Her eyes dart to the clock. 9:24 AM. Michael? Could he have...

Another knock, its tone familiar but unwelcome.

Evie selects everything across her screen, archiving the records, securing the data, and saving the files. Rising from the desk, she absently brushes against the rosary in her pocket. The phantom lingering from the night prior dissipates.

It's anything but cold outside. The morning is already warm, the sun dazzling as she opens the door. His slick mustache and broad shoulders fill the entrance.

Her voice falls flat. "Marcus."

He wears that cocky grin, the smile of someone who knows exactly how unexpected he is. "Eve," he replies, his tone both familiar and formal. "Mind if I come in?"

Her eyes narrow. "This isn't a good time."

Marcus leans against the doorframe, jovial enough. Is this his idea of being charming? "I was in the neighborhood. Thought I'd pop by to make sure you're doing okay."

"Why wouldn't I be?"

"One never knows." His grin widens.

Evie hesitates, weighing the awkwardness of the circumstance, then steps aside. He crosses the threshold with an air of ownership, taking in the repurposed living room. His gaze passes across her conspiracy wall art, following the threads, photos, and notes. Pivoting, Marcus settles next to her desktop, everything squared and neat.

"Well, when you leave," his voice drips with faux concern, "you certainly do take your work with you."

She doesn't respond, the air between them thick.

Marcus plucks a case folder from her desk. "Nice to see you've got a system," he comments, flipping it back into place. "Thought you were considering giving up the gig."

"Thought you'd catch on by now," she counters. "I don't give up."

"Yeah. No kidding. Your new algorithms have turned heads. At the very least, catching faces. Almost borders on 'Big Brother.' Can't say it's not impressive."

Evie watches, guarded. "It's not just impressive," she bites back. "It's effective."

"Is that right?" Marcus moves toward the abandoned coffee, lifts it, inspects, and sets it down. "Sure it's not going to waste?" he jeers.

She frowns, flashing her annoyance. "Was working fine up until now."

He shrugs. "You have a thing for cold cases, Eve. Am I right?"

Evie folds her arms. There is nothing clever in his technique. An interrogation? Really?? "Seems like more than my well-being is on your mind."

Marcus's grin fades to a more serious look. He reaches into his bag, pulling out a packet. "You could say that."

"What's this?"

"Thought you'd be interested in this little development." He opens the packet, laying a series of photos on the table. They're grainy and dim, but unmistakable.

Evie's midnight visit to the crime scene.

She catches herself for a split second, then recovers, keeping her voice steady. "What's this supposed to prove?"

Marcus eyes her. "You tell me."

"You want to imply something or just cut to the chase?"

"Despite not being part of my team, looks like you can't keep away."

She narrows her gaze, refusing to let him see any sign of weakness. "I can explain—"

His smirk returns, triumphant. It is the look of someone who believes he holds the upper hand. "Don't need to. You're not the only one who can track data," he says. "I've been setting motion-triggered cams with facial recognition software. One of your old tricks. Thought it'd be smarter than hanging around, staking out all night."

"So you just happened to catch me at an old scene?"

"Your algorithm," he says. "I knew someone couldn't resist. Just didn't expect it'd be you."

Evie shifts her stance, defiance simmering beneath the surface. "Oh please, now what? *I'm the killer?* C'mon, Marcus. You can't be serious. I'm not involved."

"Is that so?"

"Off the books, we're supposed to be working together. Not chasing wild geese. While I'm not a team member, I'm certainly not a lead."

Marcus leans closer, assessing, seeking cracks in her resolve. "Yeah. Not on my team, hmm? The boss says you turned him down. Not involved... *Really?* Yet, you go back to a crime scene. Funny how that works."

A familiar anger rises within her, one not felt since their last encounter. "You know me, Marcus," her voice cuts through the air. "I am thorough."

He lifts a brow, feigning consideration. "Sure. Thorough," he says, letting the sarcasm hang. He gathers the photos, sliding them back into the packet. "Find anything that interests me?"

"Find anything that makes you think... what?" Evie retorts.

He taps the packet. "Only that you might be at it again."

She stiffens. "I told you. I'm not—"

"Oh, I believe you. Not involved at all. Just happened to be on site." He watches for a reaction. Her mouth tight, posture rigid.

"Maybe you're not a suspect," he continues. "Maybe instead you've got a guilty conscience." He needles, a slow burn. "Does this mean I should reopen the old Barnett files? Wouldn't be the first time a case you previously handled had an air about it."

Her hands clench. "I should have expected this."

"Yeah," Marcus agrees. "You should've."

Evie glares, a cold fury. "If you don't want my help, then what are you doing here?"

Marcus shrugs. "Thought I'd be civil. Away from others. You know, extend the olive branch."

"How very thoughtful."

"Didn't want you taking it personally when we solve the case without you."

Evie steadies herself. "That's what you're worried about? Someone else taking the credit?"

"What I'm worried about is you mucking up another investigation." He turns to leave, his eyes catching something on the kitchen counter.

Her divorce papers.

"Looks like you've been keeping occupied in more ways than one." There's a slight sneer in his voice. "Maybe it's not just work getting under your skin."

Evie tenses, her jaw set, refusing to give him the satisfaction.

Marcus throws open the door. "Why don't you get your own house in order before screwing around with mine?"

The words hang as he exits, a final jab.

She slams the door, his musk lingering. Her mind races, the unexpected confrontation shaking her more than she lets show. He knows she's onto something, that she's not about to let this rest. The divorce papers glare back at her, like all the emptiness she refuses to face. She moves past them, past the hollow she's left herself. Evie returns to the laptop, her fingers a blur against the keys.

Shepherd or Flores—that's what it has to be.

She targets her search, more determined, more furious. Marcus' visit proves what she's afraid of. She can't be this exposed, not when they're watching her every move. She can't risk it again. Not unless she's certain.

Evie takes a breath, steadying herself. Sure. Marcus may have spotted her in the alley, but he mentioned nothing about Riverbend Manor. So then, there's no way he can know where she's going next.

She will find him before they do.

Chapter Twenty

B&E

S he sets her focus on the singularity of purpose: find evidence, build a case.

Evie pivots back to her laptop. Firing up a cursor-bright document, she fills it with all the data sets she has collected on the two remaining suspects. Qualifications: world-class. Colleagues: almost all speak to their genius. There's a stiffness to her inputs.

Brilliance can be deceiving.

Shepherd. Flores.

The names stare back at her, daring her to make accusations.

Sliding aside her ego, she opts for a more objective solution. All she needs to do is craft a request which combines both challenge and precision. The best is required, brilliance that will measure up to the intellect of surgeons. The sort that can cut through layers of encryption like a scalpel through tissue. It must seem detached, just another client looking for answers, another search easily dismissed should suspicious eyes notice. Those eyes cannot lead back to her.

A third-party solution.

They call themselves Ethos. And they will be that tool. CtrlZ, RootMuse, HeapMonk are hackers who get results, and are not interested in trophies. This white-hat group has worked well in the past—respected and known for their skill, but their services come with a hefty price tag. She'll expense it later, likely spread out over a few quarters.

Evie drafts her request, each word careful, calculated. They will dig into both suspects and provide just the facts. She proofreads the message as she finishes; they know her—what she's lost. Ethos will never reveal her hand. She's sure of it. Then, she hits send.

With that underway, now all she needs do is wait.

Evie shifts in her chair, granting herself a brief respite. She runs a hand over her face, a blend of weariness and relief washing over her. As the hours drag on, the room grows dimmer, shadows stretching across the walls. With nothing but her thoughts for company, she revisits old memories and contemplates probable outcomes. By the time the sun kisses the horizon, painting the sky in hues of orange and pink, a want stirs within—a compelling need to do something.

She just can't stand there.

Somewhere out there is evidence to be found. It's the only means she can recover a piece of herself. Evie stares at the pending digital evidence folder, determined to fill it with what she's lost. The hacker group is good. They'll find both doctor's imprints, any unseen trail she couldn't reach, and do it without risk. It's only a matter of time now.

It's just the waiting.

Knowing she's close, so very close, itches at her. Evie rises, still needing to make use of the interim space between those answers. There are other traces, other ways. The online search is not the only source of answers. What other ground goes unexhumed? What else lies in wait for her to discover?

She moves through the house, eyes scanning the quiet.

The rosary dangles on her wrist. She squeezes the beads, then releases. In the silence, Evie settles on an idea. A somewhat cooling possibility. She really shouldn't, but thus far straying from doing things by-the-book has paid off.

A certainty builds. Evie reaches for her jacket and gloves, then finds her keys. She knows both what to do and that she shouldn't. But it's another way to the truth, another chance to uncover what's been missed. Her mind toggles between Shepherd, Flores. Shepherd, Flores.

She'll pick one and see for herself.

Shepherd.

His name resonates as the immorality of her plan flares. She pushes the thought aside—it's a just risk. Think of a possible victim spared. Isn't that worth it? Her resolve tightens. Their marriage, her family, June. It's all she needs to feel this sure. She heads out the door, casting off shadows of doubt behind her.

Not this time.

The evening air is brittle; leaves skitter and spiral across the driveway. Evie presses the accelerator with a purpose that matches the roads; each turn sharper than it should be, each mile bringing her closer to the wrongs which will be righted.

'Shepherd & Associates' the sign reads with an aloof austerity. It's an older building, bordering on historic. So, not likely to be festooned with the latest security tech. She'll start here, then Flores next. Evie pulls over on the street across from the parking lot, watching and waiting. Her mind runs over the steps, the sequence of events that brought her here. Is she running out of time? Has she already lost control? Her determination is cold, assured.

From the building's glass entrance: motion.

An elderly woman, head down, exits and locks the doors. She shuffles to her car without looking up. Evie waits. She watches until the woman drives off, headlights winking into the distance, leaving the lot dark and vacant.

Now.

Evie snugs on her gloves and raises her gray scarf to her face. She moves quickly, exiting the car. The sound of her footsteps a soft crunch in the empty lot. She hesitates at the glass doors. This is wrong. She shouldn't even—

There are no wires or sensors around the doorjamb. Reaching into her jacket, she pulls a set of slender tools. The familiarity disquiets her—how easily she resorts to this. Evie's sensibilities fall away with each stage of her deft touch. Her fingers, nimble and precise, manipulate the tension wrench and pick from countless hours of practice. The first pin resists momentarily before clicking into place. Her second has a subtle give as it aligns perfectly. The third is stubborn, but her steady hand coaxes it into compliance. One by one, the pins fall, each yielding with a distinctive click, until the deadbolt retracts smoothly.

A small shudder runs through her. It almost feels like she is meant to be here—as if the world is complicit in her scheme. Her mind latches onto Shepherd's name, justifying this reckless invasion as necessary, as just. It's not a crime; it's an answer. The sound of the door clicks with a sharpness that momentarily stills her.

Then she's in.

Stepping through, she shuts the door behind and resets the latch. A rush of adrenaline drowns out any echo of trespass, heightening her cause.

Minimal lighting spills a faint glow into the hallway, softening against the modern glass partitions. Evie moves with caution, scanning for any signs of security measures. It's not as sterile as the nursing home, but it's just as cold. These offices are sparse, minimal, designed for efficiency, not comfort.

Across from this good doctor's office, Evie finds rows of filing cabinets lining the corridor. Not exactly copy/paste details to be gleaned and taken back. It is a rather antiquated way of keeping patient profiles. But who knows? She can at least search for previous victim names. If one is here, it'll be an ideal start. All she needs is a single crack in the armor—a slip, an error. Proof.

Her hand grips the cabinet handle. She pulls. Locked.

Of course.

A faint rattling of the picks fills the air. She takes a breath. Nervous much?

Simpler than the front door, this lock gives way. Evie rummages through the files, the names and dates blurring past. She needs this. She needs this to work.

Maley, Milham, Mitchells... Nope. No Miles. That rules out that victim. What next? Donaldson? The names are familiar; her lists of the dead flip by. Everything is in place except for them. She swallows. Okay, possibly not Dr. Shepherd. Still, be thorough; keep looking. There's always Flores next.

Her phone vibrates.

She freezes, a curse just under her breath.

Unlikely Ethos, but then they're hackers. Expect the unexpected. She checks the ID, and it is anything but. She crosses a line here as well.

Michael.

Evie hesitates, willing it to go to voicemail, but the buzz keeps on. She takes a moment, a breath, and then answers.

"Evie?" Michael's voice from the other end. "I couldn't sleep. Figured you'd be up."

She repositions the phone, pressing it tight to keep her breathing low. "What's up?" she asks. "I'm just... working as usual."

"Huh," a note of suspicion. "Financial crimes got you burning the midnight oil?"

She juggles the phone, making sure she's got room in her effort to twist out a manila folder. "Not exactly," Evie repeats, her words reserved. "I needed a change. I'm breaking away for a bit."

A pause. "From us or from the Bureau?"

A flare of annoyance, not unlike the flare that got her here. "You know I'm not like that."

"Like what?"

The need to give up. The need to let go. The need to... Michael's voice distracts her thought.

"Evie, are you still there?"

"I am," she replies, her voice a controlled pretense. "You know, I'm always here."

"Yeah. Question is, where's here?" There's an edge to his tone, but something else too. A bit of hope. The hope she almost had, this very night. But she couldn't risk it all, not even this.

"Is that why you're calling?" she asks. "To check if I'm working?"

"Kind of. It's about those papers," Michael confesses. "I... I thought, how could we get through this? You know, work together instead. I thought maybe we don't need to be off the hook."

Each of his words feel like that hook. "Hold up. Is it about my investigations, or you wanting me to do your investigations?"

"I didn't mean it like that."

"Then what did you mean?"

"That you don't have to follow FBI leads when we should follow our own," Michael says. "I thought maybe you were ready to see where this can take us."

"Huh," Evie lapses.

He waits, knowing her too well. "Where's it taken you now?"

She starts to simmer, but the noise in the lobby makes her stop.

Keys.

"You still there?" Michael asks.

She stares at the entrance. A silhouette flits across the frosted glass. Someone is here.

Chapter Twenty-One

Stretching the Tether

E vie thumbs her phone's power button. She squeezes it, smothering the device to shut down as she presses herself into a neighboring closet. Breath held, she peers out through the folding door slats.

A figure moves with deliberate assurance. Footsteps echo in the otherwise silent office, confident and authoritative, as if they own this place. A tall figure strides down the corridor, clad in a crisp white coat that almost glows under the fluorescents. His eyes gloss over the surroundings with a sense of familiarity. A meticulously groomed beard frames a hardened face. An air of quiet surrounds him—Dr. Shepherd. The air seems thick with her pulse as he approaches his desk. Seconds stretch, and she wills herself still, but cannot spy him further as he passes out of view.

She cracks the door, chancing a glance for a better angle.

His build seems about right. Could he be?

Now in his office, the doctor carefully reaches behind his desk and slides aside a panel from the wall, seamlessly blended into its surroundings. Standing ajar, it reveals a space she wouldn't have ever noticed. Her eyes narrow, tracking his motions. He draws out a sleek aluminum laptop.

Well, that's interesting.

Each action is measured, precise. He sits and boots up the machine. The glow of the screen casts a pale light, reflecting off the window behind him. Her pulse quickens as she studies its reflection. His fingers navigate the touchpad, opening files.

Patient records.

Wait. If he has digital records, why have all these cabinets? Unless…

They appear on the screen, rows of names and data. He scrolls through with clinical detachment, pausing only briefly to examine and annotate. Evaluating. A creeping dread fills her. These names, they're not random. It's a struggle to make them out in this reversed mirror reflection. But Evie knows what she's looking for. They are there; Miles, Donaldson, Schaffer, and the others. His calm, methodical review feels practiced—routine. This is who she is after. This is the Cartographer!

Evie strains to see, to take in every detail. She shifts slightly; the movement unsettles a mop and bucket beside her. She catches them just in time, her heart in her throat.

Don't blow this.

Through the window's reflective surface, she tracks his work. The distorted views offer glimpses of his process, his procedures. He is thorough, systematic. She stifles a gasp, a growing horror as she sees how he documents various stages of his victims. They were awake! They knew what was happening to them.

They spoke to him—pleaded, begged.

He closes one file and opens another. The pace accelerates. He examines each profile with a calculating eye, a twisted triage. Is this what the dead meant for her to see?

The walls close in, the pressure of time and exposure mounting.

He opens the next file. Can't quite make out the name on this one. The reflection is too distorted through the glass. One thing does stand out, though. Shepherd is not this patient's assigned doctor. *Of course not. Nothing connects him.* Fresh meat, she imagines. Her mind reels as he notes details, preparing for another one of his 'procedures.' A more precise harvest. Her vision blurs with the horror of knowing.

No. This cannot happen.

As she takes it all in, a shiver trickles down her spine—strangeness coils in her stomach, like a serpent awakening to the presence of its prey. Her muscles tense, the chill spreads from her core to her fingertips, gripping her with an icy authority.

Shepherd snaps his laptop shut. He rises and crosses the room, eyes scanning for something. Her panic rises, a surge of cold and fear. *Did he see her? Does he know?* He approaches, just out of sight, the threat of exposure looming. Evie holds her breath as she watches through the door's thin slats, each second an eternity.

Her heart races. He's so damn close. She can feel it.

Then, something else notices too.

A force ruptures inside her, wild and unchained.

The fluorescents shudder—a frenzied strobe playing out the scene before her like a staccato animation.

No.

It's too late. Something within surges; Evie braces herself against the closet walls as it hurls through her. The air shimmers, the closet door a mere breath against its passage. Ethereal and chilling, it streams out in silvery filaments. Gathering on the other side, unnatural shadows loom, building. Medical equipment spirals in a fanned arc. She struggles to stay grounded, each nerve a live wire.

Shepherd stares, disbelieving. The force coalesces before them, casting him in an icy light.

The room contracts with chaos, blurring the space between the living and dead. Spirals of power course out from Evie, pulsing with raw energy. Her body shudders, the cold rush claiming every inch. Her vision tunnels, darkness pooling up around the edges. *Oh, no. I'm blacking out. Can't... let that...* She fights, struggling to reclaim herself, to keep a part of her mind intact.

The desk overturns. Cabinet files scatter through the air like blown leaves. The doctor raises an arm to shield himself from whatever looms before him. He backs toward the exit, disbelief giving way to panic.

The Harbinger's form stretches, thin and insistent, a web of spectral animus. She feels it. The more she resists its tug on her, the less control it maintains. The force lengthens itself, frays. As Shepherd ducks out to the hallway, Evie pulses back into herself. The air explodes, a last surge of fury. A glass door splinters; the walls tremble from the impact.

Evie collapses, a cold sweat forming on her brow.

She snaps back, breathless, shaking. Through the last flutters of papers and post-its, Evie scans the office interior. The room is a wreckage of tipped chairs, scattered files, and splintered frames. She struggles to stand, her fingers finding purchase on the closet door.

But Shepherd...

In the distance, there's the squeal of tires on asphalt.

Shepherd is gone.

Doubt he'll be back tonight.

Oh, gawd. How close she came to losing—herself, her mind, control? Evie's breath is ragged. She can't afford this. Another surge like that. Another loss of herself. Now she knows what a haunting truly means.

Drawing a deep breath, she carefully returns her scarf to her face. It's some small comfort to hide her identity, at least a little. If anyone should see her five-foot-nothing frame though—that would certainly be a tell. Then, with caution in her step, Evie scans the exterior lot through the window.

Darkened street lamps cast dull pools of orange. There are no signs of Shepherd. Only the gaping void of shadows and silence. A cat slinks, passing beyond the drive, then vanishes into the night. Not a single car. Not a person. She waits a moment longer, the chill of her escape slowly receding. Then Evie bursts from the wrecked office.

The night embraces her as she makes her way to the curb where she parked. The taste of adrenaline is sharp on her tongue. Evie fumbles for the keys, heart still pounding from what happened inside.

She doesn't hesitate long, her fingers trembling as she throws herself into the car. Once inside, she collapses against the wheel, gasping. She is drained, energy spent. This Harbinger's recoil left her shaken, unsteady. The force was unlike anything she had imagined. Unlike anything she can fully contain.

The dead won't stop.

Chapter Twenty-Two

Do the Aftermath

Evie wakes with a start.

She glances at the clock. 10:08. Last night replays to her as a wake-up call—the doctor's face, the gamble she took. Evie has never made a mistake so risky, that bold. She considers how close it came, how much was on the line. How will what happened play out? Will her actions get reported? "Break-in." "Unidentified female." Only if someone saw her. "Suspected vandalism?"

Evie drifts out of bed, her head a haze of worry and uncertainty. The house feels unfamiliar, out of sync with her rising anxiety. She checks her desktop. No emails, no messages. She straightens her blouse, then herself. Anything to reduce her exposure.

Her mind—far away, she refocuses on what's next. Orchestrating a search, she scans the news for anything which might give her away. Armed robbery? Burglary? She clings to the warmth of her coffee, her nerves craving its solace. Her brow raised, daring herself to see the worst. But needing to know.

She had him!

She came so close.

Each rough headline gnaws at her uncertainty, each report a new threat. Might there be security camera pics, a witness reporting a vehicle and tag number to police?

Nothing.

Evie exhales, some relief returning. It doesn't appear anyone has noticed. Or if they did, there isn't anything linking back to her. The feeling isn't as reassuring as she'd hoped, not with the stakes so high. Perhaps Dr. Shepherd didn't even report what happened. Maybe that's it. Could he be that careful?

Shepherd. He's the one.

Let's see what exists outside his normative datasets. Evie pulls up media archives. She scours everything on her subject, each article a new puzzle piece. Her mind gears itself into a reassuring rhythm. This is her comfort space. Turning the subjective into detailed integers. Here is her domain.

'Dr. Shepherd's breakthrough work in consciousness mapping has pushed him to the forefront of scientific advancement,' one article gushes. 'With connections to senators and former presidents, the doctor's elite network reads as a who's who of American influence.' Evie's heart slows as she opens another. 'Seen as visionary, his research into brain plasticity garners global acclaim, earning support from tech innovators and medical boards.' No. This is too much. These are influential people. She knows their faces.

There is a pooling in her gut. It can't be. 'Shepherd's residency overlaps with innovative research teams at Northwestern, UCLA, while giving generously time to needy facilities. This and his techniques in neuroplasticity have made him invaluable.' Evie's eyes widen as she reads. His funding partners are among the wealthiest political donors. His patrons include Fortune 500 CEOs. She clenches her teeth.

No wonder. This man doesn't have a legal shield; it's a goddamn fortress.

Implications bear down. New understanding floods over her. She's not just facing some high-end killer. This is someone untouchable. Someone with an army of lawyers, news outlets, and privileged elites ready to take her down if she even dares.

Who is little FBI Evie to take this on?

Her hand fumbles for the rosary. *Oh, gawd.* Maybe Michael's right. Time to cut her losses. Time to face facts, admit she's lost. Damn logic, the dead, the truth. Seriously. This can get so much worse. It's more than lives. It's her career, family. Her sanity.

June.

These connections—they explain why any conventional justice failed. She isn't just facing a killer, but an entire system. Could she really take that on? Her fingers grip the beads. The thought of June and the other victims compels her. No matter the cost. If they can arrange her daughter's murder, they can target Michael next. Her parents. It drives deep into her, a force as powerful as the cold surge she felt back in that closet. This time, it's a different kind of haunting; harrowing, personal. She will not be so reckless. These people won't give her a second chance. She has to be sure before she makes a wrong move.

Evie races through the possibilities, the risks. She won't be deterred. She'll be ready. She'll find a way to connect him, to make sure the evidence is ironclad. He won't see her coming.

On impulse, she grabs the phone. Her fingers hesitate before dialing. He deserves to know. But what will this news do to him? She has no idea what she'll say. No idea how to break it to Michael.

This is why they took June.

That will send him spiraling into his own frenzy. She imagines his eyes, red with sleeplessness, widening at the knowledge. Desperation would drive him. She remembers the little control he had when he thought it was hopeless—how shattered he was, how broken they both were. He is a Pediatrician. Michael moves in those same circles. He'll connect the dots. Then what? He'll do something far more reckless. He'll go rogue, get himself in so deep, so fast. It'll be worse than five years ago. Much worse. But if she doesn't tell him, then he's stabbed twice over—once by the killer, again by his wife keeping the secret.

No.

She sets the phone down, a ghost of indecision tracing her movements. She knows what she has to do, but not what it'll take.

Stepping from her desk, Evie considers. Her mind is a flurry of contingencies. She needs more. This time, she won't act until she's sure. They won't see her coming if she's not there. Work remotely through others. Collect the details, and give them to Vaughn's team. Let him have the glory. Evie will keep her family safe.

She uncoils the rosary from her wrist, lets it sit idle next to the divorce papers. Last night was foolish. No more taking chances until she knows what is safe. Until she knows what is right. She stares at them, then at the papers which would end her old life. Evie spirals through potential moves, each a sequence of exposed nerves.

She's not frantic. Knows how to keep it together. She has agency.

She's...

...Evie Cross.

Holding onto her sanity, bargaining with herself, she edges into the kitchen to refresh her coffee. Evie stops cold, the mug slipping from her hands. Her attention snags on the refrigerator's sheen, on what she thinks she sees. In its stainless steel surface, a figure—stands just behind her. Evie gasps. Her body tightens, twisting abruptly. She knows what she saw. She knows what this is. Yet...

Nothing.

She's not alone. Evie's logic tells her so. The dead don't rest. They follow. They know. Her pulse spikes as she turns back to the fridge, summoning her own force of will, the same force that's driven her this far.

The reflection stares back.

It is a male in his twenties, hair matted, eyes bleeding.

Evie wheels around, heart pounding.

Still nothing.

She takes a step back, her heel clacking against the floor. The sound echoes, like an afterthought. He is there. Watching her. Maybe her own eyes can't perceive him. But he is still there. She presses her hands to the cool metal, needing proof, needing to close the distance between what she knows and what she can see.

Evie sucks in a breath. She won't flee. Not going to cower. She won't let this break her. Instead, she lets it feed her conviction. Her eyes scan the room, hyper-aware of each shadow, each flicker. But she is alone, alone and yet surrounded.

Hands falling to her sides, she exhales, fogging the stainless. She has command of her world. This is real, and she will not let it drive her to madness. She's got more resources than the dead suspect.

Evie backs away from the haunted kitchen. Her mug lies in pieces, the spilled coffee soaking into the grout. She passes the divorce papers without a glance. Later. When she's ready. She'll get to the dead, when it's on her terms. They can haunt her all they like. But she will not be afraid.

Not of ghosts. Not of herself.

Evie leaves what she can for now. Fresh air will help. Gathering her keys and jacket, running errands will help clear her head.

Chapter Twenty-Three

Her Way

Evie winds her way through the aisles again, her cart nearly empty. Each shelf stocked with the patterns of other lives, each item a reminder of how far she's come. Every choice is measured.

Plastic utensils. White bread. Ramen.

A sense of exposure tugs at her. She feels the length of her unsteady stride, the way this becomes so different from the life she once knew. The reality she once shared with Michael and June. She floats through the store, a ghost among the living. A ghost of herself.

Frozen dinners. Rice.

These are the only supplies she'll need. The thought of permanence clings. It chills her, and she feels that presence trailing her every step. It stalks, each aisle a narrow corridor she can't quite escape. She reaches for a light bulb. An unseen touch glances hers, sends static up her spine. It is deliberate—urging.

"Not now," she whispers.

Evie subdues the faintest of shivers as she places the bulb in her cart. She grips the handle, reclaiming some control. She won't let them drive her to madness. A woman with three children squeezes past, their squeals and darting movements a reminder of the life she should have.

Bananas. Milk. Single servings.

Evie takes a shallow breath. A rush of panic floods her memory. She allowed this to happen. This world is no longer logical; it's a tangle of want and guilt. A disconnect between who she once was and what she's becoming. She fled from the truth once before, from her own capacity for manipulation. How far would this Harbinger have her go?

Back through the dairy section, she reaches for a half gallon.

She's already too far for that.

The grocery store glares under garish lights, its bounty a testament to her isolation. Her unlikely suspects refused to show, not even the real Cartographer. Especially not him. Had he been there, she might have...

What?

Her mind turns back to her own analysis.

She spirals through 'what if' and 'why not' until it closes in again with the force of so many impossible choices. She can't, for all her discipline, exorcise her choices. Her intrusion into the office has left its mark. Evie had justified her violation even though it was far outside protocol. Risked her and Michael's future. But it was something. The only thing tangible she has done since the moment they found her braid.

The checkout station beeps, its conveyor rhythm steady. Evie's mind clings to the patterns, the sequences she controlled. The data. Her life. She wonders if this Harbinger will have her even break the rules of reality. Can she follow through with the deception? Does she even want to? Is she willing? Her hands are unsteady as she fumbles for her wallet.

She steps outside into the dying light of another Autumn day, more crisp than warm. She maneuvers through the parking spaces, remembering her Ford Fiesta's place. Canned soup, generic bread, and an extra blanket all sit neatly in the passenger seat.

A roughshod array of tents and tarps huddles on the fringe where the parking lot meets the woods beyond. She pauses, her mind flickering again to the one from the Bureau—his eyes wild with an indescribable intensity. It seemed an unnamable pull had reached out from him to her. Now, these figures in the distance gather like wounded phantoms.

Is that where this all leads?

Did he give in to it?

She stands frozen beside her unloaded cart. The idea is a vise tightening in her chest. Her head swims with a thousand abandoned hypotheses: following rules, breaking them, neither matters. Nothing has brought her daughter back. She is suspended between two worlds, each as empty as the other. The scent of autumn fills her lungs, drawing her toward another season's end.

She lingers there for a moment before closing the door. Evie unconsciously touches her wedding ring. Her fingers, unsteady. June. Michael. This family she can barely name as her own. She sits unmoving, the sight of the tents gnawing at her.

This too will pass.

This too she can forget.

The car's heater cranks to a hum as she pulls out of the parking lot and the past. The homeless blur in the rearview, a smudge of color and movement.

The phone buzzes in the cup holder, a digital insistence she cannot ignore.

MICHAEL: Have you signed yet?

Evie grips the steering wheel, her knuckles white against the black leather. The road unspools before her. She doesn't answer. The text lingers like everything they once believed.

The house is dim when she arrives. She methodically puts the groceries away, each item finding its place in the cabinets. As she moves through the kitchen, her foot nudges the shards of her broken coffee cup. She absently gathers the pieces, placing them next to the shattered life of her divorce papers. With a sigh, she wipes the spilled coffee from the floor, her mind elsewhere.

The phone rings. The caller ID notes her parents. She hesitates, letting it go to voicemail. As if on cue, it rings again.

"Evie, we're worried. Please pick up."

She doesn't. Instead, she mutes it. Their certainty, their concern, are more than she can bear. She can handle only one haunting at a time.

Hours bleed into night. She paces the small rooms, aimless, her thoughts a tangled knot. The digital glow of her laptop catches her eye. She opens it, but her mind is too restless to focus. The words swim, a sea of data and doubt.

From the kitchen, a cascade of tinkling glass sprawls across the silence.

She wheels around, panic spiking.

Her breath catches.

Its ceramic pieces distinctive—the mug shards from earlier—scatter across the kitchen floor.

She is not alone.

Evie backs away, grabbing the countertop for support. Her heart is a wild rhythm that drowns out her reason. She knows what this is. She knows who wants her.

They follow. They know. Her complacency just won't do.

She retreats to the bedroom, slamming the door, shutting out the impossible. Evie clutches at herself, her body curled against the edge of the bed. She doesn't need to see them to know. Shadows gather, a silent jury. The woman. The teen. Their hollow eyes watch, accusing, unblinking.

"You're not real," her voice is a brittle whisper. "You're not—"

But they are.

Evie wraps herself in her comforter, the plush fabric a thin shield. She squeezes her eyes tighter, willing it all to go away, the dead and the living.

Sleep, impossible.

Despite that, exhaustion eventually consumes her. The night is a churn, through the weight of all she's lost, all she still stands to lose. Concealed within the comforter, she fitfully tosses and turns until the dawn illuminates the fabric.

She raises her head, eyes bloodshot yet defiant. The apparitions will not leave until she does what they want. Until she finds the answers. She is going to relent in what they want. They're just going to do it her way.

Evie pushes the door open, the house confronting her with its emptiness.

Chapter Twenty-Four

Fall In to Get Out

She keeps her gaze fixed on the seam between floorboards, following its linear nature as if it might carry her into some alternate apartment, another more solitary version of this morning. Unmuting her phone, Evie checks her call history.

Her mother, twice. Michael. The number for the divorce attorney's office, which she has blocked but still leaves silent voicemails—legally, always allowed one more chance. Then, a successive chain of calls from Quantico.

Uh oh.

The doorbell jolts her. The ring is steady, expectant.

Evie opens the door, grousing, "It's seven forty-five, Collins."

"I know," he says, shifting his weight awkwardly in the doorframe. Collins holds a paper coffee cup in both hands, as though unsure whether to offer it to her or shield himself with it. "SSA Haden sent me." He attempts a smile, apologetic and fresh-faced. "He's been trying to call. Asked if you could come in early. Said it's important."

Evie gives him a look. She considers closing the door and letting him wrestle with the next directive on his own—which, knowing Haden, will be to stand outside indefinitely like a butler in a British farce. Instead, she shrugs, slips her phone into her pocket, and tugs a cardigan over her T-shirt.

"Give me two," she says, closing the door before him—not ungently, not warmly.

She's fast. Hair in a knot, small messenger bag slung crosswise, badge and lanyard retrieved from the kitchen counter. She glances at her reflection in the microwave door—a ghostly, translucent overlay of herself. It's neither reassuring nor damning. It's just there, like the rest of it.

Collins remains on her porch with the same patience one might show a feral cat. He offers her the coffee cup again. "The boss says he wants a debrief before nine," he says as they walk, trying to match her clipped stride.

"That's just an adjective stuck on 'brief,'" Evie accepts the cup, surprisingly still warm.

He blinks. "Sorry?"

She waves it off. "Never mind. It's not you."

The drive is long enough for silence to settle. Collins glances her way several times. After a few failed attempts, he manages, "Ma'am, if I can ask—" then aborts. Evie waits, but he doesn't finish. If he were any other man, she'd prod. But Collins is too polite, too raw. She lets him pick up the thread himself.

He does so gracelessly, as they cross the bridge into Quantico. "Haden says you're a legend," he blurts, cheeks coloring. "He says you're the only one who ever outdid him at simulation scenarios. That you're the only profiler he ever recruited personally."

Evie snorts. "He says that to all the damaged girls." She looks out the window. "How's the training?"

He shrugs. "Sir says it's all quicksand; take the next shallow step and hope you don't go under."

"And how's that working for you?"

He thinks about it. "I keep my head above. Most days."

Evie says nothing, but something in her nod feels almost like respect.

At Quantico, Collins parks in the visitor row. "Boss is in already," he says. "He asked me to escort you up." There's a flicker of something—pity, or maybe shared complicity—in his eyes. This isn't good. Something has taken a turn.

Collins walks her past security and through the echoing marble lobby. Haden's office glowers from the end of the row, the frosted glass panel catching a bitter slant of morning sun. No one else is here yet—not even the secretary, desk vacant.

He leaves her at the threshold, as if he's delivered a bomb and must now retreat to the minimum safe distance. Evie knocks once, then lets herself in.

Agent Haden sits behind an uncluttered desk, a manila folder open before him. His massive palms rest on either side, a show of balance. The only personal effect is his Howard University mug—steam rising.

He shares nothing as she closes the door, devoid of his usual warmth. Haden only gestures to the seat. Evie takes it, setting her borrowed coffee between them.

"'Morning, Agent Cross," Haden intones.

She waits, learning these last years: never fill the quiet first.

He gives her a long appraisal, equal parts concern and audit. "I want to talk about the Cartographer case," he says, voice even. "Specifically, the review I conducted last night of all associated case files. Including archived ViCAP and supplemental libraries." His eyes never leave her. "There's a pattern that's come to my attention. Code anomalies. Edits made amazingly with no attribution, dating to... five years ago."

Evie stiffens, unable to summon a deflection. "I see."

Haden waits, measuring her every micro-expression. His baritone softens, but not by much. "Is there anything you want to contribute before I begin a formal inquiry?"

She considers a thousand ways to spin the truth. Blame it on the system, on stress, on a corrupted workstation. Each one tastes like ash.

Instead: "I did it, sir. I altered the algorithm. I buried a signature in the clustering code to mask location congruencies." She folds her hands, knuckles white. The lift in her chest is almost laughable—confession as relief. "It was me."

Haden doesn't nod, doesn't blink. He listens, a monument.

She exhales through her nose; the words tumbling. "It was after the Cartographer's seventh escalation. Michael and my... loss. As you know, someone left evidence on my porch—the braid. But more importantly, it included a note I had not disclosed. It wasn't just a threat..." She hesitates, unwilling to say her daughter's name here, in the sharp morning. "It was an offer—a quid pro quo. We could have her back if I rerouted the Cartographer investigation. I complied, thinking I would still end up catching the killer myself, but..."

She stops. You did not. You lost her.

"I thought I could fix it after," she admits, voice thin. "But the opportunity never came."

Haden leans back, exhaling. "It's not the case integrity that concerns me most. It's you." He flips the folder closed. His massive thumb rests on the seam. "Did you ever plan to disclose it?"

"I tried," Evie says, and means it. "But it would have all been for nothing. And I—I didn't see a way to tell it after the team signed off on the conclusion."

She lets the quiet linger, expects anger, but there is only the hum of the mug's heat and the faint pop of Haden's knuckle as he considers. Then his tone shifts from disciplinary to paternal. "I see," he says, at length. His eyes are too tired for judgment. "You understand what this means, Evelyn."

She nods, feeling the weight. "You have to report this."

"It means," Haden says, "that everything you've worked for here will be gone, possibly with criminal prosecution. Even if I wanted to, I won't be able to shield you." He softens, almost imperceptibly, as though he mourns the math as much as she does. "I can only conclude you were understandably fraught at the time you acted. Clearly under duress. If you were thinking clearly, the code would have been invisible even to me. That is at least some defense. Do bear that in mind."

She resists the impulse to meet his eyes. "I can brief internal affairs myself. Give them clean logs. Save you the paperwork." The offer is almost a kindness.

"Thank you," Haden says, though he doesn't sound grateful. Instead, he regards her with a careful, almost clinical curiosity, as if weighing how many more bombshells she has left.

Evie gives one.

"I think I know who he is." She draws a slow breath, then: "The Cartographer."

Now she looks up—a sharp slat of morning sun finding an edge of triumph in her face. "Last night, I got close. Not a theory, not a rogue's gallery. An actual person: Dr. Victor Shepherd, neurosurgeon and consciousness researcher, currently consulting in Alexandria. He's not only local; he's doing multiple rotations at several facilities."

She can see Haden working through this. "Walk me through it." He leans forward.

She scans the office for a whiteboard, then realizes she doesn't need to draw it out; the logic is sequenced, as fluent as breath. "The MO changed after the original cluster—mid-four years ago. Surgical method got more refined, less trophy, more information-gathering. The killer was experimenting, not just indulging. If you compare the cuts pre- and post-escalation, the suture marks line up with neuroanatomical mapping techniques. I pulled samples, then overlaid them with Shepherd's published photo sets—his journal abstracts and conference posters. Identical angles."

She pauses for air. Haden doesn't interrupt.

"The next layer is behavioral. Shepherd cycles between elite research hospitals, additional state clinics, and what—'community service sabbaticals'? Victim recoveries are in proximity to his assigned duties, both locally and abroad. I also think he's got an enabler. Maybe more than one."

"That's all circumstantial," Haden says, but Evie hears the shift: an emphasis on rigor, not dismissal.

She presses, "It's a start. I know how to run it down further."

Haden rubs the bridge of his nose, eyes clocking through the evidence as if overlaying Evie's narration onto his own private matrix. "Were you aware Vaughn's team already included Shepherd on their suspect list?"

"I had their notes, but preferred an independent approach," Evie says. "There's nothing in this suspect's records. Not even a parking citation."

"We do things by the book, Agent Cross." Haden's words are rhetoric, but the slow tap of his thumb on the folder is not. "If you're correct, we're up against a subject with more insulation than the Bureau itself. His legal team will be goddamn bulletproof."

She shrugs, the gesture quick, a shadow of her old self. "You asked for my take. That's it."

Haden regards her anew. The disappointment is still present, but the scales are shifting—methodical concern yielding to something like recognition. "Last time you got this look, you nailed that strangler in a week. I still have the marker from the betting pool." His mouth twitches, not quite a smile. "Alright. Walk me through your expected approach, step by step. What are you thinking?"

Evie is ready. "I'll need whiteboard access." Now she stands, sleeves bunched at her forearm, already moving toward the conference area adjoining the office. Haden follows, steaming mug in hand.

Chapter Twenty-Five

Attack Vector

The boss's conference room is a seldom-used annex at the end of the main corridor, meant for closed-door briefings and the occasional classified brawl. The glass panels, etched with the Bureau crest, are smudged for private scoldings and other acts best kept quiet. Like these. Haden gestures for her to enter first. The room is chilly, even by government standards.

Yet now the temperature in the room shifts. The rules have changed. For the first time in years, she is not here to be managed, reined in, or punished. Haden stands in the doorway, a calculus of weight on his shoulders. He then closes it with a deliberate hush.

He looks her over. "You need coffee, Cross?"

"I'm fine."

He nods, then fishes out his phone, sending a message.

Within thirty minutes, the war room holds a trinity: Marcus Vaughn, Elena Reyes, and their IT lead—Cassandra. Cass boots a laptop, swipes through security layers, then projects the digital workspace onto the glass wall. Without a word, she slips to the far corner, already pulling up access logs and anonymized video feeds.

Haden cuts in, brisk but quiet. "We're off the grid. No notes, no calendar invites—nothing traceable." He leans toward Evie, voice low and almost gentle. "If you're right about Shepherd, I'd rather save lives than see one destroyed. But we need ironclad proof if that's going to happen."

Evie gives a tight nod. She knows the drill: Haden's testing her—and setting the stage. She steps to the glass whiteboard and begins sketching a timeline; the marker squeaks in the cooled air.

Her mind snaps back into focus with surgical precision. "Every victim cluster coincides with one of Shepherd's public appearances—conferences, speaking gigs, consulting trips, even holidays." She dots each on the map. "But here," she points to an isolated mark, "is a case no one ever linked: a patient in the Dominican Republic. The official story was a botched surgery." She glances at Marcus. "Shepherd was supposedly on medical leave—officially on a surf trip. In reality, he was at an unsponsored clinic, off-books. No hospital records. Body went through a local mortuary. And the incision patterns—"

She hesitates, glances at Cass, then back to Vaughn. "They match the Cartographer signature exactly. Same orbital-rim access on the left side."

Marcus crosses his arms, chin tilted. He gives that sly grin of his. "So why detour from the usual venue? What's the point?" His tone is half-casual, half-provoking—like he's baiting her to fill in the blanks.

"Practice," Evie says. "Perfecting the technique on a softer target before bringing it home."

Marcus nods, eyes sharp. "Makes sense. Always target the low-risk prototype first." He swivels slightly toward Elena. "What's next?"

Elena taps the board. "He's got a pattern in Virginia—disappearances that spike when his stress levels rise. Media attention, even grant denials."

Evie cuts in: "There's more." She flips back to her laptop and brings up a roster. "Thanks to some intel from my white-hats, I've learned Shepherd operates a second phone on a silent loop: VPN, custom OS, encrypted channels." She scrolls. "He's definitely communicating with someone—an enabler."

The room leans in. Evie continues: "Two numbers ping between 1:00 and 3:00 a.m. One's 703—local. The other bounces through Cayman proxies."

Marcus smirks, tapping his fingers on the glass. "Let's put a digital tail on those midnight conspirators." He looks to Cassandra. "Cass, trace them."

"I'm on it," she replies without looking up.

Marcus turns back to Evie. "Solid. What's our next move?"

Evie hesitates, guilt flickering behind her eyes. "We build the case quietly. Go public, and he lawyers up—or disappears."

"He certainly has the means," Elena agrees. "Or his sponsors would for sure."

Evie erases part of the timeline and redraws it. "We start with travel records—every conference, every dark window longer than twenty-four hours. Then overlay local law enforcement and coroner reports."

Haden's mouth twitches. "Do it."

Silence falls but for the tap of keys and the scratch of a marker. Maps, timelines, victim dossiers, foreign news clippings multiply on the glass. Evie orchestrates, drawing connections, issuing orders; the team moves with lean purpose.

By noon, the beginnings of a radial map emerge: Shepherd's shadow cast over the Midwest and New England. Each spoke a cluster of disappearances; each dot a fracture in someone's life.

Haden returns with sandwiches and bitter Bureau coffee. He surveys the table, then finds Evie at the floor-to-ceiling window, her hands deep in her coat pockets.

He lowers his voice. "I'm holding your confession close. I've seen careers—and lives—ruined for making impossible calls. If this is you making it right," he pauses, "then do it."

Evie can only nod. The tension in her chest shifts, though the guilt remains—her silent anchor.

The afternoon slogged by in audits and proxy queries—everything laundered through dummy accounts or pitched as routine. At 4AM, Marcus calls out: "Get this—internal memo from a Vermont hospital. Shepherd led a 'volunteer teaching session.' Right after, an eighteen-year-old with a rare CNS disorder goes missing."

Evie catches herself. "That's the trigger. He's hunting neurological outliers."

Elena goes sullen. "He's got a type: anomalies."

The whiteboard fills with fresh lines of inquiry, each more chilling than the last.

As the night rolls on , the room permeates with worn carpet and stale coffee. Sleeves are rolled, collars unbuttoned, faces drawn. Evie stands at the board, dialing in one last angle. She knows Haden's watching—pride and sorrow mingled in his posture.

When the room finally empties, Haden gestures for her to stay. He shuts the door and crosses to the glass wall, hands folded.

"You did good today," he whispers.

Evie lets it wash over her—strange and welcome.

"Five years ago, the Bureau failed you. Protocols broke, safeguards collapsed. If they'd taken my son and dangled proof of life, I'd have broken every rule," he unfolds his hands. "That's not a conceit. It's truth. You bent the rules because you had to. We're human. That said, you're exactly what we need—here," he taps his temple, "and here," then his chest.

Evie nods, eyes burning. The admission loosens something inside her, a knot that has held too tight for so long. She tries to hold it back, but the tears come anyway—a quick, furious drop, then another. She wipes them with her sleeve, mortified, but Haden only waits, steady as stone.

He leaves it there—just the two of them and the silent hum of possibility. "We do it by the book. We make it right." He lets the sentence die. "Rest up. Tomorrow's the real grind."

She wipes her name from the whiteboard corner, steps into the cold night. The chill bites, but her stride has a spark—Evie's back in the fight.

Outside, under the harsh security lights, she catches her reflection: older, a little frayed, but unbroken. Still here. Still fighting.

Chapter Twenty-Six

To Serve and Collect

In the parked sedan, the faint click of Evie's thumbnail against the steering wheel is the only sound. Haden says nothing, eyes forward, elbow planted on the window edge with practiced stillness. The street is empty but for the occasional patient's car nosing toward the gated lot. Across from them, Shepherd's clinic is sterile brick, low glass, and the minimalist signage preferred by expensive specialists. The lights inside are already lit.

They are curb parked, but eyes on.

Three figures cross from the government pool car, shoulders squared against the drizzle. Vaughn takes point, a blue folder visible in his left hand. Elena is at his right, hands at her sides, eyes scanning the entry vestibule. Cassandra brings up the rear, clutching her tablet like a riot shield.

Evie's mouth is dry. The radio in her lap is a talisman she doesn't need—audio is piped directly trough a whisper earpiece—even so, her hand goes to it as if for comfort.

Vaughn leads his team through the outer glass doors, all in clear view from the sedan. The lobby is as antiseptic as she remembers: corporate art, rubber plants, soundproofing meant to absorb everything but the low hum of health care. A receptionist in slate-gray scrubs glances up, clocking the trio within two heartbeats. A supervisor appears behind her, summoned by whatever silent panic button exists in these places. She is short, mid-fifties, with the polite steeliness of a woman who has survived three EHR transitions and a dozen 'practice mergers.'

The woman extends an open hand, eyes flicking to the warrant in Vaughn's grip. Her voice pipes through Vaughn's mic. "Good morning. May I see the paperwork and know what this is about?" Cordial, but she stands with the posture of someone who can dial an attorney in seconds.

Vaughn does not bother with theatrics. "Of course." He flips the folder open, holds it for her to read. "We're here to serve a warrant and secure records as part of a billing audit—Medicare and private insurance, past seven years. We'll need access to all current and archived ledgers, and your staff will please remain in common areas until cleared."

The manager reads. Her eyebrows lift and her lips purse, but she offers nothing but a small nod. "You'll want the file room and Dr. Shepherd's private office. I'll have the records administrator and IT lead join you. If you'd like coffee—"

"Thank you," Vaughn says, already moving. Elena splits off to flank the hall. Cassandra glides past the reception desk, badge visible, beelining for the server closet. The supervisor trails, muttering into a Bluetooth earpiece.

Haden shifts in the driver's seat, eyes still forward. "Very by-the-book," he murmurs, while parsing every inflection of the voices inside.

Evie rolls the window down half an inch, inhales the scent of wet concrete and new mulch. "You think Shepherd will show?" she asks, as much to herself as to Haden.

He grunts. "On a Saturday? It's enough that they have offices open on a weekend."

Evie tracks her team's progress through the lobby glass, the sense of intrusion almost palpable. The staff—three nurses, one PA—cluster in the open break room, their body language stiff but compliant. No one seems nervous. No one is calling their spouse to check in. Have they been through this before? Should've searched for previous investigations.

The first comm check comes, Vaughn's voice steady: "On site. No resistance. Office supervisor is assisting."

Evie's fingers tap the steering wheel, then stop, then start again. She is alert for chaos, an accusation of harassment. Instead, she gets orderly compliance and Vaughn's muted confidence. The staff assists when asked. No one mentions the prior break-in. No alarm is raised about the integrity of the office. If anything, there's a mild undertone of being inconvenienced by another round of outside scrutiny.

Elena's update is clipped: "File room secured. Records admin here. No attempt to shred or remove. Files are mainly patient docs—mostly hard copy."

Cassandra's check-in is softer, as if she's whispering directly into Evie's skull: "Server access live. Office uses an off-site cloud for most billing, but there's a local cache. Downloading now."

Haden leans back, fingers tented over his lap. "So far, so good. Anything odd?"

Evie shrugs. "It's all routine." But she can't help the spike of guilt, the knowledge of what she did just nights before. How tidy everything appears now. It's too easy, too smooth. She listens for any sign—an off note in Vaughn's tone, a trace of suspicion in the staff—but there's nothing. The staff must have covered tracks, or simply never saw any disruption.

"Doesn't bother you?" Haden's voice is low, but his gaze is clinical. He is not just asking about the operation.

She meets his eyes. "Nothing about this is normal. Not for me."

He nods, as if that's the answer he expected.

Rain spatters the windshield. Evie turns the wipers on, eyes fixed on the glass doors ahead. Through them, Vaughn and Elena patrol with disciplined focus. Cassandra sits at reception, fingers gliding over her laptop. The rest of the staff wait, subdued, in the break room.

Vaughn's voice crackles over the comm: "We've begun review. Records admin cooperative. Office locked; manager to open at 08:00 sharp."

Evie shifts in her seat. "It's too orderly. I expected some resistance."

Haden arches an eyebrow. "Why the nerves?"

She swallows. "When the pattern holds perfectly... that's when it's most dangerous."

He gives her a rueful smile.

As the minutes inch forward, a Saab pulls through the misting rain. It parks. A dark suit emerges to pop an umbrella. His beige briefcase is a stark contrast against the gray backdrop. Vaughn meets him in the lobby and displays his badge. "We were expecting the good doctor."

"Sorry, Dr. Shepherd is not in today. I'm Mr. Banner—the practice's business manager. The staff has already informed me of the situation." He shakes off his umbrella, turning it into a corner canister, and extends an open palm.

Vaughn's handshake is bland but insistent. "Appreciate your time, Mr. Banner. We'll need full access to Dr. Shepherd's office."

Banner winces, clearly not pleased to be here. "Yes," he says, "but let's be efficient. Anything not directly related to the audit—insurance, payroll, vendor contracts—I would prefer you not disturb."

Cassandra's voice is steady: "Office unlocked. No resistance. Manager cooperating fully."

Haden leans forward. "Now it gets interesting."

Evie's knuckles whiten on the wheel.

The team returns to their search. Elena escorts Banner down a corridor of frosted-glass suites. Vaughn examines logs at the central desk. Cassandra sweeps the reception area with her laptop.

Evie feels the operation's precision like a taut wire. Too easy.

Vaughn's gloved hands part rows of alphabetized files. Digital logs flicker on Cass's tablet. Evie adjusts the rearview mirror, checking her own reflection blurred by raindrops. A subtle, misplaced scent of dirt tingles at her nostrils.

Then, someone subtly shifts behind her. In the backseat, a slouched figure—pale, waxy, bearded lips drained of color. His eyes are gone, hollow holes, the mouth moving without sound. He radiates accusation... and something deeper.

She goes cold, eyes wide, every nerve paralyzed. His vagrant mouth shapes a word, lips forming syllables but making no sound.

Evie flicks her eyes to the side, seeing if Haden has noticed. He is unchanged, eyes still fixed on the office, attention wholly invested in the unfolding search. Her backseat apparition doesn't plead, doesn't beg. It simply glares. It is a measure, almost as if waiting for the scales to tip.

She wants to speak, but knows—knows better—to let the words die in her throat. Her fists clench the wheel, bloodless and rigid. A drop of rain slaloms down the windshield, warping the reflection until all that's left is a whorl of white and gray, and when she looks again...

...he's gone. The backseat is empty.

Haden follows her stare. "You see something?"

"Just thought I saw... movement," she murmurs.

He looks back, searching out the rear window. After mulling his jaw over, he recenters to continue monitoring the team. "You've been home too long. Stay focused. Don't let getting back in the saddle spook you. Thirty years in this job taught me justice and law don't always match. Sometimes we're tempted to work in the gray. But instead we stay professional. Right, Agent Cross?"

The radio crackles. "What the hell?" Vaughn's voice comes over for a beat, then, "Boss... something's up."

A scuffle, then Vaughn's breathless: "A section of wall behind the desk just shifted—frames fell. Sound of something breaking. I don't know, some latch?"

Evie's pulse spikes. She reaches for the mic, but Haden is faster. "Are you secure? Have you tabs on the staff?"

"Elena here. Yes. All present."

A pause, then Vaughn: "What the... Oh yeah. Now we're talking. Seems we've found ourselves a recessed wall compartment."

Silence.

Haden raises his eyebrows Evie's way. As if to say, did you know?

Evie's heart pounds. No. This is not good.

Elena asserts herself, sounding so positive. "Inside are a laptop, bound journals—surgical logs, hand-drawn neural diagrams, annotations."

"Evidence of crimes?" Haden asks.

Another pause. Vaughn: "Some diagrams. They match patterns from the Cartographer case. Dated notes. Detailed procedures."

Cassandra cuts in, "I'm imaging contents now. Securing evidence."

Evie closes her eyes; the vagrant's hollow stare burns into her mind. He was urging her. Demanding she act. She triggers the talk button. "What happened in there?"

Marcus replies, "Ya got me, man! It was like a mini-tremor slash tornado. Back half of the office flew apart. Then, click. Panel opens up." He sighs, leading the team back through the office. "Elena's got the evidence case."

Cassandra snapped closed her laptop, adding, "I've backed up elements on my end."

Vaughn nodded, holding up the computer. "And I've got the laptop."

Mr. Banner trailed behind them, his expression serious. "So, what? We're done then?"

Vaughn smirked. "That's one way of putting it."

Haden glances at Evie. No words—only his expression, 'Did you know?'

She meets his gaze but says nothing. She didn't plant it—but she certainly delivered it. This Harbinger doesn't whisper; it acts.

Vaughn's voice comes over the radio, calm: "We got it. Fire off the request to the judge."

Haden signals to move. Evie complies, turning onto the wet road, windshield beads tracing silent rivulets. She glances in the rearview. Empty—yet she feels that weight.

They do not rest.

No. They want.

Chapter Twenty-Seven

The Warrant

Shepherd's estate is an iron-fenced compound of engineered serenity. The drive leading to the main house is crushed granite, kept so perfectly raked that the lines might belong to a garden or a Zen crime scene. The property unfurls itself, three acres of obsessive order. His topiary hedges wind with contortions of thought, imported birches disciplined to keep their branches skyward. Then there is his lawn. It's so precisely shorn that Evie imagines each blade would wilt in despair at the first sign of disorder.

At the entrance gate, a tent sits just offside with a uniformed attendant. Evidently, the doctor is having a Saturday gathering on his agenda. The usual hush of privilege is layered with the manufactured cheer of a charity luncheon. White tents puncture the drizzle like domes of institutional innocence, from the other side of the compound fence.

The scent of grass, wet and trampled, leaks through the glass of the sedan. After Haden flashes his badge and warrant, the attendant hits a remote. The rolling gates part, and a row of dense vertical bollards retract into the drive.

Evie maintains herself in the passenger seat as they park under the eaves of a copper beech. Her badge is stowed—presence as nonofficial. She, herself, in civilian blandness: slacks, a pressed shirt, the old Burberry coat she stole from Michael when they shared a closet. It holds his scent, at least the memory of it.

Haden is outside, conferring with Marcus Vaughn and Elena. From here, the trio looks like the first act in a staged morality play: Vaughn's body language full of predatory enthusiasm, Elena's a mask of quiet dread, and Haden himself—monolithic, composed. Behind them, Cass waits in the secondary vehicle, her face lit by her tablet.

Though the estate party is already underway, it is Haden's team who are ready to get it started.

She watches movement at the tent's open flank. Shepherd holds court at the head of a long table, the kind made for deals and feasts. To his left, their State Senator—pale, balding, radiating the comfort of a man who has never known genuine fear. To the right, a woman in her early forties: platinum hair, navy fleece, the logo of a biotech firm sewn in discreet gold at her breast. Flanking them are others, each rehearsing a casualness with an intensity that belies federal law enforcement at their gathering.

Haden signals; Marcus and Elena fan out, approaching from oblique angles to minimize any sense of spectacle. It is a good plan. Evie thinks, not for the first time, how little anything about Shepherd has been left to chance.

She shifts in her seat. Her fingers drum restlessly against her thigh, then the window button, then the plastic fob left near the ignition. Each movement echoes the pulse at her neck.

From her periphery, two plainclothes units from Quantico's regional office materialize from the catering tent. Both move with the deliberate slowness of men paid to be unnoticed. One positions himself at the estate's rear, radio clipped to his hip. The other stations himself at the tent's ingress, blending with a trio of groundskeepers.

Evie wants to believe this will go smoothly, but the calculus in her mind disagrees. This is not a morning for simple resolutions. This is Shepherd's home field, and if the past has taught her anything, it's that a home advantage in Shepherd's world could be a form of asymmetric warfare.

Haden strolls the center path through the tent, flanked by Marcus and Elena. He brandishes no badge, just his grey suit and expression, both invitation and warning. The guests at the table fall silent, heads turning as if a slow-motion spill of dominoes.

Evie lowers her window two inches. The air is sharp with rain and ozone.

Their voices drift, providing stereo for her earpiece.

Haden says, "Dr. Shepherd. Sorry to interrupt, but we have a warrant for your arrest."

Shepherd stands abruptly, his posture stiffening as surprise flickers across his face. For a heartbeat, he grapples with the sudden intrusion, eyes darting to the three agents. His expression betrays a hint of uncertainty before he composes himself. "Arrest? Forgive me. I... I don't understand."

Marcus swiftly shifts to the right, anticipating any sudden moves. Elena stays back, hands clearly visible, her expression a carefully maintained blank slate.

A silence falls. The guests murmur, one or two reaching for phones in discreet panic.

Shepherd motions to the Senator and the biotech woman. "Would you excuse me for a moment? It appears I am needed elsewhere."

The guests break off, a few rising to watch from a distance that is not quite safe and not quite involved. Evie lingers on the woman in the navy fleece—she watches Shepherd with a clinical curiosity, as if studying a rare specimen. She swallows, keeping her eyes on the tableau as it unfolds.

Haden presents the warrant. He speaks with a lawyerly cadence. "This pertains to evidence recovered at your office, and an ongoing investigation into the deaths of multiple individuals in this state and others."

Shepherd glosses over the warrant. He makes a small sound—bemused perhaps, or resigned. Then he lifts his chin at Haden. "I'm not going to make this difficult for you," he says. "But I will include my attorney before we go any further."

Evie sees Haden's jaw tighten. Marcus can't quite hide that twitch of victory at the corner of his mouth. Before anyone moves to cuff Dr. Shepherd, three figures stride forward, purpose radiating from their every step.

An ivory-jacketed woman reaches Haden first, voice calm but unwavering. "Agent, we're counsel for Dr. Shepherd. Might I be allowed to review your warrant?" Her hand hovers open, expectant.

A tall, stern man—Shepherd's second attorney—pulls out his phone. "I'll have the district judge in just a moment." His tone carries the weight of finality.

Their junior lawyer holds up his phone, hand steady. "We're recording," he says, "every moment of this engagement."

Haden glances at Evie through the drizzle, a micro-tremor in his gaze. He clears his throat. "Shepherd, I—"

"No," Ivory-jacket says, stepping directly between Haden and Shepherd. "Under your own protocol, allow us to confer privately. Out of mutual respect, give us a moment."

Marcus opens his mouth, but the undertaker-eyed counsel raises a finger. Marcus stifles himself. Elena remains by the tent, her face an impassive mask.

For the first time, Shepherd exhales. Evie watches him, noting the easing of his navy quarter-zip.

Haden clears his throat again. He hands over the warrant. "Read the charges," he says, voice steady now. "Material involvement with deaths in the Commonwealth and other jurisdictions, and unlawful handling of human remains."

Ivory-jacket scans the warrant, lips pursed. She lifts her head. "May we see the supporting affidavits? We were not notified prior to this morning's filing."

Haden narrows his eyes, curious. "How do you know about the affidavits we filed?" he asks. The attorney merely gives him a smarmy look, as if to say she just knows.

His gaze flicks to the circle of guests: the State Senator, two biotech executives at the tent's entrance, and servers frozen mid-pour. Their whispers ripple through the damp air. He glances back at the counsel. "The evidence is on file at Quantico. You may review it by appointment."

"That won't do," the undertaker-counsel interjects. "There's a stay issued by a district judge. Did you confirm before arriving here?"

Ivory-jacket hands the warrant back. "No? I thought so."

The rain intensifies, drumming on the Suburban's roof like a metronome. The senator's lips twitch; a few guests lift phones to record the legal skirmish.

Ivory-jacket lowers her voice to a near-whisper; only Haden and his mic can hear: "Two nights ago, our client's office was broken into. The Wackenhut Agency documented the incident. Yet this warrant—filed post-break-in—alleges hidden compartments." She taps the paper. "Chain of custody is in question. For all we know, your team planted evidence. Anything discovered after the break-in is going to be ruled as tainted."

Haden's face goes still. He folds the warrant, tucking it away. "Understood," he says at last.

Evie's chest clenches even tighter.

Shepherd steps back. His lawyers flank him, as if escorting a dignitary rather than a suspect.

She watches them turn back toward the tent, voices low, legal strategies already spinning. The guests follow in a loose circle, curiosity ablaze. The senator shakes his head, mutters something about "next time," and raises a glass in what might be solidarity or mockery.

While the others on the team head to their respective vehicles, Haden retreats to the Suburban. He drops into the driver's seat, the bulk of him so heavy with rage and disbelief it tilts the whole car. Haden is silent for a count of five, then ten. He looks at Evie as if he wants to bite something in half. Then, before any accusations can rise, his phone vibrates again—a short, cruel hum.

He answers it. Listens. His features, never soft, sharpen further.

"Understood," he says, and hangs up.

Evie doesn't need to ask. The shape of the disaster is already clear: they have been outgunned, not just in law but in politics, in the hierarchy of who owns reality. She wants to say something—an apology, a justification, a confession—but Haden's fist against the dash cracks the silence.

"Internal Affairs," he says. "We're suspended. Full audit pending."

He doesn't look at her, but she can feel the judgment radiating from him.

Evie is numb. She understands now that Shepherd's defense was never about the legal challenge alone. It was about making the FBI look like thugs. They would be lucky if they held onto their jobs, let alone the case. Shepherd had known—must have known—what was coming. The break-in at the office. Their chain of custody. The warrant that now made Haden look like a fool and herself like a dirty cop.

She wants to say; It wasn't me. She never touched the journals, never planted anything. But she can see through the rain and the glare of her own failure that it doesn't matter.

Shepherd has won. Not in court, but in the realm that counted. The realm where power, not facts, shaped the narrative.

There is nothing that can be said. So instead, Haden presses the ignition button. The car is silent except for the rasp of the wipers. They pull away, granite crunching under tires, the estate shrinking behind the water-dropped windshield.

Chapter Twenty-Eight

It's Over

Quantico, Monday. The sun has long since burned off the last dew of morning. It now filters through the third-floor windows in a kind of sullen haze, gilding the dust motes that drift and settle over the long conference table. The Special Crimes Division is supposed to be empty by four; today, every corridor is deserted save for the one leading to Haden's office.

Inside, the air is close and static, like the inside of an evidence locker. Marcus sits nearest the window, his chair canted back just enough to keep his posture from breaking. Elena anchors the far end, hands folded tightly in her lap. Cassandra stands, arms crossed—her usual territory. Haden positions himself at the head of the table, motionless except for the slow flex of one hand.

Evie arrives last, the seconds of her entrance echoing. She slides into the only remaining chair, one with a direct line of sight to Haden. No one looks at anyone else.

On the table is a brown folder: "BULLETIN—FOR OFFICIAL USE ONLY" in red, the edges already nicked from too many hands.

For a long, airless moment, nothing happens.

Then the door opens, not with the gentle hush of an agent but the officious rattle of Legal Affairs. The woman who enters is just under five feet, gray bob, a navy suit, badge on a lanyard that reads "OIG Liaison." She walks with the assurance of someone whose business is wreckage.

She doesn't introduce herself. There isn't a need to. Instead, she sets a slim envelope atop the folder and addresses Haden in a solemn tone.

"I'm here as a formality, but let's get to the substance." Her eyes scan the room, pausing an imperceptible beat longer on Marcus—possibly because of the color in his face, possibly because she recognizes his name from an earlier career disaster. "Earlier today, we received ex parte notice from the Commonwealth Attorney's office. They've determined the material evidence recovered Saturday—namely, the surgical journals and laptop—has been ruled inadmissible."

Cassandra's lips part, just a little. Elena's jaw slackens, a ripple barely visible beneath her olive skin.

"On what grounds?" Marcus's voice is low and not remotely curious.

The woman turns to him politely. "Procedural. The initial search warrant referenced financial fraud and was signed by a magistrate outside the jurisdiction for violent crimes. It was clearly a fishing expedition with intent, and likely with foreknowledge. Any evidence not stipulated in the original warrant is ineligible for criminal proceedings, and possession thereof constitutes a breach. In plain English, we're required to return the journals and all digital images to the subject—Dr. Shepherd. Effective immediately."

The word "subject" hangs, sticky as bile.

Marcus barks a laugh, ugly and sharp. "With respect, ma'am, no one on our team had any knowledge about the hidden compartment or those records. The wall shifted on its own. If anything, it was goddamn providence!"

The OIG Liaison's face is by-the-book bland. "Providence is not a recognized legal principle," she says. "Intent is irrelevant; appearance does count. Circumstances strongly suggest you were seeking evidence outside your scope."

Marcus sits forward now, unbalanced, a spent match in human form. "You're telling me if a serial killer keeps a diary under his pillow and it falls out and hits me in the face, I have to hand it back?"

She relents a sigh. "You may use it to wipe your nose, Agent Vaughn. But under these circumstances, you may not read or retain it."

Cassandra's jaw clicks. "So we're what, supposed to apologize to Shepherd and let him keep his library of torture notes?"

"Not supposed," the Liaison says, "required. The digital forensics unit will supervise the deletion of all related files. Anything you've accessed, derived, or discussed outside the original warrant is forfeit." Her eyes flick from person to person, counting the number of careers circling the drain.

Haden stares down at his clasped hands, thumb working slow circles into the space between them. "And the rest of the inquiry?"

"On hold," she says, shifting her weight. "Unless you want to see your entire Division referred for OPR action. Which, by the way, is a possibility if you attempt to circumvent this order." She places a second envelope next to the first. "All agents present at the search are to report for administrative review, effective end of day."

Elena whispers, "You're suspending us."

"I'm saying you're on leave, with pay, pending outcome." The woman looks at each of them. "Do not access the case files. Do not communicate with the media or any parties associated with Dr. Shepherd. Any deviation will be considered grounds for termination and possible prosecution." She looks at Haden, and for a flicker she seems to soften. "I know this isn't your first rodeo, sir. My number's on the card in the envelope. If you have any doubts, I'd use it before you burn your career down."

The woman leaves as briskly as she entered; the door clicks shut with a thud.

The silence she leaves behind is a physical thing, heavy and infectious. The team sits in a semicircle of barely controlled outrage.

Marcus is the first to break. "This is such bullcrap," he spits, rising out of his chair as if ready to pace, then aborting, then sitting back down harder than before. He keeps his fists on his thighs, his neck mottled pink.

Cassandra says nothing; she only keeps her arms folded and stares at the floor, jaw locked, a muscle working in her cheek.

Elena's eyes shine. She does not cry, but it's an effort. "All those months," she says, just above a whisper. "We did everything right." Her hands tremble in her lap, fingers squeezing so tight they are bloodless.

Haden finally sits back, letting the old office chair creak. For a moment, he is unreadable, the poker face of a man who has seen too many unpunished wounds. Then he looks at his team, one by one, meeting their eyes, refusing to blink.

"I won't sugarcoat it. They've kneecapped the case, at least for now." His voice is a husk, all the energy spent in keeping himself together. "What I want you to remember is this: we forced him to surface. He won't be able to operate, at least not for a long while. And we're not dead in the water yet. There's always another angle. But for now, the Bureau wants us to get scarce."

He lets that settle. "Go home. Don't talk to each other until this cools down. If you need a lawyer, ask for one. Don't freelance it. Don't take any bait."

Marcus glances at Evie, then Cassandra, then back to the window. "He gets away with it."

"He does. But not forever," says Haden, and it almost sounds like hope.

The team stands, each moving as if their bones are too heavy for their bodies. Cassandra lingers at the screen, eyes flicking to the dormant case files. Elena follows Marcus to the door, both of them careful not to brush against each other.

Evie is the last to rise. Haden catches her with a look that is not quite an order, not quite a plea. "Stay a minute, Cross," he says, voice low.

The rest leave, their footsteps receding, the closing door a velvet knife-edge.

Evie stands, hands at her sides, badge at her hip like a failed star.

The hum of the overhead lights is all that remains.

Haden exhales, a slow deflation that settles him deeper into his chair. He loosens his tie, the gesture less relief than resignation, and pinches the bridge of his nose. When he speaks, it's as if he's talking to the floor. "You're not on suspension, Agent Cross. Technically, you were never assigned to this team."

No.

Evie shudders, jaw so tight she can hear her molars creak. She doesn't move, not even to shift her weight.

Haden's gaze lifts, unexpectedly vulnerable. "That was intentional. I wanted to shield you and protect us." The words taste bitter, even to him. "So when Internal Affairs calls, you answer, but you keep your distance. Nothing off script. Shepherd's lawyers are like sharks—you bleed even a little, they'll devour you."

Evie lets her eyes drop to her badge—physically present, but not. A token of almost-belonging, a vestige of credibility she hasn't earned in years. She waits, forcing herself to be still.

Haden rakes his hand through his close-cropped hair. He looks at Evie—really looks this time. "Listen," his voice softens, "If I file the report about what you did five years ago, it will cement every accusation against all of us. The cover-up, the breach of protocol, the motive to plant evidence—it'll destroy whatever chance we have at a second pass. I know you did it for the right reasons. I don't want to know any more than that. As much as you may want to take the hit... we simply cannot afford it."

Evie inhales, sharp and shallow. She wants to say something. Wants to confess. She cries out inside for absolution. But Haden is not a priest, and this is not a church.

The silence yawns wider.

Haden rubs his temples, voice gone hoarse. "Go back to your home office. Get lost in your financial crimes. If anything changes, I'll let you know. Otherwise, stay clear."

He stands, the movement abrupt, and begins collecting files into a cardboard box. Hands shake—just a fraction, but enough for Evie to see the toll. She watches him work, each case file a headstone for another hope buried.

He pauses, just once, to look at her. "We did our best," he says, almost inaudibly.

Evie nods, then pivots on her heel. She walks out of the office and down the empty corridor. Her shoes click hollow on the tile. In the lobby, the security guard gives her a vacant nod. The place seems stripped of its purpose—procedure over virtue.

Outside, the late light is orange and cold, striping the lot with long shadows. She finds her car. She sits in the driver's seat for a while, gaze fixed on the endless rows of windshields and the chain-link fence beyond.

Shepherd is free. The system is closed. If there is a victory, it would appear to be his.

She starts the engine. Goes nowhere, the gears in neutral, the day stuck.

Is there even a way forward?

Chapter Twenty-Nine

Devil in the Dataset

The morning sky after Quantico is gray enough to blend with the Formica countertop. Evie hunches at the kitchen island, the same space that fed her family, now a launchpad for her disappointments.

Her laptop glows in silence, tabs flaring across the browser. She scrolls through the news. Every outlet, every algorithm, every aggregator has converged: Dr. Shepherd. Today, he's anointed by the local NPR as "the mind-surgeon of the new century." CNN runs a banner trailing photos of the man with convalescent children beaming beside him. Washington Monthly's headline—"Modern Oppenheimer or Neuroscience's Salk?"—forces her jaw to clamp.

Shepherd's photo cycles across the feeds: conference panel, lab coat, TED talk. He's suddenly being quoted on half a dozen press releases. His statement, "Shouldn't it be the privilege of every scientist to risk their reputation on behalf of the vulnerable?" is smeared verbatim in three separate sources.

She digs for a different sort of story. Nothing about warrants. Nothing about the journals, or his wall compartment, or the botched warrant. Not a whisper of yesterday's truth.

The only place she finds any hint is a two-sentence "opinion" in the right margin of a paywalled blog, where a "former law enforcement analyst" suggests the "recent scrutiny of Shepherd's grant funding was politically motivated and completely exonerated." It's drowned by five paragraphs of Shepherd's alma mater and his contributions to the local firehouse.

The numbness in her knuckles, when it comes, is almost a relief.

Evie scrolls, then clicks, then scrolls again. Shepherd's warm, bearded smile is everywhere. The past week's effort has been reduced to a press cycle—a detergent wash, leaving everything hospital white.

She slaps the laptop closed; the sound is sharp enough to jolt the room. Silence follows—thick, dense, unyielding. She presses her palms flat against the countertop as if bracing for aftershocks.

It doesn't matter; she thinks. They'll not connect the bodies. They'll never have evidence. The system was designed for process, with scant chances at justice. Shepherd knew it. Haden knew it.

She presses a thumb to her temple, massaging a phantom pain.

A minute later she pops the laptop open again, to its hinge's complaint. This time, she does not browse the news. Instead, she navigates to the webmail client—a skein of encrypted links and dummy inboxes, her own contribution to the war of privacy. There's nothing from Haden. Nothing from anyone but the usual vendor spam and a single message from her old white-hat, its subject line: "You up?"

She snorts. Then types: "He's everywhere. All clean. I need something dirty, anything you can dig." Evie hits send, then sets the laptop aside, watching the cursor blink in the empty reply box. The world outside the kitchen window is still dull and gray.

She doesn't know if there is a way forward, but she'll keep scrolling until something gives.

Night again. The house is a shipwreck, adrift in a sea of unfinished coffee and roiling silence. At two in the morning, the only sounds are the tick of the fridge and the occasional flare of car headlights, smearing the blinds in spectral white.

Evie is half-sleeping on the couch, the television's flicker painting her face in washes. She dreams of the hum of machines, sterile scalpels, and the cold embrace of a coffin. His victims gather around Shepherd at his dais. He pulls a brain from a velvet sack, placing it down with reverence. It trembles, and she knows it is alive. The victims turn to look for her, their silent screams echoing. Yet, her own screams suffocate in her throat.

Her laptop's alert cuts through with a chime.

She bolts upright; the world jerking back into focus. A notification flares: 'Secure Package Delivered—Check Auth Key.' Evie blinks the sleep from her eyes, then fumbles with the keyboard. Instinctively, she punches in the VPN, routes through two foreign servers, and pings the mailbox.

The file is big—gargantuan, in fact. She downloads it to the dummy desktop, decompresses with a code, and the screen floods with PDFs, spreadsheets, and a half-dozen odd files she doesn't recognize. It's a data dump of the sort that ruins careers or governments: corporate records, transaction logs, internal memoranda.

She scrolls for twenty minutes, mind numbing as she tries to make sense of the data labyrinth. Somewhere in the middle, there's a chart labeled 'Patient Pathways—Special Grant Recipients.' Another folder, 'Mercer Holdings—Confidential,' contains a horde of scanned wire transfer slips. The sums are obscene.

The name appears over and over: Mercer. Alexander Mercer. CEO of DeepTime Technologies. Reclusive, billionaire. The blogosphere has theories about this guy's health. But the official word is "chronic illness—request privacy."

Shepherd's name appears in some as vendor and in others as payee. Sometimes as 'Herd Medical Consultants,' sometimes as an abbreviation, sometimes simply as 'V. Shepherd, MD.' It's never direct, always layered through three or four shells.

She prints them.

Evie works in silence, letting the pile thicken. Fatigue falls away as adrenaline kicks in. There are dates—transfers, appointments, public appearances. Then she pulls her old notepad from the junk drawer, flips to the Cartographer timeline, and begins to cross-reference. Her pen trembles as the patterns congeal.

June 2015. A large transfer from 'Mercer Asset Mgmt' to 'Neuro-Life Foundation.' Two weeks later, the first documented Cartographer kill.

September 2015. Same pattern, different shell company, same aftermath.

A dump of money bracketed every murder, every "disappearance" into a "nonprofit" with no website, no board, no public audit. Some names are grotesquely on-the-nose: 'Elysian Fund,' 'Mors Vitae,' 'Cure Initiates.' She shudders.

The amounts are always just enough to influence, or—maybe—to fund something that does not want the attention of a grant committee.

She stops, massaging her temples.

Evie returns to the PDF bundle, opening another: 'Immortality Project—White Paper, v.3.' She scrolls through the summary. It is written in the blithe language of technologists who assume ethics is a technical hurdle, not a question.

"Our group theorizes that, using next-generation neural mapping and organic-digital interfaces, a subject's consciousness may be instantiated beyond biological death. While prior efforts failed due to tissue decay and loss of key neural 'signatures,' newly discovered novel extraction methods show promise in preserving these patterns intact. While test subjects are currently limited to animal and ex vivo models, the ultimate goal appears to be within reach."

The technical diagrams are explicit, annotated with familiar handwriting. In each, the target region is outlined—a sweep of the temporal lobe, a web of the pons, the cruciform shape of the corpus callosum, each crosshatched in blue. "Limited extraction," the notes say. "Window: 12 minutes or less."

The blood drains from Evie's face.

Shepherd's surgical notes—Cartographer's trophies—were never random. Not the thrill of the kill. They were roadmaps. Each brain harvested was a test run for someone's digital afterlife.

Evie reads on, compelled and sickened. There are internal emails, redacted but still telling, where a knowledgeable source assures Mercer's team that "current procurement methods are optimized for minimal trace," and that "the risk to operational integrity is within parameters."

She recognizes the tone. It is the same flat, clipped precision Shepherd used in every public appearance. The man has no variance between the worlds.

Her stomach clenches. She glances at the clock. Three in the morning now. The house—this room feels crowded with invisible presences.

Evie spreads the papers on the island, creating columns and grids. She draws the lines: wire transfer, fake charity, brain harvest, rinse and repeat. The implication is so vast, so monstrous, that she almost wishes she were the one losing her mind.

This is not just Shepherd. It's Mercer. It's a cabal of those so rich and terrified of death that they would devour anything to stave off their own oblivion. The system that failed her at every turn is, in fact, working exactly as intended.

Evie traces the timeline again, once, twice, desperate to find a gap, an error, something to break the logic. There is none.

Her hands shake as she types a reply to the white-hat: "Got it. You're sure you transferred this all air-gapped? They'll come for you otherwise."

The reply is instantaneous: "We're out. Now, it's on you. Be careful."

Evie sits down, then stands, then paces the kitchen. It's too much. The edges of her vision pulse with black static. The weight of it all swirls in her gut.

She makes it to the bathroom, drops to her knees, and retches until there's nothing but bile.

The horror is not the murder. The horror is how close she had been—how unremarkable the machinery of it all.

She wipes her mouth, flushes, then leans against the cold tile. In the reflection above the sink, she looks alien: sweat-soaked, eyes rimmed with red. For a moment, she is unmoored, not sure who is looking back at whom.

She whispers, "What am I supposed to do with this?"

There is no answer. Only the steady whir of the refrigerator, the hum of the laptop, and the weight of a secret so vast it has its own gravity.

Evie staggers back to the kitchen. She collects the printouts, collates them. All the data is so spread out. None of it connects directly. She can see the whole wide picture. None of it is concrete, all slippery sand under her feet. She has nothing. The FBI isn't about to take her seriously. Not after... Haden is out of options. Marcus is probably under surveillance himself. Elena, maybe, but she's got a family to lose.

For the first time, Evie understands how the world ends: not with a bang, but with a transfer receipt and a glowing profile on morning news.

She lies on her bed, wide-eyed, as the sun rises.

Shepherd is free. Mercer is untouchable. And ghosts never sleep.

Neither can she.

Chapter Thirty

A Hand to Hold

Evie slouches on the couch, one knee drawn up, half-swaddled in a blanket she must have pulled from the dryer yesterday. Or was it the day before? Her face is sallow, ringed with grime. She hasn't left the house in over a day. The recycling bin, once reserved for water bottles and soymilk, now primarily holds whiskey bottles. Even the air smells like surrender.

The phone is at it again. She glances at the display—MOM, all caps, plus three missed. It vibrates against a mound of folders with dull, robotic insistence. She turns it facedown, exiling the living to darkness. They can wait until she's fit for the land of the living.

Evie stares at the table, at the glowering pile of files: the PDFs from her white-hat contact, the spreadsheets mapping Mercer's every financial step. The web is so complete, so impersonal, she wonders if the dead she's trying to mourn are even visible. She's linked victim to murderer to oligarch, knowing for certain that the pattern is not proof. It is a geometry of despair.

She picks up the latest bottle—a good third left, label peeling back—and pours into a chipped mug. The amber sloshes, dribbles over the rim and pools in a crevice between the printouts. She smears at it with her thumb, but it only runs, blurring out half a name. Doesn't matter. Nothing matters. She drinks, consuming empty potential and spirits.

She surveys the table for something to anchor her, the only un-stained artifact. Divorce papers. Michael's neat, judicious signature; her line still blank. She stares at it, feeling nothing. In the company of evil, bureaucracy is almost a kindness.

A rapping at the front door disrupts her. She blinks, orienting herself. Has she even locked it?

The door opens.

Michael, the husband she once knew, leans in. He raps apologet-ically on the now-open door, his gaze settling on the empty bottles behind her.

He says softly, "You look like hell."

Evie sits up. "You're the doctor," she mutters, then sinks back into the couch.

Michael stands there at the threshold, scanning the interior. When he enters, it's with the gait of a man who expects the floor to give out at any moment. He settles in across from her, arms on his knees, quiet.

Evie waits for a question, a judgment, a what the hell have you done. Instead, Michael gauges the mess, then at her—a glance at the divorce papers.

For a moment, she thinks she might break. Instead, she sips and grimaces. "I don't know how to make it stop," she says.

Michael nods. "Neither do I." His voice is hoarse. "But I can try to help, if you'll let me."

She laughs, then coughs. "No one can help. It's all too big. Like fighting gravity. They have everything. The Bureau, the law, all of it. I tried. I tried, and I lost."

Michael listens, not flinching. "I heard. You did more than anyone else. You didn't just walk away."

She shrugs. "I refused to quit. Probably should have."

"That's Evie." He folds his hands, scoffing. "Probably why you still won't sign."

She stares at the blank line. Her cheeks flush. "I don't know. Maybe. Maybe I thought if I held on, I'd keep a piece of her, a piece of you, something worth saving. But I don't think that's going to work now. Not anymore."

Michael leans forward. "Right at this moment, I'm not here about the papers." He sets his jaw. "Sign them. Don't sign them. Seems you could use some help. You don't have to do this alone."

Evie looks at her hands, their tremor. She wonders if the shaking will ever stop. "I'm scared," she says, so quietly that it doesn't sound like her at all.

Michael's gaze softens. "Me too."

For a long time, neither moves. The clock ticks. The fridge churns on.

Evie closes her eyes. She breathes, letting the presence of another human carry some small part of the burden. For the first time in days, she feels herself surface.

They sit like that, both sharing each other's space.

He doesn't reach for her right away. There's nothing in his posture to suggest he's come to scold or to reclaim. Michael sits with elbows braced to his knees. He breathes slowly, so even Evie finds herself matching his rhythm.

"You want me to take out the empties?" he asks.

She laughs, or tries to. It's just an exhale, half cough. "Let's pretend I'm recycling," she says. "At least until I have to show my face outside again."

Michael glances at the floor, then at the line of Evie's jaw. "Your parents are worried," he says.

"I'm a full-time disappointment," she replies. "I don't have any updates for them, anyway."

Michael's gaze lingers, then falls to the mess of paper. He picks up a page, glances at the numbers, the names. "What's this about Dr. Shepherd? One of your financial deep dives?"

She hesitates, picking at the edge of the mug. "It's all Shepherd. All of it."

Michael squints, the first sign of composure slipping. He flips through a couple more pages. "I thought he was just—" He pauses, as if the words can't surface. "I mean, that's just the guy from TED, right? The one on all the consciousness podcasts."

She bites her lip. "He's the Cartographer, Michael."

The words hang. She thinks maybe he'll laugh, call her cracked.

Evie sips, letting the whiskey sting the roof of her mouth. "It was always him. I ran the data. Went to Riverbend, saw him in person. His whole practice is a cover. Even his charity gigs—none of it is about treatment as much as research. The grant money, the clinics, everything is just his hunting ground. He's the one."

Michael stares at her, and for a second she sees herself as he must: unwashed, unhinged, a woman with a wild-eyed theory and days of alcohol in her veins. "You... What? Evie, I..." He's about to say more, but the words tangle up.

She shrugs, almost as a challenge. "It doesn't matter. I can't prove it. I can barely even get anyone to listen—Haden tried, but they shut him down. Put the team on probation. Wiped the evidence clean. All that's left are cash flows and white-collar misdirection. He has an all-seeing patron on high. It's quite astounding, really.

"It's all about Mercer. Shepherd's just the blade; Mercer's the one providing it." She closes her eyes, the weight of it pressing from inside. "It's always the same with these people. The world bends to them, and we just get swept under."

"What do you..." Michael stammers, paper balanced between his hands. "What do you want to do?"

Evie takes a breath, trying to summon something like resolve. "I want to destroy them. I want to take everything they love and salt the earth. But I'm not even sure how to touch them. I can't even move myself." She laughs again, and it sounds more like grief. "After this, the Bureau is probably done with me. Haden says to lie low, play dead. Even if they weather the inquiry, I'm not going to be trusted again."

He folds the paper, sets it down with more care than it deserves. "You've tried to do the right thing. All along."

She snorts, the sound ugly. "That's what got her killed. Or worse."

Evie picks at the edge of a printout, shreds a strip off and lets it fall. "I told myself if I just worked harder, if I gave them enough data, I'd come out a star. But the system isn't made for that. It's made for protecting itself." She looks at him, the first time she's really met his eyes. "We were right. Hope is a dangerous thing."

Michael sighs, a tired, old-man sound. "Maybe. But without it, what's the point?"

Evie almost laughs, but it turns into a sob she clamps down on. "You ever think about what she'd say if she saw how we turned out?"

He blinks, and for a moment his composure slips. "She'd say we're idiots. That we should stop pretending we can win, and just run away to the beach." A hint of a smile. "She always wanted to see the Pacific."

Evie finds her mug again. She drains the last of it, wipes her mouth with the back of her hand. "Neither one of us believes we can just walk away. Not from life's greatest train wreck."

He shrugs, the motion simple, sincere. "Maybe not. The world doesn't change for us. But what if we can still change for her?"

She snorts. "Now you sound like a guidance counselor."

"I'm serious, Evie." He shifts, finally bridging the space between them, his hand resting on hers. "There's no one left who'll fight for her except us."

She wants to recoil, to fight the comfort, but there's no strength left. Instead, she lets the touch ground her, slow her heart.

"I broke everything," she whispers. "Every promise. Every rule."

He shakes his head. "You broke the rules. The promises you kept."

A flush of heat climbs her throat, shame and relief colliding. "I don't know what to do next."

He considers. "You start with the truth. And then you keep telling it, even if it hurts." His hold on her tightens, just for a second. "Maybe you stop playing by their rules. Maybe we make our own."

She lifts her face, searching for sarcasm or bitterness. There's none. "You want me to go rogue?"

"I want you to make it through. I want you to outlive them. If it means burning the world down, maybe that's what it takes." He leans in, forehead to hers, a contact so intimate it hurts. "June wouldn't want you to give up. Neither do I."

She closes her eyes, lets the world tilt. In the dark, with his forehead pressed to hers, she finds a thread of calm.

"I'm scared," she says again.

Michael's voice is barely there, but it holds. "Me too."

For a long while they sit, joined in the fragile architecture of surviving. Outside, the cold creeps into night. Inside, they are just two people, tethered to nothing but memory and a last stubborn glint of hope.

Chapter Thirty-One

Come to Terms

The house reverts to its old self at Michael's morning departure—a kind of brittle hush. The living room is a bright wash. But even the light seems hesitant, caught in the dust motes above the rug. Evie sits where she has since dawn, knees drawn to her chest, the wrapped blanket still some lingering comfort.

The divorce papers are as they were. She stares at them for an interval that could be a minute, could be an hour. When she finally looks up, the doorway is empty. The edge of the rug is turned slightly from when Michael's shoe caught it on the way out. Evidence she didn't imagine the whole evening.

Back to alone, but not completely.

A cooling sensation builds at her nape, subtle as a cat's paw. It starts its migration down the cord of her spine. She recognizes this—the small, subnatural signal of a resonance inside her own. Not hunger, not thirst, not even the ache she carries for June, but something outside the continuum of need. A charge, a gathering.

Evie brings her arms around herself, fingers digging into the blanket fabric. The motion feels childlike, not comforting, more like holding herself in check. The house creaks—pipes settling, a neighbor's leaf blower, the fridge inhaling and exhaling—but none of these sounds explain the thickening air, the taste of iron that's accumulated at the back of her mouth.

There is no voice.

Instead, the presence enters through sensation: pressure behind her ribs, the slow coiling of tendons at the base of her throat, a heatless shift that glows at the core of her sternum. It is not invasive, not entirely. The sensation is almost seductive, the way alcohol traces its path to the root of your limbs.

Rage builds first, like the snap of a wire under tension. It is not the kind of anger Evie knows; not the rolling boil that followed her home from the Bureau's defeat. No, this is vaster, deeper, not merely anger directed at an individual but at the entire world—the vast sea of existence.

It passes as quickly as it ignites, and then comes the sorrow. Immense, oceanic. Evie has embraced grief—it has been all of her since the day June was taken—but this is different. It is collective, a burial mound of generations, thousands of the lost folded into one. She clutches her abdomen and keens, a sound low and private, so soft it doesn't cross the boundary of her lips. Each breath is salted, every heartbeat echoing a drum she has always carried.

On the side table, the priest's rosary is a clump of black beads and steel, left from yesterday's collapse. She eyes it with the desperation of an addict. The urge is primal: reach out, wrap the beads around her fist, let it anchor her to her own body. She extends her hand, fingertips trembling, but just as they graze the first bead she stops.

What's left to lose? The thought surfaces, not as a question but as a conclusion. The Harbinger waits, its pressure a fist inside her chest. She pulls her hand back, lets it drop into her lap, and closes her eyes.

It is a surrender, but also a leap.

The shadows in the room respond. They gather in the crooks of the armchair, pooling in the gaps between furniture. Evie feels the shift, the tiny adjustment of the world to accommodate something new—an old program kicking back online. Like some system that has always run in the background, it just needs permission to come to the fore.

She draws a breath, lets the cold expand her lungs, and it expands with it. Her vision darkens at the edges, fills with streaks of color, then with nothing at all. Is this possession, or simply the way it was always going to be? The boundaries between what is Evie and what is Other are porous, a membrane more than a wall.

The anger returns, this time not as cold but as intuition: instrument. Both hinge and blade. Sorrow is ballast; the anger is aim. The weight is familiar, as if she has carried it for lifetimes, or will.

Evie opens her eyes.

It's still her living room. The coffee table, the divorce papers still there. But now she feels the Harbinger with a clarity she has never allowed herself before, both chilling and absolute. It is not a voice, nor some spirit, but an unrelenting call: be what they cannot.

Become a reckoning.

The room's geometry collapses. Time shivers, slows, then splits. Her coffee table pulses between glass, wood, and the absence of anything at all. Her hands—small, brown, Evie's own—are overlaid with those of others: a beefy fist, callused and pocked; a taper-finger, veined with translucent skin; hands young, old, genderless and not.

Her vision descends like a dropped curtain: a damp chamber, maybe England or France. The air is tainted with the metallic scent of blood and the greasy smoke of torches. She gazes out of some medieval host. His tough skin scrapes against black leather and wool; a half-mask holds tightly over his jaw. Before her, a nobleman kneels, his vocal cords shattered by terror, wrists bound. The nobleman babbles, a jumble of titles and connections, but her mind is elsewhere—on the horrors they had witnessed because of him.

She recalls the children, pale and lifeless, their innocence stolen by this nobleman's greed. Their families torn apart by his treachery. He had bribed the sheriff, the bishop, even the family of the murdered, to bury these sins, to silence truth. But the Harbinger was not to be bought. When the axe falls, it is not just the noble's head but the very face of his cruelty that splits.

The executioner stands—not in satisfaction, but in a profound dread. The host's eyes shimmer a menacing phosphor blue, the same icy chill behind Evie's own eyelids.

Her vision rips from the chamber with a violence that leaves her stomach in her throat.

She is a nurse in a hospital, a place of starched linens and mildew. The year is impossible to name—could be 1915, 1950, a time when every woman wore her hair up and men died in beds labeled with tags. Her hands are deft, gloved, a syringe already prepped. On the cot lies a man of some stature—a judge, someone who dispensed mercy in public but purchased debauchery in secret. She works alone, but is still watched. Ghosts of the judge's victims pay witness in the corner, children and women and men with broken teeth, silent and swaying.

The nurse moves to the judge's bedside, eyeing the machine that preserves the judge's breath. She pinches the line of his IV, injects a liquid, and then calmly disconnects the pump. There is a blip, a faint alarm, then nothing. The judge does not stir. The ghosts in the corners fade as one, as the nurse closes the man's eyelids with two fingers. Precise, gentle, more than deserved.

In a whirl, the city becomes night. Bombed-out tarps and hungry sky replace roofs. Evie is a young woman now, perhaps nineteen, maybe fifty, hunger gnawing out her cheeks. She moves through the alleys, hands wrapped around a Luger pistol too large for her grip. The city is under occupation, and every step is a gamble. She ducks behind a tangle of bicycles, waits, counts the paces of jackboots beyond the ironwork, then sprints across a square. The air smells of sour milk, gun oil, and piss.

Her destination is a narrow window above a bakery. She scales the fire escape, feet finding each rung in muscle memory. Inside, a man sleeps in a room lined with foreign books—her people's books, looted from the university. He is a collaborator, a small functionary who bargains with lives. He is deep at rest, dreaming when she presses the barrel to his temple... and pulls the trigger.

Seconds later, she sits in his chair and rifles through his desk. The names on the lists are there—dozens, hundreds—names she knows, or once did. She pockets the lists, wipes the blood from her cheek, and vanishes into the night.

When Evie returns to herself, the intense weight drives her to gag. The world strobes of then and now, a parade of hosts stretching back and forward, each a vessel of this same purpose.

This Harbinger is not a demon or a devil. It is old. Older than law, older than the thin scaffolding men build to keep their kind in check. It is a recursion, a brute-force algorithm: when all else fails, the Harbinger is made manifest. Sometimes it's an executioner, sometimes a healer, sometimes a weapon disguised as a girl with a gun. In each case, the host is never a puppet. Each time, they choose.

That is the horror, and the blessing.

She rises from the couch. Every nerve is awake, every sense tuned. The fibers of the floorboards are like fingerprints; the tick of the wall clock plays as if each second is an opportunity. The air has a taste—copper and ozone, or maybe the burnt tang of something too-long repressed.

Her body is both familiar and not, a vessel newly requisitioned. Evie walks through the house, deliberate steps, as if mapping the terrain for the first time. Carpet fibers yield under her toes; the archway to the kitchen frames her as both guest and occupier.

She can feel it now—the Harbinger—its hunger and disdain.

With a turn, June's door is before her. It is closed as always, but the aura is different. No longer a space of loss, but of stillness—an old cauterized wound. She touches the wood, fingertips hovering along the grain. The spirit's reaction is subtle, a withdrawal rather than an advance. This is not its domain. Here, there is only memory—mercy. She lingers, listening for some sign, pressing her own demand. Evie runs her palm down the frame, then turns bereft.

She knows now, June will not be solved—not the way she imagined.

Not with a courtroom or a press release or the right combination of empathy and data.

That is not what the Harbinger brings.

She returns to the living room. The old blanket on the armchair is still warm from her body. She presses her palm to it, then folds it along its seams and places it on the backrest. Evie goes about collecting the empty bottles. The gesture is unremarkable, but it feels like the closing of a chapter. Or at least the shelving of it.

The mirror beside the coat rack reflects back at her. She stands in profile, shoulders squared, chin slightly lifted. There is no hint of ghosts here—just a woman, a little older, a little more tired, but standing. She allows herself a brief inventory: cheekbones, eyes, mouth. All present, all accounted for.

It is only when she turns to the window that she sees it.

Outside, the day is already ending with a speed she hadn't antici-pated. The houses are painted in long warm shadows, their windows catching the last golden rays. She steps to her window, parts the cur-tain, and leans close.

For a moment, the dual panes share two faces: her own, and another behind it—gaunt, hollow-eyed, echoes of an executioner, a nurse, the freedom fighter. The effect is fleeting, but leaves a residue, a certainty. She is not alone in this. She never was.

Its presence settles in, not as a burden but as a perfect fit. Armor, not parasite. Its clarity is total. There will be no more bargaining, no more running. She is the last appeal, the last resort.

This is what it means to be chosen.

This is what it means to finally embrace the monster within.

Chapter Thirty-Two

It's On

Night has smothered the house, lending to a silence so complete. Emboldened, Evie pivots to next steps. She sits rigid at her desk, spine bent, knees drawn toward the battered chair, one hand holding her chin as she delves.

Among the heap of PDFs and images comprising Ethos' mass data dump, was a diverse inventory of real estate holdings. Several along the New England coast. One in particular stood out.

Her screen is filled with a god's-eye view of her Virginia region. A rural expanse—wooded hills, a snake-curved river, a single dirt drive coiling through the trees to a clearing that holds what looks like an expansive cabin, small outbuildings. A vacation property, if one were an oligarch, or an exile. She toggles a slider; the image time-travels through six seasons, snow melting into thaw, summer grass obliterating winter scars, the drive never changing.

A quiet retreat, rarely used.

She overlays grid coordinates, then blinks slowly, as her mind parses the data she's pulled. Most see only the geography; her gaze registers the other, less obvious layers—the subtle scars in the ground, the faint discolorations where earth has been disturbed and replanted, the subtext of the terrain itself. To a profiler, every scene is a confessional, if you know the right questions to ask.

She pushes her mug aside—empty, rim etched with the grind of old coffee—and taps at the keys. Another window opens, a spreadsheet of energy consumption for the outlying county. Every parcel mapped to an address, each with a column for kilowatt usage. Most are exactly what you expect: farms, barns, a cell tower pulling down what it needs for holiday lights. But one—tangentially affiliated with a Mercer account, 'Spruce Bend Retreat'—is an anomaly.

Evie lets her finger hover over the number. The consumption is large, orders of magnitude above a household or even a rural business. The usage matches more closely with a climate-controlled data center.

She opens a new tab, calls up the most recent property filings. The retreat is nominally owned by 'Elysian Residential LLC, which connects, through a daisy-chain of Delaware shells, to a familiar address in the Caymans—the same cluster of entities that funded Shepherd's first patent. She doesn't bother to smile. Evie had expected this; she always expects this. Despite that, the satisfaction is a faint warmth, registered but not unwelcome.

A highlight in the bottom right notes, "Fiber install map. Zoom to node #2110." She does, and there it is—a fiber optic backbone, pure overkill for the supposed weekend cabin. Why would you need sub-millisecond bandwidth unless you were moving petabytes of imaging or offloading vast sums at a scale that would shame a regional hospital?

Evie leans back, the chair groaning. The darkness beyond the screen feels absolute, yet she is untroubled by the void now. In the afterlife of her old self, that which goes bump in the night no longer troubles her.

She brings up a map of the property and begins to annotate. Entry points: the main gate, a buried culvert, a half-mile fence line that opens into unmonitored forest. She layers in a thermal satellite image, scans for heat blooms, finds two: one at the main house, as expected, and another, larger, deeper, thirty yards from the edge of a decorative pond. The signature is so strong it bleeds into the surrounding soil. Whatever is down there runs hot—probably ventilated. A bunker or a theater.

Evie moves fast, her brain a live wire. She prints each image, lays them side by side on the desk, marks the likely locations for exterior cameras (solar-powered, pole-mount, low-profile), and circles in red the spots where such surveillance can be best intercepted. The software has shown her this pattern before—a perimeter designed less to repel, more to detect approach.

She pulls a final window: a satellite snapshot from yesterday, high enough resolution to count the number of solar panels. She leans in, searching for movement, for signs of activity. In the north outbuilding, a fresh scrape of earth, a series of stacked crates, and, outside, a tangle of heavy cable. Someone has been prepping. She overlays the date of the most recent shipment—one charity hadn't received a pallet of "medical disposables" just two days previously. The timing works out.

Finishing her notes, she prints three copies and tucks them into an old manila folder labeled only with a question mark. Evie opens her desk drawer and finds her badge—cold, heavy, all the power of the state compressed into a hollow disc. She turns it over, then sets it face-down.

There is no need for it.

Evie turns back to the screen, her hands folding in her lap. The pattern is clear: the murders, the data, the shell companies, all of it converges here. This bunker is the Cartographer's gallery. Shepherd could be there, or at least his work. Mercer probably not, likely only interested in results. The oligarch went to great lengths to provide Shepherd with a wide berth, far from him.

Evie's chest tightens—not with fear, but anticipation she has never known. It stirs within her, an animal in its cage, eager and ready.

She powers down the monitor, darkness reclaiming the room. Sitting in it for a while, her eyes adjust, letting her pulse slow. She is alone, but not.

Evie breathes once, then rises.

Time to hunt.

She moves through the house, each step guided by intent. It's not the old discipline—bureau, badge, evidence and chain of custody—but a new clarity distilled into necessity. No wasted breath, no pause for memory or regret.

In her closet: black tactical turtleneck, sturdy jeans, nondescript boots, gloves so thin you could feel the skin beneath. From the bedside lockbox: her service weapon, a Glock, cradled in its foam holster. She pauses only long enough to check the magazine. She takes less than a minute to change. The new clothes fit closer than skin, the weight of the gear distributed so well that she feels lighter, less present. She cinches the boots tight, tucks the picks into a side pocket.

In the bathroom, she checks her reflection—not for vanity, but for proof that she is still there. Who looks back is nobody's agent, nobody's wife, no one's mother. Her face is a negative, shadow where light should be. A five-foot nothing of a woman that no one was ever intimidated by, yet now seems to impossibly loom.

She shoulders an empty duffel bag and marches downstairs to fill it. Her utility room cabinet contains the real implements: bolt cutters, two grades of lock picks. A pouch of bypass tools for electronic locks—wafers, shims, a contraband WiFi-jammer.

As she makes her way back, the temperature in the house drops—sharply, immediate. The fine hairs on her arms rise.

It begins at the periphery. At first, just a thickening of the shadows near the baseboard, a murk that refuses to be explained by an absence of light alone. As she zips her bag shut, it coheres—first one, then two, then several. A line of figures spaced along the path to the front door. They are more present than any ghost she's seen before: each with a face, or at least the suggestion of one, eyes hollow but searching. They stand in silence, a congregation of lost souls, not demanding but paying witness.

Evie does not flinch. She knows them. Some she recognizes from the case files, from photos no one else would ever see, the postmortems of the Cartographer's decades of work. Others are strangers, but their wounds so similar—punctured at the skull, cranial breaches of vanished lives.

She meets their gaze and bows her head—a slow lowering. It is neither an apology nor permission, but simply an acknowledgment. Evie sees now how the Harbinger operates: it is a quiet rage. It's inertia, a compulsion born of unanswered cries... of lost pleas.

There is no question or doubt, nor any wrongly accused.

She secures the bag, her breath releasing small tufts into the cold. The dead initially do not move, but as she takes a step forward, they recede in concert—opening to her a lane to the door.

As she passes through the foyer, the air grows colder. Her senses sharpen; every detail is amplified, each sense heightened to the edge of too much.

She stops at the front door. Hands tighten on the strap, her holster, the keys. She listens once, for their voices, but there are none. Instead, there is only certainty. This is not a mission, not a rescue, not even revenge. It is a rectification, the last measure when all else has failed.

Evie steps out into the night.

Chapter Thirty-Three

He Deserves to Know

At the threshold of her husband's condominium, Evie stands with her knuckles poised after her knock. There is a hesitation behind the door—a shift in movement, a heartbeat's delay before the bolt is drawn and Michael appears.

He's in sweatpants and a faded Virginia Cavaliers tee. His arms crossed tight as if still unsure if he's awake or dreaming. His hair is the kind of mussed that only comes from pulling at it.

Michael blinks. "Evie?"

"Hi," she says quietly. There is nothing left to soften, so she doesn't try.

He stands aside, allowing her in. The gesture is more instinct than invitation. The door clicks closed behind her. Inside his five-year separation condo is almost offensively unchanged. There are photos of June on every wall, arranged not as a shrine, but as if she were simply in the next room. On the table, old case files are fanned out in a near-geometric array, some annotated with Michael's blocky, over-careful handwriting. The couch is topped with a quilt—Evie's mother's, she realizes, from Christmases long ago.

Michael walks to a neighboring kitchen island, gathers two mugs, then sets them back down. "You want coffee?"

She shakes her head. "No time. I can't stay long."

He returns to the living room, folds his arms and studies her. "Did you learn something new about Dr. Shepherd?" he asks. "Or is it this Mercer guy? Never really paid much attention to the news before. Now, I can't help but see Shepherd being made into a blasted celebrity."

Evie feels a twinge of pride—he's accepting the truth. Too bad it's about to be smothered by the weight of what she's brought with her. "I'm not here for work, Michael," she says. "At least not the Bureau kind."

He waits. He's always been good at waiting.

"I wanted to see you before I go," she says, and is startled by the sound of it—final, not future tense.

He abruptly registers the tactical outfit, the boots, the gloves looped through a carabiner at her hip. His eyes note her Glock holstered inside her waistband. Recognition lands in his posture. His body hardens, feet plant, as if bracing against a physical blow.

"Are you going somewhere?" he asks.

"Tonight." Evie nods. "After I leave here."

He moves forward, closing the gap between them in three steps. "If this is about—if you're going after them—" He stops, presses his lips together. "Let me help. I can help. I know the region, I can—"

"Michael." Her voice is even, even as it strains. "No. Not for this. Not for what's coming."

He shakes his head as if to clear it. "You're going to do something stupid. Something reckless. And you came here why—what, to say goodbye?" He laughs, a short and wounded sound. "You can't. What if I say no? I'm not going to let you."

Evie steps closer, her height diminished further by the way she looks up to him. She sees the way they used to be when he was most himself—on the pediatric ward, or reading to June in bed. His hand lifts as if to touch her, but stops.

"I judged you," she says. The words catch in her throat. "All these years, I told myself I was the strong one. That you were weak for not letting go. But it was you who kept hope alive." Her voice trembles, and she grits her teeth to hold it. "You kept a door open I slammed shut."

He exhales, the sound half sob, half anger. "That hope was the only thing I had, Evie. There was nothing else left."

She isn't about to dispute him, because it's true. "I'm sorry."

He glances down at her holster. "You don't have to do this alone," he says. "Whatever it is. I'm her father. I won't be left out, not after—" His voice cracks. He swallows. "I won't."

He is across the foyer in an instant, a standing roadblock before the door.

She closes her eyes. "You have a practice and so many people that depend on you. No matter how this goes, it will not end up well. You cannot afford that. I need you to be safe. For her."

"Don't," he says, "don't put that on me. I will not watch you just go."

Evie sighs. "It's already done."

He is trembling now, fists at his sides. He braces against the door, then steadies himself. "Five years, Evie. For five years I've been looking for her. If you know something, if you have a way—if there's even a chance—you have to let me be there."

She almost relents. Almost. Her old life pulsing in her veins, an impulse to fold, to yield, to hope. But a pressure behind her sternum spikes—a cold, metallic edge, a knife of purpose that brushes her longing aside.

She places a hand flat against his chest. Feels the thrum of his heart, fast and shallow. "You did your best," she whispers. "You did everything right."

The Harbinger uncoils within her. A chilling static charge bleeds up her arm and into her hand, through his shirt, into the muscle and bone beneath. Michael's eyes widen; he stares at her, confused, then dazed.

"Evie?" he says. It has already started—his head tilts, as if seeking balance from an upending world. Weariness seems to pull on his bones, draining him. His knees buckle. He lurches sideways, catching himself on the edge of the living room entry. Michael gasps, tries to speak, but the words don't come.

Evie clasps the doorknob. "I'm sorry," she says again.

He steadies himself, shakes his head, tries to clear the fog. "What—what was that?" He sounds panicked, less at the sensation than that she's already lost to him.

"You'll be fine," she says. "It'll pass." She looks back one last time. It isn't how she wants to remember him, but he is alive. "You were right about me before. I am a ghost. One who has been haunting the wrong people for far too long. Time I changed that. Goodbye, Michael."

She opens the door, steps onto the porch and lets it swing shut behind her.

Striding away from the landing, she can hear him scramble, attempting to recover. He's not going to give up. It means too much to him.

Michael's car sits in the drive.

Evie stands beside the BMW, resting a hand on the curve of its hood. The paint is cold, the finish so spotless. The Glock feels heavier in her grip. This is no longer about defense, or performing duty. This is the arithmetic of necessity.

She levels the muzzle at the driver's front tire. Inhales, holds, then squeezes the trigger.

The gunshot is impossibly loud, compounded by the blown tire. It cracks, echoing between rows of parked cars and the hard faces of the condo buildings. The tire slumps instantly.

Evie holsters the Glock.

From the condo, a commotion—Michael's voice, indistinct, a note of panic sharpening each syllable. She does not turn. She walks north, away from the parking lot and into the clutch of streetlights that mark the spine of the neighborhood. Her shadow lengthens, trailing behind her, then fades out as the bulbs space farther and farther apart.

Chapter Thirty-Four

Infiltration

Night has remade the woods into a shadowy corridor. Her Ford Fiesta is far behind, more than a half-mile back on a dirt road. As Evie rounds each hill, the trunks lurch closer, and every breeze whispers through the leaves. She flows with them; her steps a science of tread and pressure, learned in Quantico halls, now animated by something that is not her alone.

The property boundary is just a contour in her mind's map. This is not a simple perimeter. It's a security array, woven into the woods with the cunning of the very rich. Few know the signs: a post too straight, the camera lens so disguised it only registers to someone who knows where to look.

Evie knows where to look. And not just because of training.

She stops. At first, it's the temperature that shifts—a bloom of cold against the dew-wet air. Then their shapes register: three figures in the undergrowth, faces barely resolved. The closest is a stark man, mid-forties, his skullcap missing. Beside him, a woman in a patient gown, blood matting her hair; and behind them, the smallest—a teenage girl, eyes bleeding but still searching.

Wordless, the man stares at the rough wedge of a cedar, six meters ahead. A slight glint bounces from what's inside—a lens, fiber-optic, likely streaming IR. She can almost feel the sensor, the way a blindfolded animal can sense a predator. The dead do not move. They direct. Not here to haunt, but to ward.

Evie crouches, lowers her profile, and veers along the dead's suggested path. She keeps the pace slow, calculating the intervals of camera sweeps.

The property is a marvel of modern paranoia. At the foot of the hill, the woods abruptly recede into a sweep of emerald lawn, so flat and vivid it seems the sky above has bled down and stained the grass blue. In the near distance stands the solitary resort—its architecture a contradiction of log-cabin affectation and glass-walled bravado. The windows are wide, the beams massive, the stonework so precise it could serve as a monastery. It's a house built to be both seen and not. It's the ones who want to be immortal would choose, a monument of their own continuity.

She stops behind a birch at the edge of the mowed boundary. The dead gather at the margins, spread out along the perimeter. Some are the same; others are new. None cross onto the lawn. They are deserving spectators in unearthly anticipation.

From her pack, she slides out a wafer-thin rectangle: the WiFi jammer, matte and black. She powers it up, and the green LEDs blink in silent sequence. Instantly, there is a subtle shift—the static falls away as if a hundred wireless connections go silent. The network of cameras, alarms, sensors—blinded.

She holds up her phone and tries to ping the cabin's WiFi. Nothing. A thrill—a small, illicit one—curls at the base of her spine.

This is it. Time to—

A faint snap—ground twigs, not far behind. The dead dissipate; their absence is there but not. Evie's hand is on her holster before her brain can even complete the command.

Someone speaks, calm as a metronome: "For someone your size, you've got quite the pair. Knew you'd lead me somewhere interesting, Cross."

She doesn't turn at first. It's a standoff reflex. But then she knows the voice. Even five years removed from the case, the lilt of sarcasm and grudge remains lazily in her memory.

"Vaughn," she says, and lets the word hang.

He's a silhouette at first, but as he steps from the tree line, moonlight renders his face: stubble, crows-feet, the cut of his mustache set in a line intended to mean 'winning.' He has a black windbreaker, tactical pants, and his own service weapon held low.

"Considering how that whole case collapsed into feces, I figured you'd do something spectacular," he says, eyes on her pack, then the jammer, then her face. "Didn't think it'd be this. Plan on ending it all by throwing yourself on the Cartographer's doorstep?" The words are almost kind, in the language of old adversaries.

Evie lets out a breath, slow. Her grip on the Glock relaxes but does not release.

"I'm not just here for Shepherd—not only him," she says.

He lifts his chin. "Then why are you here, Cross?"

It isn't a question.

She nods once.

He steps closer, never breaking eye contact. "Trust me. You don't want to do this alone. The Bureau's not watching. No one would know if we pulled it off clean."

Evie almost laughs. "What? You think you're here for the same reasons?"

He gives her a look edged with pity. "I spent five years convinced I had nailed him down. Then Haden got me drunk, shared the new files. It all blew up in my face. The bastard got away with it then. Looks like he's doing it again. Afterward, he—what?—gets to retire with all the accolades? You know, something about that doesn't sit right. Just galls me way too much."

Evie's mind races. The house, the dead, the two of them: all pieces on the same board, all condemned by the same moves. Vaughn is a good profiler, a decent cop—but it won't matter here.

"You followed me," she says.

He shrugs. "You made it easy. I just waited for you to get desperate."

She scans the property for any movement. There are none, but her every instinct says they're being watched. Vaughn followed her, but did he step where she stepped? *No, of course not.*

"You bring backup?" she asks.

He smirks. "Wouldn't dream of it. Not after what you did to Haden's team."

She frowns, offering a bitter smile.

Vaughn crouches closer. For a long moment, they become old partners—not enemies, now something more complicated. Evie listens for the dead, but they are silent.

Evie shoulders her pack, lets the jammer pulse through the field.

"If you're going to do this," Vaughn says, "then consider me backup. Cover me?"

She studies him—the angles of his face, the battered dignity. Nothing left to hate.

She nods. "Lead the way."

Together they slip from behind the birch, skirting the edge of the lawn. Immediate cameras down. Sensors blind. For now, only the cold, the two of them, and the massive cabin wait ahead.

Evie's other companion is there, taut as a tripwire. Ready. And for the first time, she isn't afraid to unleash it.

The air between them stays sharp. Marcus shifts his weight, then settles beside her. Evie can smell old aftershave and fresh nerves. He keeps his eyes on the cabin. "You gonna tell me what we're walking into, or should I improvise?"

"Honestly, there is no way you can possibly know what you've walked into. But I'm guessing you're going to find out." Evie scans the windows. "Shepherd's inside. Or at least was. Satellite shows the power draw hasn't dipped in the last forty-eight hours—someone's maintaining this place. He could be here packing up, or maybe he's starting something new. Either way, whatever is underground isn't a panic room. It's a data center. Some kind of experiment."

Marcus nods. "So he's alone."

"Correct."

He flicks a sideways grin. "You always did have the best algorithms."

She doesn't rise to it. "Sensors—motion, IR, sound. The jammer kills comms, but it doesn't stop physical detection."

He shrugs. "That's why you included me, right?"

Evie glances at him. "If you're here to drag me before Quantico, say so now."

Marcus shakes his head. "No one's waiting for you there. The Bureau's written this off." He softens just a fraction. "This is your call, Cross. Always has been."

She nods. "We go in quiet. Engage only when sure."

"Never liked noise anyway," he says.

They slide along the windfall's lee, keeping low. Marcus checks his pockets, palm-concealing a small canister of knock-off CS. "In case hospitality turns rough," he whispers.

Evie smirks. "You have your toys; I have mine."

He winks, and for a second she sees the old Marcus—hungry, reckless, never cruel. Just a man trying to prove himself.

They reach the cut between grass and flagstone patio. Automated lights highlight geometry, not perimeter. They crouch by a planter of black mondo grass—no accounting for taste.

It's a sprint to the patio shadows. Marcus is faster, but Evie's steps are silent. She glances back at the woods—nothing. They duck under a kitchen window. Through the glass, she sees the edge of a gunmetal fridge and knives on a magnetic strip.

Evie focuses on the basement bulkhead. Last night's blueprints showed a service entrance for electricians—simple cylinder lock, three pins. She holds up a gloved finger, touches the handle, and works her picks with quiet precision.

Marcus's eyes widen. "You break into many billionaire bunkers on your off days?"

She cracks the lock, meets his gaze, deadpan. "Only the interesting ones."

He grins, and for the first time they fall into an old rhythm. She pushes the door open a hair and smells the interior: cool, dry, rustic. No voices. Just the distant hum of fans and their own breathing.

Chapter Thirty-Five

Enter the Fray

Inside, the retreat is a rustic mausoleum for the living. The air is conditioned to perfection. She and Marcus keep to opposite sides of the entry vestibule—he moves with predatory confidence, scanning for human threats; she drifts, letting her senses splay outward. The house is a study in contradictions: mid-century modern lines finished in fossilized woods and Italian marble, but beneath the cosmetic warmth is an undertow of clinical aloofness. It's a place meant to project comfort, but built under tight control.

Marcus holds up two fingers and nods toward the grand staircase. "Up or down?"

"Neither," she says, without looking at him. "We sweep the ground floor. If he's here, he'll be prepping to run."

He grins. "Are you hoping he'll run?"

"I'd rather he not have the chance," Evie says. She moves past him, rubber soles silent on the black slate tiles.

She moves through the open-plan living area. Everything just so: cashmere throws, hand-woven rugs, a driftwood art piece above the hearth. But none of it feels used. No cups on the table, no clutter on the bookshelves. It's the life of a man who lives elsewhere—a showcase, only surface.

She passes a glass wall and feels a feather brush across her leg: spectral wisps, faint as the breath on a window, curling in slow arcs. At first, she thinks some sort of fog. But the air is dry. Then one strand dips, trailing pale blue across her field of vision.

Her training would urge her to check the closets, the side exits, the pantry with its double-thick steel hinges, but she goes with this instead. Evie drifts into the gallery corridor, with its oversized canvases lining the wall. She studies nothing for more than a moment. Then continues along the spectral line.

It draws her to the far end, where the corridor doglegs behind decorative stone. The air is distinct here—cooler, as if the climate system is fighting a losing battle. The wall on her left is plain, flush-painted in matte. Evie's hand presses the surface. She feels a pulse beneath, a subtle change in pressure.

Stepping back, she squints and taps her knuckles on the plaster. The sound is off. Hollow, deeper than it should be. She traces the seam with her thumb, then applies weight. The panel slips inward with a soft, pneumatic sigh.

Beyond is a stairwell, swallowing all light. It descends a precise twenty-two-degree angle into poured concrete. A stairwell that is entirely at odds with the rest of the house: no walnut treads, no brass. The floor is raw, speckled with flecks of rebar. The air is colder here, and reeks of sanitizer.

Evie stands at the breach. Unafraid, she lifts her foot to the threshold—

A figure bursts up from the black before her, so close she reels.

A silent warning from a matted beard looms up at her, emptiness glaring—imploring. The homeless one. Up close now, he comes into stark focus: skin stretched thin over a bony skull, eye sockets dark and hollow, and a jaw hanging open. The figure is so immediate she stumbles back a step. Her pulse spikes. The vagrant's semi-substantial form hovers in before her, then dives, desperately gripping at the walls. The act makes her look, forcing her gaze along the steps, banister, the wall surface.

There, just where the doorframe meets drywall, a faint metallic reflection. Evie glances once, then again. Embedded in the gap is a canister—a cylinder, no larger than a thumb, but with a soldered seam. Farther down, more of them. Piping that should feed a radiant floor instead bends in weird detours, flexing down the stairwell. She drops to a crouch, fingers splayed over the raw floor, feeling for vibration, for heat. None—but there's a chemical tang.

She's seen this before. Then, it was a covert burn guard for a data center, a C4-studded crawlspace in Vienna. It is a failsafe, a purge. The stairs are lined with micro-charges, thermite or something worse, packed around a pressurized gas line. If tripped, the entire lower floor would incinerate, sterilize, collapse—a hundred thousand dollars in custom stone instantly slagged.

The vagrant hovers lower. His warning delivered, he fades back into the dark.

Evie rocks onto her heel, scans the upper lip of the hidden stair, and then withdraws. She moves at a half-run, tracking Marcus back the way she came.

He is at the far side of the kitchen, sweeping his SIG in patient arcs across the island and the wine wall. He almost shoots her when she rounds the corner. "Cross, wholly shi—" He lowers his weapon. "Anything?"

"Plenty," she says. "Don't take another step. Shepherd doesn't have a panic button; he has a nuclear one. A thermite rigging. C'mon."

Marcus gapes. "Thermite?"

"Thermite connected to gas lines and maybe hydrofluoride. I counted four in a stairwell. There's likely more."

That earns a side-eye, and a swallow of whatever retort he primed. "Show me."

She leads him back, her movements crisp. Reaching the seam, Evie presses her thumb to the trigger point and lets the panel inhale.

The chemical cold breathes up at them. Marcus says nothing, but his jaw sets, a tendon flickering along his cheek. He checks the wall gaps of the stairwell, the corridor behind them, then meets her gaze. With a slight throat clearing, he says, "It's not a classic booby trap. Doesn't seem to be any trip lines or pressure plates. That wouldn't be practical for daily use. So, probably a remote failsafe. I think we're good."

She nods. He then follows her down.

They descend in silence, save for the touch of boots on poured cement and the hum of a power draw below. At the landing, Evie points to the gap at the baseboard, wordlessly inviting Marcus to kneel. He does, his large hands careful as he lifts the loose panel. When he confirms the thermite brick, his mouth forms a thin, compressed line.

"He's prepared to burn everything down," Evie murmurs.

Marcus nods, thoughtful. "Gas line runs under the server racks. Thermite will drop when heat triggers the relays. No chance for evidence, or even DNA." He glances at her.

She shrugs, all nerves. "We're assuming it's Shepherd. Could very well be his patron covering their involvement."

Marcus puts the panel back, slow and precise, and stands. "Either way, that's a lose/lose for us."

They both stare at the steel fire door, the keypad a nervous blinking blue in the dark. Marcus draws his SIG, checks the load, then looks at her.

"Ready?" he asks.

Evie nods. "Ready."

She pulls out her requisitioned Cellebrite UFED, letting it whir softly in her hands. The gadget processed the numbers; it quickly settles in on 271828. That pops the lock. She presses the door open.

The lab is transformed. Every overhead is alive, surgical halogen so bright as they step inside. The hum is louder now, almost tactile, and the smell is strong—a layered assault of formalin, bleach.

Marcus sweeps the room, weapon ready but down. "Jesus," he mutters, scanning the reliquary.

Evie moves straight for a glass wall. Before her, preserved brains float in columns of clear fluid, each one ringed by fiber-optic umbilicals. She can feel the hum through her fingertips as she nears the first canister. The glass is thick, maybe three centimeters, but the curve of it warps her reflection into a haunted mask.

She points. "These are the missing parts from the victims," she whispers. Her breath fogs the glass.

Marcus does a slow pan of the room. The wall opposite is a bank of servers. Quantum, she thinks, given the way the heat sinks bristle with exotic metal. In the center of the room: a surgical chair. Stainless steel, no padding, ringed with articulated arms. Pneumatic medical drills and saws are wheeled off to the corner. Two racks of surgical tools and braces wait beside it, arranged in symmetrical perfection. Partition curtains on ceiling rails are tied back to the chamber walls.

He moves to the server stack, eyes the cables, then frowns. "These aren't just storage. They're active."

Evie looks at the 3D model spinning on the monitor, the nodes flashing in a wild, meaningless sequence. "He's running them, keeping them... alive?" She doesn't mean it literally, but the implication is so monstrous she nearly steps back from the glass.

Marcus's voice is low, hushed in the hum. "Why? Why not just destroy the evidence?"

Evie thinks, mind racing. "Maybe this is *his evidence*. Maybe he needs it to prove his theory. If the neural map can be read after death—"

"Then he's what—a pioneer, not just a butcher?" Marcus says.

She shakes her head. "He's both."

Behind them, the air stirs.

She turns just in time to catch a wisp, then a full-blown apparition. A girl, maybe eighteen, face pale and blurred, lets out a soundless scream. Her arm stretches out behind Evie.

Evie jumps, but not in time. There's a sharp sting under her jaw, right side. She is spun, hands up. The world tilts sideways, and her arm is seized before she can resist.

Marcus' hand slaps onto his sidearm.

"Don't!"

Shepherd's breath is in her ear. He presses her into himself, her back to his chest—a human shield. His other hand tenses on the hypodermic in her neck. *Oh gawd. If that's in the carotid and not the jugular, she'll be dead before she hits the floor.*

"Don't move," Shepherd continues, voice so level it almost calms.

Marcus holds himself, calculating. Eyeing for any window.

"Drop it," Shepherd says.

Marcus hesitates, eyes flicking from Shepherd's hand on Evie to the hypodermic, to her.

Evie can barely feel the skin of her own throat, but she manages a shake of the head: Don't do it.

Shepherd's tone is gentle, almost paternal. "This is not a negotiation, Agent. The solution in her neck is ten times the clinical dose. You can play along. Or…"

There is a minute burning sensation in her neck.

Marcus' eyes go wide at the sight. Shepherd is slowly squeezing the plunger! She feels herself going, vision tunneling in and out. Still, she tries to stay upright.

Then the clatter of metal on tile. Evie looks down at Marcus' service weapon at his feet.

Shepherd pauses. "Good. Now, take the cuffs out of your left cargo pocket and secure yourself to that chair. Use both hands—lock the second cuff around the frame."

Marcus doesn't move. He's calculating, weighing, desperate for anything other than complying. "You realize our backup will be here any moment, right?"

"Please," Shepherd drools out. "Not after your team's little infamy. You've been disowned. No one is coming for you. That's why you skulked in to begin with." He tightens his hold on Evie.

She gasps, and the world narrows to a razor line.

"She can still die," Shepherd says. "Your choice."

Marcus does as told, steps to the chair, and sits. The click of the first cuff is loud in the silence. The second click is even louder.

Evie wants to say something to him, but her tongue is heavy, thick as a boot sole. She manages only, "Don't wor… ry."

Marcus looks at her, and his eyes—usually full of venom—now soften, only frightened.

Shepherd bends her arm behind her back, then, with practiced care, injects the plunger.

As the world tunnels away to darkness, Evie catches the dead girl, hands splayed around the glass canister. She wonders about its floating, fiber-plugged contents. Might that be hers?

Chapter Thirty-Six

This is Pre-Op

Her waking dream sets her in a cathedral of light and concrete, with the chill hum of filtered air and the percussive whir of recirculators. Evie rouses to a soft beeping, a monitor registering a heartbeat. Every sense is occluded; her eyelids feel weighted. The world sharpens slowly, from black into the blinding spectrum of surgical halogen.

The leather restraints in this chair are snug. Wrists, ankles, her every limb immobilized. The room has changed from what she glimpsed before, reconfigured into an operating theater: all the furnishings pressed to the margins, gleaming instrument tables circling her. There is no pretense of humanity here—only a neatness of purpose. A clock, white and analog, ticks by the seconds.

Across from her: a bald man with a mustache. He slumps in a matching chair, head down. His windbreaker has been cut away, both shirt and undershirt peeled back to expose his shoulders. *Oh, gawd. Marcus.* Around the crown of his head, Shepherd draws a surgical marker in slow, loving arcs, mapping incision lines. Marcus's mouth hangs. A nasal cannula delivers oxygen; his chest rises and falls, untroubled, unknowing.

Evie's own skin tingles with a thousand ants. Her tongue is sandpaper, her jaw wants to clench, but the rest of her is deadweight. Her vision flickers at the periphery, blurring every edge.

Shepherd works, his voice barely above a whisper. "You're awake," he notes without looking. "Given your diminutive size, I'm surprised you're already with me. I wondered if you'd metabolize that quickly. Honestly, it really wasn't ten times the dose. Even so, impressive."

Evie's first attempt at speech is a rasp, little more than an exhale. She focuses on the slow in and out, then shapes the words with effort. "How... long?"

He shrugs, capping the marker. "About ninety minutes since your arrival. I like to do a double-check on the preps. Don't like surprises." He wipes Marcus's scalp with an alcohol pad, then steps away, snapping the gloves free from his fingers. He disposes of them in a steel pedal bin and returns with a new pair.

She tries to orient. "Why... not just... kill us?"

He laughs—a clean, clear chuckle. "That's not the point. Don't worry. You're both going to pull through. Things will just be... different." He walks to her, checks the IV in her left forearm, adjusts the flow. "Like you, Agent Marcus here has a custom blend—fast onset, short half-life, a bit like propofol but less dissociative. Can't map a mind if the subject can't participate."

She blinks hard, forcing the world into focus. "You... could've been... a legend. Instead... just a murderer."

He cocks his head, hands steepled. "Oh, legends are determined by those who write history books, my dear," he says. "My narrative is already determined. I'm building something here. And you—you get to be an early adopter."

She struggles against the restraints, a full-body convulsion that brings stars to her eyes. She fights to lift her arm, but the leather will not give. The only thing that moves is the pulse at her throat.

He studies her face almost kindly. "I have admired you, Mrs. Cross. Even after you cost me five years and many experiments. You're the only one who ever got close." He leans in, a faint antiseptic smell coming from his gloves. "You deserve to witness the next phase. I want you to know what it means."

Shepherd turns back to Marcus. "This one has been a fixture of mine for years. Always standing behind you, always looking over your shoulder. The Bureau's 'brilliant second best.' That's what they should call him." Shepherd runs a finger along the blue lines of his scalp. "He'll be a good test. You'll see. I've never had an audience for this procedure before."

Evie's heart stutters, a rabbit's thump. She needs to say something, anything! "What about my daughter!? What about June?" she blurts. "Don't I deserve to know?"

Shepherd stops, the smile fading.

For a moment he is perfectly still, as if the room has run out of air.

Then he waves a hand, dismissive. "Your daughter. Yes. Sadly for you, I'm afraid I had very little to do with that. You see, like most medical researchers, I work under a benefactor, someone who appreciates my research. This marvelous and undocumented facility is one of theirs. Not mine. When my patron realized these vital studies were about to be... *exposed,* they felt it important to bring in a third party. I have no idea who. Plausible deniability, and all that." He picks up the next instrument, a small, forked device. "That turned your June into a bargaining chip. And I was merely told to lie low. Which I did. In time, the Bureau lost interest. My case was closed."

He pauses, looks at her with a flicker of wonderment. "It's interesting, now that you mention it. Children's brains are far more elastic. Trickier to map, but possibly easier to preserve. Perhaps that's a next direction. I wonder what would happen if I started younger." He turns away offhandedly. "Thank you for the idea, Mrs. Cross."

The words slam into her like a bullet. *No.* Evie's rage explodes; she feels every vein in her neck pulse. Her teeth grind. She howls, a wordless animal, as if she could shatter the surrounding glass.

The strain is intense; her world goes red at the edges.

Shepherd glances back. "You'll see it soon. You'll understand."

He returns to Marcus, places a hand on his shoulder. For a moment he looks almost priestly, his features lit from below by the sterile glow of the monitors.

Helpless to watch, Evie breathes through. The drugs try to drag her down, but the horror of what Shepherd said—what he will do—scalds away the chemical haze. He's not lying about June, she knows; but she also knows that Shepherd is utterly capable of testing his hypotheses on children. Her body, frail and bound, has no leverage against the bonds, but her mind claws at the walls for any foothold.

Reality snaps back.

It stirs.

How could she forget?

It coils at the base of her skull—a creeping frost, a black wind that shifts from the corners of the room. It's always been there, pulsing behind her heartbeat. She knows what it wants. It wants her to yield, not in fractions, but in totality.

Shepherd is locking down Marcus' head brace, maneuvering the pinions to their ideal positions. The process is very delicate. His drill, so final. "A thing of beauty," he murmurs.

Evie's fury is elemental, unmodulated by pain or fear. The restraints bite deeper as she flexes, the leather groaning, but her body cannot rise. Her mouth, dry and metallic, shapes a silent plea.

The Harbinger listens.

In the blackest core of her being, Evie offers a silent pact. Her heart pounds as she whispers within. *I'm done. It's all for you. Do what you want with me. Make him pay. Make him suffer.* Her eyes go wide, pleading. *Just spare my partner.*

Lights flicker—a soft stutter, just enough to cast the shadows into jagged relief. Even Dr. Shepherd notices, looking up with a frown. "Odd. The backup generator shouldn't be cycling."

He glances at her, checking if she's passed back out.

Her gaze is locked on the monitor. Evie's pupils dilate to the edge, swallowing almost all color. Her chest rises and falls, slow, but every breath is purposeful.

She feels herself unwinding, as if her being is a thread, and the Harbinger is spooling it out. The sensation is not one of loss, but of becoming thin, hollow. Her vision clarifies; the world turns high-definition. They have come. They are here with her now—to bear witness.

Shepherd cannot see the way the dead gather at the margins of the glass—silent, their numbers swelling. He doesn't notice the chill that radiates from behind Evie. The frost crawling from the HVAC vents, the static that builds along the stainless rails.

Evie's thoughts fragment and then reassemble, sharper than before. Every moment she ever doubted, every time she clung to procedure and rule. It was never about justice. It was about control. About knowing the shape of the world and believing she could control it, tame it.

The Harbinger has no such illusions.

She feels it rise, slide along her nerves, taking an inventory of muscles and bones, sampling the shorn edges of her memories. It finds everything it needs. Then, something ephemeral is implied. They're not so much... words as an agreement.

For this one, we will not kill. We have something far more deserving in mind. Thank you, Evie Cross.

The world contracts, then expands.

Shepherd looks at her, waiting for something—an insult, a prayer, a last confession. Instead, he sees her eyes close, her breathing shallow out. He shakes his head, turns away, certain that he will have to decrease the dose for her harvest.

But inside, Evie is not gone.

She is simply not the subject he expects.

Chapter Thirty-Seven

The Harbinger

Dr. Victor Shepherd prefers beginning his incisions early. Control is always in the opening cuts. By the time a subject is opened, the nature of the procedure is established—the will, the artistry, the intent. This separates Shepherd from the butchers who populate his profession. The difference between purpose and pathology relies heavily on a steady hand.

Today's theater is as close to ideal as circumstance allows: a chilled room beneath his personal retreat, clean to surgical spec. His lighting system is set to simulate full daylight. Subject #24, Marcus Vaughn, is already in position, body strapped at wrists, chest, and ankles. The man's breathing is regular, his face a blank wash under the anesthesia. Shepherd even shaves the scalp himself—he prefers to lay out the field with his own hands, especially for a specimen as antagonistic as Agent Vaughn.

His only wildcard is Mrs. Evie Cross.

She is immobilized in the secondary chair, a good two meters away, perpendicular to Subject #24. Her restraints are strict, her arms braced at the elbows and wrists, her ankles locked in to prevent even the illusion of leverage. He has double-checked her IV twice—propofol, with a supplementary drip of midazolam. Really was impressive that she came out so early.

He regards her as he passes. Her chin down, hair falling like curling eddies over one cheek. She looks younger than he remembers; the last time he saw her, she was a shattered professional sitting in a sedan. She probably doesn't realize he noticed her at his home. Shepherd finds it almost enticing to see Evie like this—vulnerable, her legend unwound.

His focus returns to Vaughn.

Shepherd dons the operating loupe, adjusting the headband until it bites into his temples. He reviews the surgical field: the scalp, the blue lines drawn with surgical marker, the neat row of hemostats at the ready. His hands do not tremble. They never have. He lifts the number ten blade, aligns it with the first dotted guide, and prepares to cut.

A tremor rattles the table. Not his hands, not the patient—a vibration through the metal.

He frowns and resets his grip.

Another tremor. This time, a metallic clink as one hemostat shifts a fraction of a centimeter on the tray. He glances at the light overhead. The illumination pulses, a frequency stutter perceptible to Shepherd's obsessive attention to detail.

He pauses. It does not repeat.

"Power surge," he mutters. The infrastructure here is supposed to be isolated from the main grid, but rural contractors are notoriously unreliable. He files the anomaly away and sets blade to flesh.

The edge of the scalpel catches on Vaughn's skin, meets resistance, then parts the dermis with satisfying smoothness. He has always found the opening phase the most elegant. The rest—retracting the skin, drilling the bone, accessing the dura—is mechanics. The cut is everything.

The temperature drops.

He notices it in the way condensation builds in the mask. His skin, usually impervious to the lab's chill, prickles with cold. He hesitates, tilts his head, and examines the ceiling vent. The airflow is as always. No audible shift in the HVAC. Yet, a thin mist forms around the surgical tray.

A low hum fills the room. It's a frequency just below hearing, but Shepherd feels it in his teeth. He looks at Cross.

She remains slumped, her head down. But the angle has changed. Her chin is now tucked into her chest. Her hair curtains her face. The monitors above her display a steady, elevated pulse—much higher than expected for someone so sedated.

Shepherd steps away from Vaughn, wipes his gloves on the blue pad, and approaches Evie.

He checks the line at her wrist. The IV is intact. The needle is seated. But her eyelids flutter, a rapid, almost frantic twitch.

Something is off.

Correlation forms. It's her—she's causing this, just like the vagrant before. Has to be. Amazing!

He inhales, steadies himself, and returns to the surgical tray. Victor picks up a syringe and another vial of propofol. This worked once, will do so again. As he turns, the smell of wet earth fills his nostrils. His mask dampens with condensation. Shepherd tugs it down with his gloved hand.

Then, he hears.

"Dr. Shepherd…"

It is not a voice. Not quite. It comes from everywhere at once: as if speakers in the ceiling, vibration in the equipment, the hollow between his ribs. The consonants are so crisp he almost misses the distortion, its impossible resonance.

He looks at Evie.

She sits upright, eyes open.

No: eyes are wrong. The whites are gone, just only black—so deep it is as if her skull has been cored and filled with void. She stares at him, unmoving.

He steps back; the syringe slipping from his grip.

Evie's jaw works, mouth opening in a rictus that should hurt, but takes on a delighted grin.

She continues, "We've been expecting you."

An ethereal plume exhales from her lips. At first, it is a faint wisp. It thickens, gathering into a column, then splitting into branching tendrils. The plumes move, deliberate, touching the surrounding spaces. It slides along the armrest, pools over the surgical steel, then lifts, high and higher, gathering density as it forms.

From this mass, a shape emerges. Two hollows—eyes, or an echo of them—open within the cloud. The mouth forms next, a maw of icy vapor. The visage is not that of Evie Cross. It is archetypal, a mask drawn from every feared death in the dark.

It turns. It looks back… at him.

Victor nearly loses his footing on the slick, chilling tiles. His heart is a drum in his chest. He's shaking. His hands—these hands—are not steady. For a heartbeat, it registers as humiliation. In all his years, not once has the work outpaced his composure.

He sprints for the exit, knocking a cascade of trays and stands against the wall.

The air grows denser as he moves. At the door, he tears off his gloves and mask. His fingers stab at the access point, and glance over his shoulder.

The entity stands over Evie Cross, expanding until it nearly brushes the ceiling, its arms—arms?—lengthening and tapering into spectral claws.

This is taking too damn long. The readout shows as 'UNRECOGNIZED' twice before accepting. The door unlocks with a pneumatic hiss. Then, in a single, liquid movement, the entity sweeps toward him, covering the distance in a fraction of a second.

Its expansive claw hits Shepherd with force. His eardrums pop, vision whites out for a second. There is the cracking of glass, the shriek of metal.

His feet come off the floor as he is dragged up, pinned against an adjacent wall. His head jerks sideways, forced to watch as the being stretches its neck—absurd, impossible—and brings its empty gaze level with Shepherd's. He cannot look away. Victor tries to scream, but the sound is eaten by the air.

It can't end like this. All my work, everything I've accomplished. Can't let them...

He jabs a hand into his lab coat, feeling for the hard plastic pad. Finding the remote, he whips it out, slides back its single button cover, and presses.

A klaxon sounds—the lights turn red.

The entity's hollow eyes expand. Its face roars as it presses against Victor's. Hated darkness consumes all his perceptions... and then retracts. The thing looks at the lights, back to both patients #24 and #25. Marcus is beginning to stir. Evie strains against her leather restraints.

It makes a choice.

Victor crumples to the floor as the entity turns back.

Spectral claws latch onto Marcus's wrist straps and cleave them. The restraints—three-ply leather—shear like wet cloth. His hands snap free first, then the legs. The pressure collar around his neck groans. Another stroke of the claws and the carbon-fiber brace splinters, raining composite shrapnel onto the floor. Marcus's head lolls, then jerks upright, eyes fighting to open—cognition flickering.

Scrambling back, Victor barely registers any of this. Instead, friction burns his palms as he crab-walks toward the exit stairwell. His mind races, rehearsing every scenario for loss of containment, none of which involved a supernatural ejection from his own lab. Regardless, he knows... the clock is ticking.

The entity pivots to Evie. It looms, its heatless face whiting out the reflection in her monitor. One tapered claw, more elegant than efficient, traces the line of the buckle, lifting the thick nylon as if it were a single human hair. The buckles simply unfasten. A talon touches the IV at her wrist, and the needle slides free, bloodless, the vein unscarred. Evie shudders, then folds over into its distended arms.

With the door ajar, Victor finds his feet. He rises to take to the stairs.

Reverberation thrums through him.

He looks back.

Both Evie and Marcus are cradled in the entity's arms, impossibly ethereal mass somehow lifting them together. Its distended head swivels to glare at Victor.

Its layered voice fills the lab. "There is no place you can hide. No door you can close that will keep us out."

"Run, Doctor."

Chapter Thirty-Eight

Countdown

The klaxon shudders through the marrow of his bones. Victor stumbles, shoulder smacking the door frame as he bolts from the sub-basement. Red emergency strobes divide the corridor into film-strip fragments. The smell of ozone and chemical accelerant is everywhere, wafting in dry, acrid waves.

Sixty seconds. That's how long the failsafe is designed to run: first, to warn, then to ignite every molecule of flammable gas and incinerate all evidence to plasma and ash. It was a condition of his patron saint, choosing the loss of a life's work over exposure. It feels less like insurance and more like a verdict.

At the stair top, he checks left—then right.

At the intersection, a figure waits. Stretched thin as paper, translucent, but manifest all the same. Bristling beard, blue knit cap, and a shirt reading "Property of Fairfax County—Morgue." Hollow eye sockets fix on Victor.

He knows the face. Subject #23. The homeless one who'd raved about seeing "the dead." Victor harvested his brain two weeks ago, and, in the end, the subject thanked him. He stands there now, arms hanging loose, drool hanging from the corner of his mouth.

Victor checks his forward motion. *Can't be happening. No. This is a...* Then—the failsafe, the failsafe—he pivots and heads the opposite direction.

Fifty seconds...

He bursts through the first unlocked door—a study, wall-to-wall with medical texts. The windows flicker a mad shadow play from the power cycling. Every lamp and screen flash on, then off, then on again. Monitors stutter to life, one then another, screens of flickering faces. All of them stare, eyes milky. For a fraction, he recognizes the curve of a cheek, the curl of a lip—subjects #11 and #14, from the archive.

He barrels across the room, grabbing for the opposite door.

Back in the hall, the strobe lights have shifted. Now, they paint everything as if pulsing blood. The temperature keeps dropping—he can see his breath, heavy and ragged.

A voice threads through the corridor. "Doctor Shepherd..."

He lurches forward. At the end of the hallway, the air grows dense. Shepherd leans into it, using every scrap of will to keep moving.

Forty seconds...

Behind him, he hears the slick, wet sound of something dragging. Not boots, not shoes—skin and hair, bodies hauled across linoleum. He dares to look.

The thing fills the corridor. It stretches, moving not like a man but like a lung, a white membrane drawing the world toward itself. At its core, it holds something. No—two somethings. Victor recognizes them: the little profiler, still inert, slumped in its impossible embrace; the other agent, Marcus, head lolling as if being dragged from deep sleep.

That Thing—whatever it is—does not rush. It advances with an inevitability that is worse than speed. Its limbs bifurcate, weaving around doorways and ceiling vents, feeling the way a fungus creeps along a root. The temperature falls another ten degrees. Victor breathes out clouds.

Thirty seconds...

He bolts into the great room, the custom parquet floor so polished his footing slides out from under him. His right groin muscle rages at him from the sudden strain. He skates the first two yards, colliding with the back of a Danish settee. The furniture does not move. Victor bounces off, the wind knocked out of him.

The lights fail. Only the red strobes at floor level remain, painting the space in a dreadful underglow. The grand piano at the room's center rocks, then slides—four hundred pounds of black lacquered wood, gliding into his path as if the cabin tilted sideways.

Victor yelps—an involuntary, animal bark.

He rounds past the piano. There, in the open, stands a nurse, her hair wet. The red light implies why, and it's too thick to be water. *Not real.* Her uniform ripples though the air is still. Her skin, waxy and pale, lips mottled blue. She opens her arms to embrace him.

Victor screams again—this time, in denial. "Not real. Not real!"

He heads for the main doors, and in his periphery he sees another. An old man, still in robes. Next, a boy of maybe nineteen, his hair stiff around the crown. Each blinks into existence just ahead, then to the side, never in the same place twice. They do not block him. They herd him, a cattle run of dead.

The sliding glass doors loom ahead. On a normal day, he'd curse himself for choosing a backup deadbolt, but now he has no time for regret. He grabs a paperweight from the credenza—a sculpted head, iron, at least six pounds. He swings it hard, then hurls its full momentum into the glass.

Twenty seconds...

A head-sized hole bursts through; there's a crack, then the glass all caves in. Shards rain down onto the porch. After covering his own head with his lab coat, he shoves through the opening. Shoes find the glass pebbles slick on the deck. He staggers down the patio steps onto the lawn...

...then looks back.

Behind him, the entity pushes through the ruined doorway. It unfurls with impossible grace, its core tendrils wrapping around the forms of Evie and Marcus. It looms up over him, too damn close.

That horror lifts its face, and a cascade of vapor billows from the cavity within. It stretches, arms wide, as if to embrace the entire night. Stepping up to him, it lays its burden on the grass with a kind of ceremony, arranging its arms just so. Victor watches, transfixed by its gentleness—its almost loving care.

Then, it turns to him.

Ten seconds...

Victor runs—then sprints for the garage at the far end of the property.

He slaps at the garage keypad. Fingers jabbing at the numbers. The door groans open. He dives inside, hits the clicker, and feels the cargo doors roll up behind him. He falls against the wall, shivering, lungs burning. His watch buzzes: five seconds left. Then four. Then three. He crawls behind the shadow of the Range Rover, burying his face in his hands.

The final seconds he counts with the precision of a man who has lived his entire existence in the fractions.

He expects the explosion to be instant, total. But the architects did their work well: the initial burst is muffled, contained in the sub-basement. But then the shockwave follows, rolling through the earth, slamming the slab foundation with a force that lifts the entire structure a quarter inch, then drops it. The windows of the house bulge, then burst in a storm of shrapnel and smoke. The air is instantly full of glass, wood, and a vaporized thousand terabytes of a life's work.

Victor Shepherd opens his eyes to his world on fire.

He stands staggered, and looks beyond the garage doors. The house—his research—is gone. Nothing but a smoldering crater and a halo of burning lawn. Yet in the center of the devastation, the entity stands—untouched, unmoved, its shape more substantial now, less mist than bone. Evie and Marcus lie at its feet, the surrounding grass unburned, marked only by a perfect circle of black.

Victor feels the urge to fall, to weep. But there's no time for that. Instead, he walks to the car, opens the driver's side, and sits. He grips the steering wheel, but does not start the engine. Simply waits, hands clenched, pulse racing. All that's left is to witness the inferno before him.

Will that thing vanish with the smoke, lose interest in the mortal world?

It does not. It turns its head, watching him. Its face, though featureless, is unmistakably full of recognition.

"Not real," he whispers.

But the creeping frost on the glass says otherwise.

The Range Rover rumbles to life, dashboard cycling through its startup. Victor guns it, wheels spinning on the gravel and debris. He aims for the side drive, the only way out, a path lined with birch trees now half stripped by the explosion.

Behind him, the world is orange. The first eruption had turned the sub-basement into a blast furnace; now, the fire eats up through the upper floors. The entity advances from the ruins. Backlit by the inferno, its arms branch and arc across the yard, stretching not skyward but toward him.

He slams on the accelerator. Rocks and birch bark clatter against the undercarriage. The headlights catch the far end of the drive. He's three hundred yards from the road. Two hundred. The entity grows distant in his rearview—but he swears he can see its head track him. Its face—*is that even a face?*—splits into the suggestion of a howl. It stretches, extending itself, fire reflecting through its maw.

The Range Rover hits the tarmac at sixty-five. Victor doesn't brake, not even to check for cross-traffic; this is a private access road, no one else out here for miles. He makes the first corner on two wheels, the chassis groaning in protest.

He should feel relief. The house, any evidence, even that thing—he left them all behind.

But as he straightens out onto the road, Victor sees them.

They line the shoulders, spaced at intervals, each one's head bowed as if in mourning. The first is the vagrant, his blue cap and beard frosted with rime. Next, the nurse and her blood-drenched hair. Then, the teenager, his upper scalp removed, blood trailing from his nose. Each a victim, a subject, a failure.

Victor grips the wheel. "Not real," he says. "Not real. Not real."

He tries not to look. He tries, but peripheral vision betrays him. At the last bend before the main road, the line thickens into a mass. Fifty, sixty, a hundred spectral bodies—all standing in silence, all turned to face him. They stare accusingly without a sound. Only the wind, only the engine.

Shepherd laughs—high, sharp, manic. "You can't hurt me. None of you can hurt me."

The Range Rover doesn't slow. If anything, he accelerates, sixty, then seventy, then eighty. The cluster of phantoms at the exit is impossible to miss.

He closes his eyes.

The vehicle plows through the barricade of dead.

For a moment, Victor feels a pressure, as if he's driven into a puddle of mud. A coldness washes through the interior. His lungs refuse to expand, as if submerged in ice.

Then he's through.

The Range Rover bursts onto the highway. Victor gasps, coughs, bends forward over the wheel. The air is thin, but warming. He risks a glance behind. Nothing. The access road is empty, save for the swirl of leaves and dust in the SUV's wake.

He slows just a little. His pulse returns to baseline, hands regaining color.

Victor erupts with a triumphant "Ha!"

Relief! He has survived the impossible. Wiping his face on the sleeve of his shirt, he straightens and resumes forward. Heart settling back into its normal rhythm. He considers that maybe Mercer was right. Nothing back there will connect to either of them. It's all a mound of slagged concrete and metal. He's still in the clear.

His historical findings are a loss. But the techniques—he's mastered those. If anything, that makes him even more valuable. Only Dr. Shepherd can recreate such ingenuity.

Somewhere in the cold dark of the Range Rover, comes the faintest of sounds—a staccato click, like a scalpel tapping on glass.

It is a countdown, and it has only just begun.

Chapter Thirty-Nine

What Happened

S he wakes with the taste of ash and the world on fire.

Her first breath is a searing—heat, chemicals, the char of vaporized insulation and lacquered wood. For an instant, she's convinced she's still in the operating theater. Then she's slapped by the banshee wail of burning air, and the horrendous collapse of the cabin resort.

On her back, the sky above Evie Cross is a rolling bruise. Smoke pillars up from the retreat. Her skin is peppered with grit and something stickier. The grass beneath her is flattened, crisped in patches. She can't feel her legs at first. Her left arm is numb past the elbow; her right vibrates with the memory of some impact.

She inhales again, a little less frantic, and realizes the Harbinger has passed. Not gone—retreated, condensed into a weightless knot behind her heart. There is clarity in the circumstances. Not hers. They left her trace memories of what happened while she was out.

The lab is a super-heated corona behind her. The cabin is now a pyre. Fire climbs the split-levels, gnawing through joists. Somewhere below, a secondary line ruptures, sending up a geyser of flame.

A groan to her right. Evie turns—a feat that takes all her focus. Marcus lies supine in the grass, body twisted as if dropped from a ladder. His head is bare, scalp clean shaven, and across his crown, those blue surgical lines. He blinks at nothing, the whites of his eyes stark in the chaos of red and orange light. His lips work, forming words, but the only sounds are the roar of the fire and the throb of the wind.

Evie claws her fingers into the turf and forces herself upright. Her vision blurs at the edges, but she pushes through, bracing on her good arm.

With effort, she half-crawls closer to Marcus. Ragged abrasions mark his wrists, clearly from the restraints. There's a line of blood at his temple, a small incision wound. His pupils are pinpoints—whatever Shepherd loaded him with is still working its way out.

Evie kneels beside him, breath hitching. She slaps his face. "Marcus."

Nothing.

She tries again, this time with more force. "Hey! Marcus, focus."

He turns his head, mouth slack. "What's—where's—"

She checks his pulse, finds it weak but steady. The roar of the inferno intensifies behind them, an impetus calling for distance. Evie shakes Marcus. "We have to go," she hisses. "Now."

Marcus squints back, confused. His mouth twitches in what might be a smile. "How'd we do?" he whispers. "We get him?"

Evie shakes her head, eyes darting anywhere but to him. "No. No, not yet."

She scans the horizon. The main road is distant, but accessible. Her Ford is parked a half-mile through the woods. Somehow they've got to get there. Wiping her mouth, she spits out the cinders. Evie gets Marcus back on his feet again. They stagger forward, two wounded animals escaping a trap.

Breaching the far edge of the lawn, they stumble into the cover of brush. The fire's heat diminishes, replaced by the chilled autumn night. The pain in her body is acute, but manageable. They collapse again against a tree trunk.

Marcus breathes, slow and ragged, but his eyes are clearer now. He coughs, then manages to sit, fingers probing the line of his jaw as if making sure it's all still attached. Then his hand lands on the stubble above his ear.

He frowns, rubs the bare skin, and blinks at the unfamiliar smoothness. For a moment he is lost, a dog with a new collar. He looks at her, searching for the words.

"Stay seated," she says. "How's your head? Any dizziness?"

Marcus considers this. "Just feels... off. Like my skull isn't mine."

Evie scoots closer. Whipping out her cell, she shines its flashlight into his eyes. His pupil response is not great, but it's there. She checks the back of his head, palpates the nape. "Not much bleeding. No soft spots." She sits back on her haunches. "You lucked out. Shepherd didn't get far."

At that, Marcus looks startled. "Shepherd—where's Shepherd?" He looks over her shoulder, scanning the woods, the fire-lit horizon. He takes in the burning house, the rising pillars of smoke.

Evie replies, "Gone."

He rubs his wrists, then wipes his mouth. His tongue comes away black. "I don't remember much after the stairs," he says. "You were behind me. Then... he jumped you."

Evie shrugs. "He offered us a nip/tuck."

Marcus tries to smile, but it's a grimace. "You with the jokes."

She shakes her head, the movement weary and incomplete. "Yeah. A sick one. We were about to join his tests. A couple of control subjects."

He snorts. "A hell of a control." Marcus takes a breath, letting it out slow. "How'd we get out?"

Evie examines her hands, the filth under each nail. She feels the knot of the Harbinger dormant. "Not sure," she says, and lets it hang. "Let's just count our blessings."

They sit in silence for a while, the only sounds being the hush of the distant blaze and the soft tick of cooling metal from the ruined house. The congregation of ghosts stays at the boundary, neither coming closer nor fading away.

Marcus finally looks at her full on. "You okay?"

She shakes her head. "No. But not for lack of trying."

Marcus starts to rise again, and this time Evie helps him. She stands with him, steadying his balance. "Can you walk?"

He tries, nearly topples, but regains it. "I'll manage."

They move together, not toward the road, but toward a shallow ditch just beyond the first line of birches.

When they reach the ditch, Marcus sits and stares into the darkness. "You want to tell me what happened in there?" he says. "The real version."

Evie sits beside him, close but not touching. She studies the patterns in the sky, the shifting of clouds, the flicker of blue and orange reflected from the burning bones of the house. When she speaks, it's slow, deliberate.

"Officially, neither of us was ever at this location," she says.

He snorts. "Of course. That's not what I meant."

She turns to face him, her expression unreadable in the half-light. "You want the rest?"

"Yeah."

She leans back, letting her head rest against the trunk. "He was going to open us up," she says. "You first."

Marcus is silent.

"He lost control of the experiment. The variable changed." She pauses, considering how much to say. "I changed it."

He glances at her, one brow raised. "How?"

She shrugs. "I stopped believing in the system. For a minute. Maybe that was all it took."

He laughs, bitter and small. "Some variable."

They lapse into silence.

Marcus, after a time, asks, "And Shepherd?"

Evie doesn't answer right away. She looks out at the night, her eyes catching on a faint glimmer at the far end of the lawn. She feels the Harbinger's chill, its silent arithmetic, its patience.

She says, "He's done. He just doesn't know it yet."

Her tone is final, not hopeful—not even angry. A flat certainty, an executioner's sentence.

Marcus hears it and is silent.

Evie draws in the cold air and lets it fill her, both entity and the woman welded together now, not opposites but partners. She stands, offers a hand to Marcus, and pulls him up. Together, they walk out of the ditch.

She leans back, staring up at the choked sky. The burning house is a receding nightmare, the dead a silent audience at the margins. Somewhere, deep in her chest, the Harbinger settles, a cold promise.

It's not over.

Not yet.

Chapter Forty

Perfect Memory

The last thing Victor wants to hear is another countdown. But that's what it feels like—the clicks, the numbers, the speeding frequency of his own heart in his chest. Even after the Range Rover engine drowns it, the metronome persists in his bones. He checks the rearview, then the mirrors, then the side glass, certain he'll find a face there, pressed and grinning.

Still, there is nothing.

He drives fast, faster than he ought to, skidding the first left, gripping the wheel so tight. Behind him, his benefactor's palatial cabin is a distant glowing beacon: black smoke, orange bloom. Good. Eradicated. Everything is clean, as promised.

Victor's hands shake on the wheel. It's still not enough. If he is to come back from this, it's going to require so much greater distance. A span to lie low. He curses and fumbles a half-crushed packet of beta-blockers from his breast pocket, pops three, swallows them dry. They stick in his throat. He huffs through clenched teeth, gaze flicking back to the mirror. Time for a sabbatical, he thinks.

Victor keeps driving, checking behind.

Nothing.

After what seems like forever and a half hour, Victor's grand estate rolls into view. He clicks the gates open by depressing the rearview mirror's remote button. He pauses long enough for the decorative bars to part and the security bollards to retract into the ground. Then guns it again up the drive.

For once, his rearview reassures as security protocols reassert the gates and bollards.

He rushes from room to room, retrieving his old surgical kit under one arm and a duffel bag in the other. Victor throws clothes in at random: two custom jackets, three Oxford shirts, a bag of Merino-wool socks, shoes by the pair. He ransacks the office for paper files, research, the flash drives from the locked drawer, the hard copy of Mercer's last contract—anything that might matter. No time for sentiment.

He finishes the packing efficiently. A suitcase won't quite close. He gives up, tears out a clutch of dress shirts, and stuffs them into a trash bag. In the bathroom, he grabs all his medications, shoveling everything into his travel kit. He glimpses himself in the mirror.

"You're fine. You've got this."

He kills the lights, moves to the safe behind the painting. The combination lock is cool to the touch. He rotates through the sequence and swings the door open. Inside: a banded clutch of cash, and his passport. He tucks the passport into his shirt, and the cash—well, he stuffs the bills into the hidden compartment of his carry-on.

A whisper slithers into his ear. It isn't clear, but the chill is distinctive. It's coming. *No place to hide.*

He zips, double-checks, and then hauls everything down the corridor.

The front door is still. The glass is flawless, but thin condensation creeps around its frame. He paid far too much for the nitrogen-sealed double panes for that to be natural. Victor puts a hand to the wood and feels it vibrate, just a little. Static builds, then fades. He sets down his luggage and flexes his fingers. Pressing the tips to his carotid—pulse: 130.

"Not real," he repeats.

Retrieving the bags, he forces the door. The night air slaps him: not just cold, but raw. Must be the wind. His birches sway in the driveway, a rolling cascade of branches.

He scans the property for threats, armed or otherwise. The driveway is a sweep of blue-gray stone, illuminated by the lawn's landscape lights. His footsteps echo much too loud. At the curb, his yellow Porsche Cayenne waits. The car chirps when he clicks unlock; the sound is too cheery, offensive.

Victor crosses the walk, puts the suitcase in the back, tosses the trash bag onto the passenger seat, and double-checks his home is secured. He glances up instinctively...

...that's when he sees it.

Atop the roof, between the pitch and the gutter, a drifting fog just a shade too thick. It's not a trick of the night. He can see the outline. Limbs that sprawl in impossible geometry, a head cocked at a studious angle. The shape moves not with the grace of a predator but with the casual, methodical crawl of a spider. It's not just there to threaten. It is observing.

Victor's gut plummets. He stares, blinks twice, but it remains.

He grabs a revolver and points it, hand trembling so hard the sight line vibrates. He knows instantly he could not hit anything with a hand that unsteady.

The form on the roof lifts a single limb—an arm, a leg, who knows? It gently shifts closer.

Aw hell. What can bullets do against something like that?!

Victor's bladder wants to void, but he clamps it down with professional hatred. He dives into the Cayenne, slamming the door with a violence that hurts his wrist. He shoves the start button, mashes the pedal, and the engine barks to life. The display screen wakes, blue and white. The headlights cut the drive in two distinct lanes.

He burns rubber, reversing so hard the tail nearly swings into the juniper hedge. He straightens, throws it in drive, and peels up the curved exit, toward the main road. To hell with checking the rearview!

The night thickens as he goes. The security gate looms. Victor jabs the clicker, expecting the customary whir. Instead, nothing. The distant gate does not move. He tries again—there is a moment's hesitation, then the gates start their roll back.

He hears it before he sees: a breath, like a nest of snakes shaking out their tongues. He swivels his head, looking for a threat, but the drive is empty. Victor punches the dash. Each exhale puffs out in front of his face, swirling in the interior like smoke.

The whispers come again, this time from inside the car. He can't make out words, just syllables, sss, ttt, nnngh. Has he gone utterly mad?

It is only when the headlights sweep over the threshold that he sees what waits before the gate.

They are lined up on the drive. Twenty, thirty, maybe more, all clustered before the parted gates. Their shambling appearance leaves nothing to doubt. His halogen beams catch the faces: too white, too flat, eyes hollow, jaws slack, mouths black pits. Each is dressed as they were in life: some in hospital gowns, some in street clothes, one in a blue knit cap. They stand motionless, blocking the way out.

He slams on the accelerator, tearing down the asphalt, the speedometer climbing, his hands slick with sweat despite the chill.

Victor risks a glance in the mirror.

Behind him, nothing. No lights, no movement. Just the gleam of the receding manor.

He allows himself a breath. "Not real," he whispers. "Hallucination. Stress. It's just—" His voice breaks, so he tries again. "Nothing can get through carbon and steel. Nothing can get through this."

He rounds the final bend, headlights blazing up the dead mass before him. *Bastards.* He clicks the high beams on.

There's a figure standing on the other side, dead center.

She is small, maybe five-two. Black turtleneck and windbreaker, black jeans, hair wild and lashing in the wind. Her eyes are closed, as if she is waiting to be hit.

Victor's hands jerk. For a split second, he fights the urge to swerve. The rational mind says she's not there. She can't be. The part of him that's always won—the part that makes him god—wants to barrel through.

He stomps the accelerator.

The Cayenne's engine howls, a beast in a cage. His car rockets forward, tires tearing at the asphalt. The figure in the road does not move.

As he roars up, time slows. Victor registers every frame: the dead congregation holding mass, the wind curling the cuffs of her jacket, the way her hair lifts, the skin around her eyes seems darker than any shadow he's ever cut into. She stands perfectly still. She is not afraid. Not even resigned.

At the last instant, her eyes open.

They are black—impossibly black, but registering within are pinpricks of icy blue. They're so deep they make the onrushing grill of the Cayenne seem trivial, the threat of impact irrelevant.

In the instant before collision—his world fractures instead.

Impact! The dashboard shatters in his hands. The windshield hurls up at him. He registers his face smashing through, windshield exploding. Jagged edges slice his cheeks, forearms, and the wettest rush of blood.

He's airborne.

The night is cold. His own headlights illuminate his trajectory. A bodied projectile, arcing over the drive, past the small agent who follows with her black eyes. Asphalt seems to whip by under him, drawing closer. He lands on the road with a sound like meat on marble, a crunch so loud it is a thunderclap in his ears. He skids. Momentum carries him several meters before coming to rest face down.

He tastes blood, grit, and the acid bite of adrenaline.

He's alive.

Victor tries to move. Nothing happens. He tries again, and the only response is a dry pop in his left shoulder.

He lifts his head, vision laced with agony. The world tilts, and he sees them—his subjects—gathering in a ring around him. They crowd the driveway. Their faces are no longer slack, but intent, almost focused. They stare down at him, but there is no accusation. Instead, they regard him as he would a specimen, a rat in the tray. Those with eyes blink; most do not.

He tries to speak. All that comes is an agonizing gurgle.

Then, a hand reaches for him. The hand is ashen, skin tight over bone, with a surgical scar crossing the metacarpal. It grabs him by the lapel and lifts him up.

He is surrounded by hands now. Not cruel. They move with the deliberation of nurses prepping a patient for triage. One cradles his head. Another straightens his right arm carefully, as if arranging it. A third wipes the blood from his mouth with the hem of a tattered dress.

They make him look up.

Standing above him is the woman from the road. Evie Cross. Her black eyes are slicks of oil feeding tiny flames of blue. The air around her shifts; something else looms behind her—a mist, a mask, a halo of luminous suffering. It's taller than she is, and it bends to examine him, its face forming from the fog.

Shepherd wants to scream. Raw terror climbs in his throat, clawing at his tongue.

Instead, calm descends. Not his own. Not welcome.

It is Evie—no, that thing—which speaks in a voice that is not hers, and yet exactly hers. "You have always been meticulous, Doctor," it says. "It makes you feel... special."

Victor trembles, teeth chattering uncontrollably.

The woman/entity leans close until their faces are nearly pressed to his. Black eyes widen, their cold centers pulling him in. There is a sensation not unlike a needle entering his skull—at the foramen magnum, then spiraling upward, tapping every old dread along the way.

"Thus, you are deserving of special treatment," it says. "You will not die, Victor Shepherd. Not for a very long time."

The hands holding him tighten.

"You will remain. Every synapse. Every memory. Every horror you have delivered to others."

The woman/entity traces a finger along his scalp, right where he had mapped the blue lines on Marcus Vaughn. Victor feels the cold, then nothing at all. His vision falters, then tunnels.

The entity leans back. In its place, Evie stands up. Her eyes still black, but her expression now her own—sorrowful, not for him but for what must be done.

The other hands let go. Victor collapses onto the pavement, agony rushing back in full.

He tries to crawl. His arms are rubber. His spine on fire.

He turns, just enough to see the crowd of dead encircle him, their faces pale lanterns in the frost.

Evie turns away. She walks to the gate's security console. Disconnects some device. Then she strolls to the twisted wreckage of the Cayenne, piled upon the bollards. Reaching through the driver-side window, her gloved hand shuts off the headlights.

The spectral entity hovers over him, extending a tendril, needle-thin and perfect. It inserts it through Victor's right eye.

The world dissolves, reforms, dissolves again. He is not in the driveway now, but in the lab, the old lab, the one beneath the retreat. The entity is there, too, only it is everywhere: in the lights, in the power's hum, in the teeth of the drill as it whines to life.

He is the subject now, not the operator. The entity, this Harbinger thing, brings him to the surgical chair, secures the wrists, arranges the head. Victor tries to fight, but the bindings are total. The blackness overflows; it fills his nose, his mouth, seeps into the marrow of every bone.

He feels every incision, every point of pain, every slow, meticulous unspooling of the nervous system he once commanded.

He screams, but there is no voice.

He demands oblivion. Instead, the Harbinger gives him perfect memory. He replays the experiment over and over, each cycle more precise, more refined. Perfecting its technique. Each time, he is forced to witness himself as his victims did: as a silhouette, a mask, a halo of luminous suffering. The dead gather, a jury of many, all silent, all watching.

There is no mercy. There is only the enduring of seconds, minutes, hours... days... years.

When at last the Harbinger withdraws, Victor lies in the driveway, face planted in the cold. The world is silent, save for his ragged breathing.

Above him, the sky is blank.

He blinks. Once, twice, and the blackness in his vision is slow to recede. He goes to lift his hand—it doesn't.

He tries to move. He cannot.

He tries to scream. Nothing comes out.

Paralysis! He lies there, time bleeding away, as the dead fade into a silent vigil.

Only Evie remains on the road, her eyes closed again, the wind settling her hair against her cheek. She stands for a long time, just breathing... in and out.

Then she walks away.

The world does not end. It only continues, one breath at a time, with Dr. Victor Shepherd left to count them.

One.

Two.

Three.

Counting, forever.

Chapter Forty-One

The Uncaught

Evie strolls along the edge of the road, breath fogging out in short, almost ritual bursts. Farther behind her, the stillness is a pending crime scene: Shepherd's Cayenne a twisted heap of metal, glass, and blood.

She thumbs her remote device, a hacker's multi-tool. A moment's admiration flickers—the Harbinger, somehow working through her, had known precisely which sequence to run: disable the gates, leave the anti-ram bollards up, create the illusion of an escape route but leave the final gauntlet intact. Elegant, ruthless. Better than anything the Bureau inspired her with.

She tucks the device into her duffel, the zipper's rasp the only audible break in the night. There is a burnt sweetness to the air, a finish of petroleum and plastic.

At the edge of vision, something glimmers ahead, emerging from a fog.

They assemble.

Not as they were before—no longer the fractured, postmortem grotesques that had stalked the Cartographer's margins. Now, they are different. They have the color and volume of memory: clear eyes, unbroken heads, wounds gone or never made. The blue-capped va-grant who first haunted her is front and center. His face is not caved in, just bearded and proud. The nurse, hair slicked and uniform pressed, stands straight, her skin an ordinary pallor. The nineteen-year-old boy—she had seen his photo in files—no longer leaks anything; he is dressed for a holiday, all jeans and conviction.

They form a ring around her, quiet as a closed church.

One by one, they approach. The nurse bows her head, lips pressed together in a line of absolute understanding. She passes through Evie, cold as water but gone in a shimmer, not a shudder. An old man nods—twice, slowly—then follows. The teenager looks up, smiles an uncertain, gap-toothed grin, and then evaporates with a whiff of ozone. Dozens of them, the whole census of Shepherd's atrocities, file past: each offering what they can, some a gesture, some a nod, some only a weightless silence as they join the queue out of existence.

It's a processional, a litany of absences put to rest.

When the last of them—save for the vagrant—have gone, Evie is left alone in the road. The vagrant shuffles close, dropping the air of crazy he wore in life. He bows, not a feint or a parody but a deep, honest bow. When he straightens, there is a slip of paper in his hand: filthy, tattered, creased with the memory of a thousand pockets.

He holds it out to her, shaking only a little. She takes it, not know-ing why. The note, in a pen so faint it nearly vanishes, simply says, "Bless you."

Evie's throat closes—too hard to swallow. She nods back, and the vagrant grins, tips his cap, and dissolves—leaving behind only a shim-mer, and the echo of his gratitude.

She stands there for a span, the note fading in her fingers, cold eating through the layers of her jacket. The wind pushes embers and the scent of burning oil from behind. In the middle distance, Shepherd's body is a sack of wet bones, his face twisted not in pain, but in terror and awe.

Evie's hands tremble. She's unsure if it's cold, adrenaline, or what's become of her. The satisfaction is not pure. There is loss in it, and exhaustion, and the dull, permanent ache of something she will never fully recover.

But also... relief.

An oddity slips into her mind, harking with a statistic: 30%–40%.

It was Haden who'd first quoted it to her. "You know, thirty to forty percent of serials never get caught. Ever." He'd said it with a mixture of defeat and drive, as if they could all do better.

Evie whispers it aloud. "Thirty to forty percent." She lets the words condense in the air, visible only to her. She imagines the Harbinger hearing and understanding.

Another cluster of headlights stains the far horizon. Sirens now—distant, but coming. Time to vanish.

She slings the duffel over her shoulder, checks the grip of her Glock out of habit, and moves through the back gardens, away from the spectacle. The blue and red of the rescue rigs bounce off the tree trunks, giving the woods the feeling of a theater. She moves silently, every step calculated to leave no imprint in the mud or the memory of onlookers.

Once she's in the woods, the night absorbs her.

She travels the half mile by internal compass and feel, letting the Harbinger guide her through the thicket. The entity is not hungry now; its presence is a low, a companionable hum behind her ribs. Not gone, not sleeping—just satisfied, for the moment.

Is that how this works?

She finds her car where she left it, parked on a fire road behind a curtain of birch and holly. It's untouched, save for the frost on the windows. The distant glow of police lights halos over the other side of the forest. She gets in, waits for a minute, then another.

Inside the car, the silence is total.

She rests her head on the wheel. Exhales once, then again.

"Now what?" she says, not really asking, just marking the moment.

The Harbinger is quiet, but she feels its answer in the prickle at her neck, the slight narrowing of her pulse.

That number is still in her head, turning over and over.

Thirty to forty percent.

She understands in a way she never did before.

She thinks she knows why now. Why some are never found—never caught. There is a contentment, a satisfaction in that understanding.

Evie starts the engine. The Ford Fiesta's cylinders catch, steady and resilient. She pulls onto the unlit road, makes a three-point turn, and heads into the darkness, one mile at a time.

As the last of the emergency lights fade behind her, she lets herself feel the weight of what's inside.

She was always going to be this.

The world does not end. It continues, one breath at a time.

So does she.

Chapter Forty-Two

The Open Road

At 8:15AM sharp, the badge scanner at the end of the hall chirps a weak confirmation and grants Evie Cross her last scheduled audience with the Bureau. The overheads in Haden's office burn fluorescent, a hue so sterile it's more chemical than light. She stands at parade rest, eyes drawn to the old behavioral charts framed behind his desk: timeline of the DC sniper, pin map from the Monster of Belleville, a printout of the Zodiac's coded letter—anachronisms of a world that once believed in the rationality of monsters.

Agent Haden, even after thirty-five years, retains the low center of gravity and the jowled composure that says "cop" first and "administrator" second. Today, though, he doesn't even pretend. His white shirt is open at the neck, tie loose. He gestures to the single chair.

"Agent Cross." He says it like a question. His eyes flick from the envelope in her hand to her face, and for the first time in all their years, he seems tired enough to forgo the opening banter.

She sits, chair legs scraping the tile.

He folds his hands. "I already know why you're here."

Evie places the envelope on the desk, sliding it with two fingers until it touches the edge of his notepad. "It's overdue, sir. I should have—"

He waves her off. "Doesn't matter when. I'm only sad you feel you must." He opens the envelope, removes a single page. It's not even a full resignation letter; she knows he won't need one. He reads it, lips moving slightly, then sets it aside.

She waits.

Haden looks up. "Anything you want to get off your chest, Cross?"

She flexes her hand, knuckles whitening, then releases it to her lap. "You already know I falsified the old Cartographer data sets. The trace I submitted—I pinned to that deceased killer. It was the only hope I had to get my daughter's body. I told myself it was for the greater good. But that wasn't enough. I skirted things even recently. Ways that make me undeserving of carrying that badge." She lets the sentence die, knowing there's nothing to follow it.

He digests this. It's the kind of secret that should detonate a career, but in this office, at this hour, it's almost a courtesy. "You know, I once planted a fiber of nylon in a suspect's car. Drove all the way to Richmond to cut a patch out of an identical floor mat. We caught the bastard." He glances up, a smile like a broken shoelace. "They didn't fire me either."

Evie feels the tremor in her chest ease by a hair.

He leans back, hands behind his head. "You know what the hardest part of this job is, Cross? Not the cases. Not the paperwork. Not even in the politics. It's realizing there are no pure motives. Sometimes there's just what needs to be done, even when it shouldn't."

She looks at him, surprised by the confession.

"Don't look so shocked," Haden says. "You're not the only one who wanted to believe there was a right way." He opens a drawer, produces a padded envelope. He scoops up her letter and badge and drops them inside, sealing it with the heel of his hand. "Let's call this a mutual parting."

She nods. "Thank you."

He regards her for a long moment. Then, with the air of a man crossing an item off a list, says, "Did you hear? Our Dr. Shepherd's in the hospital now as a patient."

She shakes her head. "Didn't read that in the feed."

"His car collided with his own security system. Don't know what his blood alcohol level was, but he must have been pretty out of it. They say he won't wake up. Vegetative." Haden's jaw works a moment, a grindstone thought. "Makes ya wonder if somehow his past caught up with him."

Evie exhales, the last of the tension leaving her.

Haden glances at the wall clock. "That's about all, I guess. See you to the elevator?"

He walks with her the length of the office corridor. In the liminal space of the sparse hall, their footsteps tap off the linoleum. Every few bulbs are out, casting patches of floor into alternating gloom. It feels like the world is already forgetting her.

They stop at the other end, just before the elevator double doors.

"I hesitate to say this," Haden says. "But if it were my son, I would have burned the damned world down. Who knows how many I would've taken with me. Even those who might not have deserved it. Despite all that, you maintained control, Cross. I find that commendable."

"Thank you," Evie is just able to manage.

He holds the door long enough for her to enter. Then Haden returns to his office. The pneumatic hiss seals her out.

The reception lobby is glass and steel, a bureaucratic aquarium. Sunlight tries but mostly fails to infiltrate the tint, leaving the place in a lingering twilight. Marcus Vaughn has propped himself against the check-in counter, arms folded, suit a smidge too tight across his shoulders. His head is shaved clean, the old vanity finally dispensed with, but he's kept the mustache. In the bright overheads, it looks like a comic exaggeration, but somehow it fits.

"Jesus, Cross," he says. "You could have at least thrown a party. Or left a cake in the break room."

She shrugs. "Not big on closure."

He grins, but it's not the old predator grin. "You see Haden?"

"Yeah."

"He do the lecture?"

"Skipped it."

Marcus shakes his head, almost impressed. "That's a first."

She studies him. "You keeping the look?"

He runs a hand over his scalp, a gesture both vain and self-effacing. "Growing on me. My wife says it makes me look less like a cop, more like a rock star."

Evie almost laughs. "Maybe you should change careers."

Marcus ignores that, gaze drifting to the lobby windows. "You hear about Shepherd?"

She nods. "Haden told me."

"Any theories?" he asks. His tone is loose, not the old prosecutorial tension.

"None I care to share," she says. "Some things just happen."

He snorts. "Heard they found him in his own blood. No one else in the car. It's poetic, almost."

"Almost," she agrees.

They stand in companionable silence, neither willing to leave the comfort of a ritual.

Marcus' characteristic smirk emerges. "You know, the property where the fire was—nobody's claimed the loss. Not a word in the news about anyone being connected. It's like the world doesn't care." He studies her as if expecting a reaction.

She gives none.

"Some nameless shell company lawyers are tying up the estate. Us feds still don't see much of a call to be too involved. Some billionaire wants to torch his place, gonna piss off a fire marshal, but not much else. So long as they don't make an insurance claim. Guess some people really are untouchable."

Evie looks past him, to the doors, to the glare of the parking lot beyond. "Maybe not as untouchable as they think," she says.

He steps aside, giving her a clear path.

"You leaving town?" he asks.

"For a while."

He nods, as if he knew it already.

As she passes him, touching his arm. "Take care, Marcus. Don't let them make you into something you're not."

He tips an imaginary hat. "You too, Cross."

She steps through the doors, into the dazzling light, and does not look back.

The house feels smaller in the afternoon, as if the siding and insulation have grown tight against the change of season. There is a layer of dust on the shoe bench inside the door, two pairs of sneakers slouched side by side: Evie's battered old Nikes, and a pair of Michael's, still untied. She steps around them, careful not to disturb.

In the kitchen, the table has been arranged with that envelope alongside a pen. The chair before it sits askew—likely Michael, whose faint cologne lingers. There is also a glass tumbler with an amber footprint dried to its base.

Evie takes her seat at the table. The signature line glares up at her. Her hands, unsteady, flatten each page in sequence. She scans the text, but the words are only legal shadow. It's the finality, not the language, that matters.

Her hand no longer shakes. She picks up the pen, twirls it once—a fidget she's had since Quantico. She signs, first name, then last, never more deliberate.

Evie rests both palms on the table, ring finger still circled by gold. She stares at it. After a moment, she spins the ring, twists it, and then tugs until it slips free. It rests in her palm, a cool and weightless cipher.

She leaves it atop the papers.

Her phone vibrates in her pocket—a text. Michael, no doubt.

Evie taps out her message: "Signed. Sell the house. Wire half to my account." She adds a line, then deletes it. Adds another—"The rest is yours. It's cleaner this way." She hits send before she can edit again.

The reply is instant: "Okay. Thank you."

There is nothing else.

The house is silent except for the clock in the living room, ticking in polite, constant increments. The clock belonged to her mother; it is one of the few things Evie allowed to survive the move. She listens to it now, counting the seconds as if it's a safety measure.

In the low light, she walks the perimeter of the kitchen, touching nothing but letting her fingers trace the outlines of counters, the handle of the fridge, the seam of the wall where a hairline crack splits the paint. Each move is a cataloguing, an inventory against forgetting.

By the window, she looks out at the backyard. The maple tree is nearly done with autumn, a thousand yellow leaves drifting down over the patchy grass. June's old tire swing hangs, unmoving, the rope gone gray with weather. She expects to feel the urge to cry, but the sensation is muted, as if the rawest nerve was burned out long ago.

The sun is low, spilling a slant of gold through the window. She blinks, and her eyes sting.

There are practicalities to tend to. In the hall closet, she retrieves a duffel, the canvas still stiff from the last time she packed it for an overnight. She fills it with only the essentials: two changes of clothes, her battered laptop, chargers, a zip bag with a single toothbrush and travel-size toothpaste. She adds a flashlight.

In the living room, she pauses by her wedding photo, their arms around each other's shoulders, squinting into the sun. She leaves that.

At the hallway's end, the door to June's room is closed. Evie rests her palm against the wood, fingers spread, feeling the cool texture. She does not cry, does not speak. Instead, she takes a deep breath, then turns the knob.

Inside, the room remains untouched. The bed is made, the blankets a stack of purple and blue. The walls are littered with posters: a world map, a vintage NASA print, a hand-drawn constellation chart. On the desk, a scattering of colored pencils, a pile of dog-eared composition books. The air is tinged with the scent of lavender and paper.

Evie crosses to the closet, hesitating only once. She opens the door, and in the shadows finds June's favorite scarf: a thick twist of violet, soft and slightly frayed at the ends. She presses it to her face, inhaling deeply, then wraps it once around her shoulders.

She stands in the doorway, scanning the room one last time, as if hoping to imprint it on her retinas. Then Evie closes the door, firm but not final.

The last of the light is vanishing. In the entryway, she pulls on her jacket, zips it to the throat. She grabs her keys, tucks the duffel under her arm, and shoulders open the door.

Outside, the sky is a fever of orange and purple. She stands on the porch, letting the cold enter her lungs. For a moment, the world is nothing but the wind on her face, and the shuffling of leaves on the driveway.

She walks to the car, unlocks it, places the duffel in the passenger seat, and starts the engine. Evie sits, hands in her lap, watching the horizon as the colors bleed out of the day.

The Harbinger is there, low and steady, humming in the marrow of her bones. It is not hungry nor angry. It is simply there, as she is.

"We're not done yet," she whispers.

The words are not dramatic. They are a truth, uttered only for herself and the presence inside.

She lifts her head and pulls away from the curb, leaving the old life to the ticking of clocks and the settling of dust.

Ahead, the road is open. She drives one mile at a time, into whatever comes next.

Chapter Forty-Three

Final Assessment

The day begins at the exact moment the nurse presses the code to disable the room's outer alarm, a click of plastic and a hiss of negative pressure. Saint Aldwyn Estate, third floor, suite 302: it is a rectangle of glass and engineered wood. Every surface is smooth, every corner rounded for the comfort of high-end clients and those who visit them. The bed dominates. Victor Shepherd lies in it, his body arranged as if for a portrait—face turned fifteen degrees to the left, hands folded in textbook repose. Eyes open. Mouth just slack enough to deny him dignity.

A woman sits in the visitor's chair. Her shoes are black leather, the kind you buy at a place with a single sign in the window. They shine against the bluish floor. Her hair is a cascade of silver strands, hinting at her late forties, although her bright eyes suggest a wisdom that transcends age. The tailored blazer, a deep navy blue, hugs her shoulders perfectly, while the dark pants are snug. Around her neck, a muted cravat drapes elegantly, its subtle patterns blending into the fabric of her blazer, adding a touch of sophistication. Her badge—plastic, unmemorable—hangs from a lanyard tucked beneath the lapel.

Shepherd's room is calibrated for comfort, but there is none here. The air hangs with disinfectant used on the door handles. A wall-mounted display registers his heart rate, the oxygen saturation, the pressure in his brain's ventricular system. Everything is within normal range, except Dr. Shepherd himself.

The woman lifts her phone, taps the screen, and begins to record.

"Patient is unresponsive," she says, accent even but inflected with something Baltic. "Spontaneous breathing, but otherwise complete absence of volitional movement." Her voice is sharp, clipped, the kind that makes English sound like a second or third language. "All reflexes intact. No signs of decerebrate posturing or pain withdrawal. Pupils responsive to light. EEG shows minimal higher function. Recommend continued supportive care."

She pans the phone across the bed, steady hands taking in Shepherd's features. It's not quite the face of a preeminent surgeon: scarred heavily, jaw swollen, skin grafts layering his nose.

Shepherd's eyes are a grey so pale they seem colorless in daylight. They follow nothing, not even the movement of the phone. His breathing is so regular a machine might perform it. His lips, parted just enough, sometimes catch a fleck of saliva; a nurse passes by every hour to clean it away, but it always returns.

The woman pauses the recording. She glances at the bed, then at the nurse, who stands just outside the doorway, checking an iPad. "Leave us," the woman says.

The nurse, unsurprised, nods and retreats.

The woman resumes. "Attending states that the patient exhibits no evidence of locked-in syndrome. All autonomic functions intact. MRI negative for infarct or diffuse axonal injury. No organic basis for persistent vegetative state. No psychogenic or metabolic cause identified."

She lowers the phone, lips compressed.

A vibration in her purse. The woman pulls out a second phone, heavy, matte black. She unlocks it with a thumbprint and brings it to her ear. No greeting, just silence, until a voice—thin, male, no traceable accent—speaks from the other end.

"Status?"

The woman glances at Shepherd. "Stable. No improvement. No awareness."

"Have you double-checked the case files?" the voice asks. "Any telltale signs?"

She nods, though the caller cannot see. "Thorough review. Police reports, hospital logs, security footage. The accident is fully contained. There is no criminal case, no open investigation. The Bureau was only marginally involved and has since closed his file. Family is compliant."

The voice is silent for two full seconds, enough to let her know he's thinking. "And the other party?"

"No sign of her," the woman says. "Cross resigned from her position. There is no documentation of her involvement. The official narrative holds: Shepherd had a sudden psychotic break, possibly induced by prescription interactions and long-standing stressors. He accelerated into the property gates at high speed, without his headlights active. Toxicology is negative. Nothing else suggests foul play."

The voice responds, "Good."

There is an implied finality, but the woman waits, as any competent subordinate should. The voice continues, "When you have concluded your observations, send the footage and your notes. Afterward, you will return to D.C. Brief directly to the Office. Keep no personal records."

"Yes, sir," the woman says.

The call disconnects.

Shepherd's eyes have not moved. On their milky surface, the reflection of the woman wavers, and nothing more.

She rises, walks to the bed, and stands so close that she could touch his cheek if she wanted. She doesn't. Instead, she leans in, lowering her voice to a frequency that only the comatose or the truly intimate could distinguish.

"I never liked you," she says, the words crisp and almost tender. "No one should ever be as clever as you think you are."

She straightens, dusting lint off her sleeve.

Her phone dings—a reminder to submit her daily wellness check to the Center's online portal. She ignores it, but types out a text: "All clear. Will report as planned."

She looks once more at Shepherd. For a moment, it appears as if his breathing hitches, a slight catch in the rhythm. Maybe a trick of the lighting, or just a muscle spasm. She leans down, places her palm—flat, gentle—on his shoulder. To any observer, the gesture would read as compassion, a ritual of bedside solace. She digs in her thumb, burrowing for a nerve.

In truth, she checks for resistance. A twitch, a flinch, even the faintest tremor of will. There is nothing. Shepherd's body yields only the minimum, the compliance of the truly lost.

She removes her hand, straightens his gown, and walks out. The door swings closed behind her with a hydraulic sigh.

Back in the bed, Shepherd's eyes remain open, locked on the crack where the ceiling meets the wall. They see nothing. Or perhaps they see everything, but the mind behind them is gone, left only with the endless parade of seconds, the data points of a life no longer lived.

The wall display ticks upward. Heart rate: 52. SpO2: 97%. Brain activity: minimal, but present.

The dead leer down at Victor.

Ready for another round. Their cranial dismembering techniques will always need perfecting.

Spectral Hunter Book 2

When the dead lead the hunt, justice finds a way.

From the ashes of her harrowing experience, ex-FBI agent Evie Cross' world is turned upside down. Now, she finds herself bound to a powerful entity—the Harbinger—forced to confront victims of killers. With seemingly unconnected bodies spread across several states, Evie must embrace her eerie connection to discover a disturbing link among them.

At the heart of this chilling puzzle is 'The Deliverer,' a meticulous killer who targets for a price. Bids rise based on the purity of their targets. As Evie delves into the shadows to unmask the one pulling the strings, she must grapple with a haunting dilemma: once you step into darkness to catch a predator, can you find your way back into the light?

In a terrifying supernatural showdown, there comes a line between seeking justice and exacting revenge.

Is it hers to cross?

Prepare for a bone-chilling journey through vengeance, morality, and the blurred boundaries between humanity and monstrosity in this heart-stopping paranormal thriller from the acclaimed author of THE HARBINGER.

Spectral Hunter Series: Book Two

Amazon: Dec. 5, 2025

Submit a Review

If The Harbinger resonated with you, a short review on Amazon would mean the world to me. It helps other readers discover the story and supports my work. Share what you loved most (a favorite scene, character, or moment that stayed with you) and whether you'd recommend it; even a sentence or two makes a huge difference.

Amazon Review Link

Thank you for taking a moment to leave your thoughts—your voice helps this book find its next reader.

Also from ALVS

The Books of Ruein

Death has its own kind of grace.

When the gods stopped listening, Ruein learned to whisper to the dead.

Once a mother, wife, and reluctant necromancer, she has clawed her way through curses, godless realms, and divine betrayals to protect the one thing that still matters—her family. But every spell cast in love carries a shadow, and Ruein's has begun to stir.

From the smoke of Vandraport's streets to the frozen citadels of Haraden, Ruein is hunted by powers both mortal and celestial. To save her son, she'll forge impossible alliances: with dragons, killers, and even the Lightbringer sworn to destroy her. Yet the deeper she delves into the underworld of magic, the more she risks becoming what she most fears.

Because the dead are never done with you.

Wickedly funny, brutal, and unflinchingly human, The Books of Ruein is a dark fantasy saga of necromancy, faith, and the cost of love in a world that eats its own gods.

For readers of The Witcher, The First Law, and The Sandman, who prefer their fantasy rich with blood, ash, and gallows humor.

Now Available on Ama-zon

UFO Science
Unraveling the Phenomena

Step beyond speculation and into discovery. The UFO Science Series takes you on an unprecedented exploration of the evidence, physics, and mysteries shaping humanity's understanding of Unidentified Anomalous Phenomena and the enigmatic patterns that appear in our fields.

In Book One, uncover the revolutionary science that may drive advanced UAP craft. From declassified Pentagon encounters to breakthrough theories by pioneers like T. Townsend Brown and Jack Sarfatti, you'll gain a clear and comprehensive view of the physics that could be redefining reality itself.

In Book Two, delve into the geometric and biological mysteries of crop circles—where intricate designs meet scientific data. Explore soil anomalies, eyewitness accounts, and the unexplained precision behind these vast formations that continue to defy conventional reasoning.

Blending research, case studies, and cutting-edge hypotheses, this series challenges readers to look closer, think deeper, and question what they thought they knew about the world around them.

The frontier of discovery is here.

Are you ready to see what's been hiding in plain sight?

Now Available on Amazon